MY FIRST SATYRNALIA

Michael Rumaker

MY FIRST SATYRNALIA

Grey Fox Press
San Francisco

Library of Congress Cataloging in Publication Data

Rumaker, Michael, 1932-
  My first satyrnalia.

  I. Title
PS3568.U43M9   813'.54   81-1489
ISBN 0-912516150-X   AACR2
ISBN 0-912516-51-8 (pbk.)

Distributed by The Subterranean Company,
P.O. Box 10233, Eugene, Oregon 97440

MY FIRST SATYRNALIA

As I ran up out of the West 4th Street subway stop, a bone-chilling blast of wind caught me from behind and shoved me across Sixth Avenue to the corner of Christopher Street, past Village Produce, its sidewalk stands, usually piled high with fruits and vegetables in all kinds of weather, empty this afternoon with the temperature dropping to near zero. Later, I would stop back on my way crosstown to the Saturnalia to pick up apples and oranges, my share of the food for this evening's festivities.

Only the chance to take part in such an event, my first, with all its tantalizing possibilities, could bring me down to Manhattan on such a bitterly cold day. One other matter roused my keen curiosity—what I hoped to find in the windows of the Oscar Wilde Memorial Bookshop as soon as I rounded the corner. The powerful wind, knifing through the streets from the Hudson River, slashed through the rips in my old ski jacket and leaky down vest, cut at my eyes and nose, all that stuck out of the face mask of my sock hat.

And there was the faded and, given the weather, appealingly warm red brick facade of the bookshop, and there, to my amazed eyes, in the center of a display of new books, was the pale blue paperback cover of my first gay novel, published, rightly enough, on the Halloween just past. All the painful discomfort of the cold eased as I silently crowed for several long moments, clenching my gloved hands at my chest, suddenly warmed by a surge of pride, seeing it out in the world at last.

Excited, anxious to get inside and see if the book was also on display there, another blustery wind pushed me up the steps and into the vestibule. Despite my flush of pleasure at seeing my book in the window, I was grateful to get in out of the cold, on this coldest day of the winter so far, and the shortest one, too, the day of the winter solstice, which my friends and I would be celebrating that night in Saturnalian ritual and song.

I slipped the drawstrings of my duffel bag more securely up over my shoulder and automatically turned the knob, which of course didn't budge since I'd forgotten the door was kept locked now, as were the doors of many other merchants along the street, because of increasing fears of robbery and harassment.

Christopher Street, like MacDougal when it was the main drag of the Village a generation ago, was crowded now with street pushers and drunks and hustlers, and exhibitionists in increasingly bizarre getups who made the street their stage: the eccentrics and out-casts and throwaways from every borough of the city, many of them on drugs. The worst were the gangs from other parts of the city or the suburbs across the river in Jersey, who periodically invaded the street to mug and beat up "the queers." A young bartender had, a year or so before, been slain in an afterhours holdup in Uncle Paul's Tavern just up from Gay Street, across the way from the bookshop, an *alleged* holdup some said, the mob wanting to muscle in on one of the few independent, and lucra-tive, gay-owned bars in the Village. Recently a rock had been thrown through one of the bookshop's windows by a street crazy. Now, anyone coming to the door was scrutinized carefully through the small window before being let in.

As I waited, and to attract the attention of the sales clerks inside, I stamped my feet and slapped my leather gloves together to shake off the cold. Through the little window I could see one of the women behind the counter look up, her bright blonde hair bobbed neatly. She moved briskly to the door to peer out at me, a look of uncertainty in her eyes behind her tinted glasses as she studied my face, or what could be seen of it. I realized I must have looked like a prospective robber and quickly rolled up my face mask into the brim of the sock hat as I tried my best to give a convincing smile. Her face relaxed, perhaps because I looked familiar, too, having been here a number of times before, and she unlocked the door.

"Hello," I said as I entered the delightful warmth of the shop.

"Hello yourself," she replied, "Come on in and thaw out," and rejoined the other woman behind the counter.

2

It was such a cramped place even the few customers browsing in the extremely narrow aisles made it seem crowded. After the raw weather of the streets, the shop had an even more cozy air than usual. My eyes flitted quickly about the shelves, searching for my book. Every inch of space was crammed with books and magazines and record albums, newspapers and pamphlets, even T-shirts, all of it in intelligent and attractive order, plus boxes of hundreds and hundreds of buttons—GOD IS COMING AND IS *SHE* PISSED and LIBERATED MEN [WOMEN] ARE MORE FUN and I OWN MY BODY BUT I SHARE and MOTHER NATURE IS A LESBIAN—along with the pink triangles worn in Nazi death camps, made of ceramic; the lesbian books and material evenly divided on one side, where the fireplace was, the gay male on the other, by the entrance.

Being one of a multitude of poor writers, I rarely ever had money, as now, to buy anything, but enjoyed browsing through the latest publications anyhow, never once having felt hassled here, or even asked to check my duffel bag behind the counter as I had to in all the other bookstores in the city. Despite the small quarters, and the necessity of the locked door, the space seemed always filled with a large and welcoming friendliness. I felt, even though I was a stranger, that I belonged, that it was not only a bookshop but a meetingplace and information center for all of us.

In fact, it was through a notice I'd seen tacked on the floor-to-ceiling bulletin board at the back of the store a month earlier, announcing simply, "Faery Circle forming," with an address to write to, that I'd come into contact with the group of men I'd be spending the evening with. And only that summer I'd received a flyer through the mail from a visionary writer-friend out in San Francisco, announcing, "A Call to Gay Brothers" for "A Spiritual Conference for Radical Fairies . . . to be held at a desert sanctuary near Tucson" over the coming Labor Day weekend, but, intensely curious and excited as I was by the prospect—"exploring breakthroughs in gay consciousness, sharing gay visions, the spiritual dimensions of gayness"—and even though the handbill said "No one will be denied participation in the conference because of inability to pay," I was too broke to get there, without even the few bucks I'd need to hitchhike the long distance. But for days afterward I dreamed of the alluring promises listed in the flyer: "To dance in the moonlight . . . To hold, protect, nurture and caress one another . . . To find the healing place inside our hearts . . . To soar like an eagle . . . to sing, sing, sing . . . ."

3

Well, I sighed, thinking about it again, perhaps I would find something of that tonight at our Saturnalia, as I'd found parts of it already at several of the gatherings of the Fairy Circle I'd been to.

But I wouldn't be meeting with them til quarter to eight, and I had purposely arrived in New York a few hours ahead of time to try to get to as many bookstores in the Village as I could, partly out of vanity, partly to spread the word about it, hoping, since I was actually shy about hawking it, to see my new novel on display in as many shops as possible, which I didn't expect would be an overwhelming number, since it had been published by a small press out in California.

I was secretly pleased now not only to spot my book here at Oscar Wilde, but to see that it was also prominently visible on the shelves near the counter, along with, as in the window, other recently released titles.

I glanced timidly at the women behind the counter, who were talking quietly to each other. They seemed, as always, amicable and certainly obliging to the customers, including myself whenever I dropped in on my rare visits to the city and asked them for information on this or that book or magazine, wishing I could afford some of the books I could only leaf through, promising myself now that with my first royalty check, however small—and it would probably be just that since the first printing, of necessity, had been small—I'd make a special trip down and splurge as much as I could. I didn't know their names yet, nor they mine, nor had I told them I was a writer, being shy about that, too, so naturally they had no way of knowing my book was for sale in their shop.

I was dying to know if it was selling and, if so, how many copies they'd sold so far, but was afraid to ask for fear of finding out they hadn't sold any at all!

Inhibiting me more than this, though, was the doubly imposed habit of invisibility, a carryover from a deeply entrenched closet mentality, as invisible faggot, as invisible writer, which I was slowly, like rigid and artificial boundaries, erasing in myself, but which was still operating here I found, even in this amiable, open bookshop, where I didn't need it at all, this wanting to see without being seen, this keenly developed lifelong habit of observing while being unobserved, of perceiving the world as accurately as possible for the sake of survival, without really being in it, without really feeling a part of it. A slow and patient process, but for some time now I've felt the fragmented face, the splintered spirit, slowly knitting, the hostile, alien boundaries in myself dissolving. But I realized, in that moment of hesitation, unable to ask that simplest question of the women behind the counter, how far a way I still had to go.

And what if I was to make myself known to them, offer to sign copies as a gesture of friendliness and to help maybe boost sales, there was still another consideration: Wary as to who they let in, the two women might think I was an impostor, just another crackpot off the street going around posing as an author, and how could I prove, even though they'd let me in now several times, that I wasn't one more nut?

So I kept my mouth shut and moved quietly and anonymously among the shelves of books, squeezing my way between the other browsers, until I came to the paperback with the photo of the entrance to the old Everard Baths on its dusk-blue cover (suggesting "blue movies," the publisher had joked), stacked on the top shelf—not far from the cash register, I noted with satisfaction.

I beamed at it, my first openly gay book, like a cherished newborn child, mightily pleased, and pretended to study the covers of the other works around it, even picked up the one next to it—*A Lover's Cock, and Other Gay Poems* written by Verlaine and Rimbaud—and idly leafed through it, but only as a ruse so that I could actually peer eager-eyed over the tops of its pages, keeping close watch on my own book, waiting impatiently for what I knew must be, never having experienced it before, that exhilarating moment when a curious browser, a total stranger—I could foresee the moment charged with the same erotic excitement as a chance pickup in cruising—would not only pick up a copy of my novel and read, with avid interest, of course, here and there through it, but actually take it to the cash register and shell out the four bucks to *buy* it.

At that thought, *A Lover's Cock*, opened randomly to Arthur and Paul's "Sonnet to the Asshole," trembled excitedly in my hand.

Although there were at least a half dozen other customers in the shop—a sizable crowd for the crimped quarters of the Oscar Wilde, the two or three women, bundled up, sensibly enough, like Eskimos, sticking, also sensibly enough, with the lesbian books on the other side—the men passed by my book with blind indifference, if they came near it at all, which most didn't. Most of them picked up the recently released paperback edition of the successful *Dancer from the Dance* and waltzed with it up to the cash register, I observed, with a pinch of that envy which, along with poverty, is a bane to writers.

The doorknob rattled and the other woman behind the counter—they seemed to take turns opening the door—the one with shoulder-length brown hair and an intense amiability, darted up to peer through the glass, then, apparently satisfied, unlocked the door.

Over the edge of *A Lover's Cock* I saw a youth with slicked down hair of the fifties wearing a sheepskin jacket, straightleg Wranglers and cowboy boots, looking like he'd just ridden in from the Boots & Saddle bar down the block, come hurrying through the door without a word, rubbing his bare hands together from the cold and apparent self-consciousness. He glanced at me quickly from under his brows and I, just as quickly, stared down at the book in my hands, not wanting to blow my cover. "Dark, puckered hole . . ." I began to read, the opening line of Paul and Arthur's sonnet, but was too distracted to concentrate and, afraid of missing anything, lifted my eyes over the page again to peer surreptitiously at my own book and then at the youth who had just come bustling in.

He exuded a harried, nervous energy and appeared flustered, when, after a cursory glance at the other books lined along the top shelf, much to my amazement, my heart pounding, my face flushing in inconspicuous delight, his hand reached straight to where my book was stacked and he took down a copy, scanned the cover, flipped it over, briefly read a line or two of Ginsberg's statement on the back, then, abruptly self-conscious again, his eyes shifting nervously—perhaps he sensed my watchful eyes boring in on him from behind—as he went to thrust the book back on the shelf, it suddenly slipped from his hand.

I gave an inward gasp and had all I could do to restrain myself from thrusting out my own hands to catch the book, much as a parent would a falling child. Clumsily, a little red in the face, glancing apprehensively at the clerks as if he might be scolded, he snatched the book off the floor and slapping it quickly—brutally, I thought, wincing—back in place, turned on his high booted heel and skedaddled out the door as fast as he'd entered.

I watched him go, puzzled by his behavior, wishing he hadn't been such a rattled cowpoke, who, from the looks of his cowboy drag, had probably never been farther West than West New York, New Jersey, and who was maybe a little confused being in a big city gay bookstore, no matter how pint-size, maybe for the first time.

Anyway, he was the closest anyone came to even glancing at my book, let alone touching it, and I decided, for the small comfort it gave me, that that brief moment, however highstrung and nerve-wracking, was at least better than nothing. Some attention had been paid.

It was now just after four, the light outside the shop windows fading fast in the abbreviated day, the sun setting at 4:29 today according to this morning's *Times,* and I realized if I wanted to check out some of the other bookstores in the neighborhood before going to the Saturnalia (we'd been told to get there promptly for the ritual massage), I'd better get started.

Reluctantly, hating to leave so comfortable a place, shivering already at the thought of how cold it would be just outside the vestibule door, I slipped *A Lover's Cock* back on the shelf, hitched up my duffel bag, went around and took a quick look at new titles on the women's side, making note of Judy Grahn's *The Work of a Common Woman* and Sally Gearhart's *The Wanderground*, impecuniously gathered up all the free lesbian and gay newspapers and literature scattered across the very bottom shelf near the door, crammed them into my bag, waved goodbye to the women at the counter, who smiled and waved in return, and headed out the door, vowing that next time I'd be nervy enough to make myself known to them. Having stepped out of practically all my other closets, my book about the baths just about closing all those doors behind me forever, it was high time I stepped out of this one too, particularly in a place I felt so much at home in. Old habits of invisibility die hard.

Once outside on the steps, a rush of wind caught me off balance, so that I had to grip the wrought-iron railing for support, its metal as cold as an icicle. Flurries were forecast with northwesterly winds up to thirty miles an hour, with stronger gusts, the temperature in the teens, a conservative prediction since the elements felt at that moment, to my bones at least, in a deeper freeze than that. I quickly rolled down my face mask, slipped on my wool-lined gloves and trotted down the steps, starting off toward Greenwich Avenue at a fast walk. Next stop was the Three Lives Bookstore up at Seventh Avenue and 10th Street, figuring I'd hit the Saint Mark's and East Side bookshops over on St. Mark's Place later, on my way crosstown. As I hurried along, I thought of

Wilentz's Eighth Street Bookstore and still mourned its closing after more than thirty years in business, selfishly perhaps, knowing they would have put my book in the side window reserved for small press publications.

Stopping suddenly in the middle of the sidewalk, I was hit with the idea of the backroom bookshop down at the corner of Christopher and West which, with its hardcore films, magazines, toys and peepshow booths in the rear, was mainly a sex shop, I knew, but I remembered they also sold a lot of paperbacks, strictly porn, as I recalled, not having been there for two or three years, but I began to wonder if, on a wild off chance, they just might have stocked my book. I remembered I'd even suggested the possibility to my publisher and had sent him their address from *Gayellow Pages*. After all, my novel did have a number of erotic passages in it, didn't it? and I thought that would be a cinch to interest their clientele.

It was ridiculous, standing there stiff with cold and straining to see in my mind's eye what I could remember of some of the books for sale there way back then. I could only vaguely recall the graphic graffiti of most of the covers, nothing at all like the cover of my book, which was staid by comparison, and nothing at all of the other kinds of books they sold, the serious and substantial kind, say, that the little Oscar Wilde supplied in generous abundance.

I glanced at my watch. It would probably be a waste of time but, since it wasn't too far out of the way, it wouldn't hurt to take a fast look inside, give it a try just to be sure. Besides, I was pretty curious to see what the place looked like now and what it might have to offer since my last trip there.

And so, even though it was a long hike in the cold, I turned around and headed west on Christopher, toward the river, back past the Oscar Wilde, giving one last appreciative glance at my book in the window, determining to circle back to the Three Lives afterwards, and then continue across town to the East 2nd Street loft where the Saturnalia was to be held, eager to get moving again in that rigor mortis wind.

I was surprised, in spite of the frigid temperatures, to see so many people on the street. Every couple of feet or so, young pushers sidled up to me, peddling, *sotto voce*, "Loose joints, loose joints." A Puerto Rican youth, hands shoved deep in his pockets, eyes tearing in the wind, murmured close in my ear, "Hey, my man, uppers, downers? Hash? I got 'em all."

"Black Beauties? Red devils? Yellow jackets? *Accc-idddd*," the last from a slim black in an emphatic hiss so tantalizingly whispered the word sizzled out of his mouth as it hit the cold air.

I hunched sideways in the wind as I scurried past, telling him no thanks, I was clean and dry and wanted to stay that way, that drugs had almost killed me once, and he replied, tailing me close, insistent—a bad day for business, no doubt about it—his silken, whispery voice carrying in the wind, "Li'l marijuana can't hurt you, man, proven scientific fact. How 'bout a joint or two? C'mon, man, get h-i-i-i-i-gh."

But I'd heard all that before, believed it myself once, had to, unable then to quit any of it, not knowing how and scared to, unable to envision a day without it, or how to get through a day, and maybe what he said was true, but I knew for me it wasn't and just kept on walking.

I passed the Bagel And cafeteria, its steamy windows filled with lush hanging plants, site, along with the Bowl and Board next-door, of the original Stonewall Inn, a blank spot on its brick facade where the wooden plaque commemorating the rebellion of June 1969 had once been before it was forcibly ripped off the wall and stolen, word goes, by a gay man who, for sóme unexplained reason, refuses to return it.

Across triangular Christopher Park in Sheridan Square, its benches and curbs as empty today of the usual daily crowd of winos and other addicts as the wintery white oaks within its iron-fenced enclosure were naked of leaves, through the bare branches and a thicket of street signs beyond the stiffly posed statue, green as mold, of Union General Philip Henry Sheridan himself (1831-88) in full military splendor, over on Grove Street above the Chemical Bank, I spotted the second floor offices of the Gay Men's Health Project and thought if the place only opened earlier—its hours started at 7:30 p.m. when I'd be well on my way crosstown—I would've stopped in for a VD checkup, something I always make a point of doing every few months when I'm down in the vicinity. I laughed to myself as I scuttled along, recalling the huge poster on one wall of the clinic with a blownup photo of Queen Victoria in full regalia, as severely disapproving as the bronze visage of General Sheridan in the Square below, and under it the caption: "Even Queens Get the Clap."

Opposite the entrance to the park the early rush-hour crowds were beginning to pour up the steps of the Sheridan Square subway station and fan out hurriedly down Seventh Avenue into the narrow streets, faces bent, coat collars clutched against the razor-sharp wind. Intermittent scatterings of snow blew down from the blackening, heavily clouded skies.

I cast a wary, sidelong glance down the well-worn steps leading into the Lion's Head, a writer's bar I used to hang out in, a "writer," like so many of the other habitués screwed to the barstools at the time, who could no longer write. I'd walked down those steps, and staggered up them, many a time, with an endless thirst all the bourbon Manhattans in the world could never satisfy, searching from bar to bar along Christopher, always uncertain what I was looking for, thinking it was sex, or what passed for sex in my condition then, and always ending up in strange rooms in the arms of men who were strangers, often never knowing how I got there or where I was.

Back over my shoulder was the flatiron-shaped Northern Dispensary (founded 1827) where Poe went for treatment, poor alcoholic, drug-addicted Poe, I thought, grateful to be sober myself that day after years of my own long and losing battle with the bottle, and felt sharp vibrations of pain emanate from the peeling brick walls, Poe's pain, and the pain of all the drunks, including myself, who had ever walked this street, before and since.

A skinny black youth hurried by me, hair in corn rows braided with a thin gold chain fastened at the top with a gold pin the shape of a flower, arms in a skimpy jacket folded tight across his chest, his sensitive, handsome face, inky blue, decorated with a scattering of tiny multicolored pasted-on sequins, glittering like stars in a nighttime sky.

It was so cold I didn't even pause to glance, as I usually did, in the windows of the numerous shops along the way, most of them trendily chic and camp, selling everything from movie memorabilia to the latest cuts in leather fashions; some, with their rarified air and profusion of *objets d'art*, modish carryovers of the tasteful shops that once catered to the stylish inmates of the pisselegant closets of the fifties. There were shops with names like The Scarlet Leather and the New York Leather Company and Leather Man and New York Man, and restaurants like Rumbul's and Duff's and *Le Petit Prés*; and there was the Christopher Street Flea Market, which was actually a smart and expensive-looking antique shop. There was a bakery called Kiss My Cookies, and another farther down the block, The Erotic Baker II, with a pair of enormous orange neon lips, parted wide, blazing in the window, a touch of warmth in the cold and darkening air.

When I came to David's Pot Belly beyond Seventh Avenue, I had to cross the street, never able to resist looking in the window. Nor had I ever gone inside, not only because I'd never been able to afford it but also not wanting to spoil the picturebox illusion from the streetside of the plate-glass window, if illusion it was, of the long narrow restaurant with its rich chocolate-dark interior gleaming with golden votive candles on tiny tables lining either wall, at which, as now, sat couples, mainly male, chatting animatedly, the place, as always, so cozy and inviting, especially now in this freezing twilight.

Warming me even more was a scene my mind flashed back to on a hot Sunday afternoon last summer when, right here on the sidewalk in front of the Pot Belly, a small crowd had gathered around a golden tanned, crewcut youth in tank top and sawed-off levis as he stood nonchalantly by the curb with a fat, somnolent python draped like a boa languidly around his bare shoulders, its mottled skin, green as pond scum, shining in the August sun.

I'd seen many gimmicks used over the years on Christopher Street and in Washington Square in the high art of cruising, from exotic canines to as much nudity as the law allowed, but, as other equally bronzed young men had crowded around to gingerly touch the serpent's skin, that was the first time I'd ever seen anybody not only airing but wearing their pet snake for tricking.

A sudden flurry of snowflakes stung my cheeks, bringing me abruptly back to the day, as I hurried on past Boots & Saddle with its three leonine gargoyles over the entrance, and looked quickly into the windows where red lights flickered in the dimly lit bar and young men—reminding me of the sheepskin-jacketed lad at Oscar Wilde—wearing fancy cowboy hats with curled brims, their long lean legs sheathed in tight denim, sat propped up in the windows like fantasy mannequins on display. Eyes narrowed to slits, they casually cruised a scant but hardier number of other costume cowboys in buckskin moseying by in the street below, who seemed purposely to slow their walk to glance up coyly in return and then, once past the windows, picked up speed to keep moving in the cold. Even out on the sidewalk I could hear the muted jukebox vibrating through the glass, the Village People shouting their way through "Macho Man."

It was another surprise, as always to me, to see the bars along the way so crowded so early, and on a weekday too, in contrast to my own drinking days in the Village in the fifties and sixties when I increasingly needed a constant supply of booze to fuel my own particular fantasies: in that mirror behind the bar I could be any-one or anything I wanted to be, except who or what I actually was. In those days, gay bar-life didn't get actively cruisy til later in the evening, and then mostly on weekends. But now, drinking and cruising seemed more of a full-time preoccupation.

Across from Ty's bar was the Solartone Sun Tan parlor—"Get Tanned Fast All Year Long!"—the clear, spare light of its window, with its rainbow arcing over the glass, brilliant as artificial sun-shine in a street that now, as I looked down along the river, was growing rapidly dusky as the faint and dying edge of the real sun shrunk down between the buildings.

Impossible to think, in the quickening dark, as the cold wind snapped against my face and occasional snow pelted it, of sum-mer sun ever returning to naturally bronze my own or anybody's skin again.

In the huge windows of Ty's, dark as sunglasses—perhaps, I fancifully imagined, to cut down the glare from the sun tan parlor across the street—I glimpsed the usual standup clientele, their boots and leathers and lumberjack drag making it look very much like a male impersonator's hangout; they appeared to be a crowd standing in an enormous waiting room with Western decor. Even their expressions were similar, like their outfits, as somber and stiff as the stuffed head of the antelope with its spiral horns and black leather patch some wag had placed over one of its glass eyes, mounted high up on the bare brick wall above their heads.

Down the block from Boots & Saddle, just before Bleecker, I recrossed the street and passed the Gessner tenements (built 1872), the facade, like the other buildings surrounding it, a grim, metallic tangle of fire escapes, and came upon three drunks lean-ing against its front.

One of them, stubble-faced, staggered toward me with the sly, contemptuous grin of the drunken panhandler, stuck out a puffy hand, lavender from wine and the cold, and muttered in a slurred voice, "How 'bout a quarter, pal?"

As I shook my head he guffawed something back over his shoul-der at his cronies about "fuckin' stingy queers," but I hurried on, thinking, Poor sonofabitch, quickening my step as an additional shiver, not from the weather this time, went through me, knowing how it was to need a drink. If I'd had it to spare, I'd have given it to him, but I knew I needed every cent I had to put up at the baths for the night after the Saturnalia, since I wouldn't make the last bus, and for subway and bus fare home the next morning.

A young black man ambled toward me, dressed in shawls and skirts, even an elaborate headdress, all crudely sewn together from soiled bath mats and carpet runners, obviously found in the trash. The whole improvised patchwork gown, heavy-woven rag rugs ideal for the weather, was so loosely basted together it looked, as he sashayed along, lifting his feet dainty as a cat in wet grass, in imminent danger of becoming unstitched and collapsing in a pile around his ankles with every step he took. Not to mention the wind, which snatched at the rugs and flapped them up and down, giving them a good shaking.

Four glistening black sausage curls, two on either side of his forehead, peeped out from beneath the carpet turban, bouncing against his brow as he swayed along, for all the cold, in his dignified, unhurried gait, cooing and talking to himself, his big dark eyes rolling in impish and humorous flirtation at every male he passed, running his tongue over his lips, the dark rich skin of his cheeks tinged gray in the biting air.

But he didn't seem to mind the cold, or even notice it at all. In one hand he clutched a plastic shopping bag crammed with what looked like all that he ever owned, and I thought of the shopping bag ladies, trudging ghosts of fiercely independent women, who lived on the streets and slept in doorways and the waiting rooms of bus and train stations, when the cops didn't run them off, and wondered if this young man wasn't a new, and certainly original, variation, if you'll forgive me, a bag fag in carpet drag on Christopher Street.

Walking stately in his carpet scraps as if wearing the loveliest of diaphanous raiment, he murmured affectionate phrases to everyone he met, women and men alike, even the foulmouthed children from the nearby schools on Hudson Street, clutching their books, eyeing him merrily and mockingly as they scampered around him, a street-character evidently well known to them. In the deepening dusk, everybody seemed to be hurrying to get home out of the cold as quick as possible. He crooned to me, too, as I scurried along, "Well, *hello*, darling!" and I waved and smiled, then ducked in a doorway to get out of the wind and whipped my notepad and ballpoint pen out of my duffel bag, writing down a quick sketch of him. *Very* quick, since, within seconds, my bare fingers—my gloves were too thick to write with them on—were so stiff with cold I could barely hold the pen. Already the brief day was beginning to close down entirely, making it hard even to see what I was writing, but I did manage to scribble a few key phrases I could flesh out later on, when I found warmer quarters.

I stowed the pen and pad back in the bag and clapped my hands together briskly to get the circulation going in my fingers, and started off once more, now swinging my arms in wide circles to keep the blood pumping fast.

A flock of sparrows scrabbled noisily over a pizza crust tossed in the gutter. All of us barometers of blood, I thought, watching them peck hungrily, lifting and falling in all weathers, like these frantic birds sensing the minute changes in pressure in the thin hollows of their bones, instinctively knowing that if they don't get enough to eat on a day like this, they die. Like the panhandling drunks, street-sparrows of another kind, needing their pints of wine, their blood, just to stay alive through this coming night. I shuddered, thinking, so many kinds of death, here, on the street, so much feeding off scraps, off each other, like the pushers, feeding off addicted blood.

The wind rushed between the buildings with the roar of a subway express, scattering the birds, knocking me momentarily backwards, but I slung my bag over my shoulder and faced into it, bending double at the waist, and pushed on toward the river, a patch of water the color of steel locked frozen between the spires of St. Veronica's and the old waterfront Christopher Hotel down near the Morton Street Pier in the distance.

Hard to believe this same narrow street, now so bleakly cold and relatively empty, could be packed from curb to curb from the river to Sheridan Square the last hot, sunny Sunday each June (in ten years, it's never rained on the day of our parade) with tens of thousands of exuberant lesbians and gay people of all ages and colors lining up to move out in the annual Christopher Street Liberation Day March up Fifth Avenue.

Even in such weather, there was a crisp flirtiness in the eyes of men passing me, eyes shining with cold, the bold, open glance locking mine for just that split second longer than any casual observance; nakedly, drily cruising or clear-eyed and direct in recognitions which were swift unspoken exchanges of visual greeting and appraisal. They warmed my heart.

How different these eyes were, I thought, from the victimized eyes of my youth, my own included, on this very same street, in harder times, pre-Stonewall, the life of the street then lived largely underground, visible only through windows, unobstructed by law, of gay bars such as Mary's and the Main Street and the Colony over on 8th Street, the San Remo down on MacDougal, the Stonewall here on Christopher, Julius' on West 10th, bars that were cages actually, illusory sanctuaries.

Behind those windows, like fishtanks on the real world, we literally drank like the proverbial fish, staring glassy-eyed through those panes which, no matter how small and screened with neon beer signs, seemed always too large and exposed to keep out prying outside eyes, enemy eyes in faces that always resembled our mothers and fathers, brothers, sisters, our aunts and uncles; the life moving past out on the dangerous street a visual reminder of all the estranged and hostile streets waiting for us just the other side of the glass, the enemy territory we all grew up in, the bars, outside our closets, really only slightly larger closets, the only places left to hide in. And danger always there inside, of police raids, of police entrapment, of picking up a charming thief or extortionist, or a rabidly homophobic murderer disguised as trade—or worse, as even one of ourselves, prey and fair game to any and all. And for lesbians much worse: total invisibility through erasure, another kind of murder.

We drowned ourselves nightly in these falsely safe aquariums, and, sadly, still do, alcohol, drugs, always there to blur in underwater vagueness what lay beyond the neon-lighted windows, getting blind so as not to see, if only for a few hours—except to envision the host of fantasy selves appearing in an increasingly drunken kaleidoscope in the mirror behind the bar, or, distortedly, tipsily romantic, in the fractured eyes of each other. The police, when they weren't raiding such places, strutting freely in among us, stiff-faced, stiff-gaited, always silently menacing, their thick guns strapped on their hips, come in for their "protection" money, the legal shrinkage of our lives, their profit; and none of us protected, none of us safe, anywhere, at anytime.

Pinched lives then, lived behind walls in isolated, glittering closets behind these same charming early nineteenth-century brick facades here on Christopher, if you had money enough. The Puerto Rican street-queen, the street-faggot and the street-dyke, with nothing left to lose, circa 1969 and before, the real guerrillas, starting the running battles at Stonewall and elsewhere for what little ground has been gained up til now. But in those days, out on the street, the glances that met yours were furtive and harried, exact fear always standing bugged behind those sneakily cruising eyes with the large unasked question: Can I trust you? Will you hurt me? There were so few to trust, and many of us, in terminal self-punishment, always out on the final cruise, unconsciously searching for our murderer.

And yet, faggots, from Gay Street to the West Side Highway, were the first to keep attack dogs in their apartments. Resilient, cunning, adaptive, all of it rooted in the safekeeping of pleasure and affection, these quicksilver guardians, I sometimes think, will be the last survivors.

"Loose joints, loose joints," whispered a youth with gold-tinted glasses and sparse beard, leaning, in his thick-knit maroon sock hat, against a parking meter, one leg of his grimy painter's pants tied with a bandana handkerchief at the knee, his extra supply bulging above it; not only a practical way to hold his stash, but in the event of a street-bust, a quick slip of the knot and a kick of his leg under the car parked at the meter and the evidence was gone in the gutter.

"Loose joints!"

I turned my head away and kept on walking.

In contrast to the number of men, there were very few women on the street; even in balmier weather, Christopher Street had become primarily a gay male ghetto. But even these women, many of them bundled up in practical heavy coats and substantial baggy jeans, had a different look from those of even a few years back, a new expression in their eyes, bold and assertive, walking by jauntily in purposeful, assured strides, sturdy shoulder bags swinging, open faces free of the tightening masks of concealing makeup. They, too, like most of the faggots they passed, no longer chose to be victims, many of them young, vital, healthy-spirited lesbians, unlike the stereotype butches and femmes walking these same streets a decade or more ago who were forced to hang out in places like Mona's, across from Tony Pastor's, over on Waverly Place. In those days, unable to dance with each other since same-sex dancing was against the law in the fifties—as was our very presence in such a bar in New York City where no more than five "homosexuals" were permitted to gather in a public place serving liquor—we gay guys danced with the femmes with their Maybelline eyes and flimsy, crushable cocktail gowns, while their cigar-smoking butches, in windsor-knotted ties and pinstripe business suits with padded shoulders and wide lapels, sat at the little round tables beside the dance floor in the dingy backroom, looking on with grim-faced pride at their women dancing in our arms.

Now a familiar figure approached, his corpulent body, bloated from booze, dressed only in a thin black raincoat, its front stiff with grease, its buttons missing, so that he kept his fists clenched in the pockets to hold the flaps closed. He had panhandled me a few times in the past, here and on adjoining streets, and each time I'd given him whatever I could, knowing, as I said before, what it is to need a drink. Once, in talking with him, he told me they called him "Bambi," and I could immediately see why, because his eyes were large and doe-shaped, like the fawn's in Disney's animated cartoon, prettily lashed eyes he could easily and quickly work a look into of sadness and pathos, enough to soften the hardest heart and loosen the tightest wallet.

He snatched a hand out of his pocket now and thrust it at me, the wrist poking out through the frayed cuff so thickly swollen it was creased with fat, his enormous bloodshot eyes giving me one of those hurt and vulnerable looks I'd seen leap so rapidly into his eyes before, even a large tear welling up in each, whether by design or from the cold I wasn't certain, and so I wasn't all that moved. And yet, much as I wanted to help him, I knew, as with the other drunk, I couldn't, not if I wanted a cheap place to stay for the night and to get back home tomorrow, and took his hand, the flesh of it bluish from wine and the near-zero wind, and told him I hadn't a dime to spare.

"Aw thass awright, honey," he mumbled, a smile cracking his chapped lips, his voice as gentle as his bleary eyes, in its tone remnants of an unmistakable gay timbre, besottedly muted, and all but lost in the fierce noise of the wind careening through the street.

I hastened on, eager to get away, not only because of the discomfort of the cold, but mostly because of the still green and vivid memories he, and all such street drunks, aroused in me, of the hopeless drunk I once was myself, on these very same streets, and was thankful to be no longer.

As I rushed along in the thickly gathering dusk, I breathed a silent prayer to Bacchus that Bambi, and all the other drunks along Christopher, and along all the streets and avenues throughout the city, would collect enough quarters to buy their bottles before nightfall when the longest cold dark of the year would set in, iron-hard with arctic winter.

Spotted here and there along the way, an occasional hustler leaned against a railing or against the corner of a building, each dressed in variations of leather and levis to suit every conceivable taste. One, in a black stetson, with red cheeks and nose, broad shoulders scrunched up, his hands tucked deep in his pockets against the cold, provocatively waggled his fingers either side the bulge in his tight levis at passing prospects. Mostly these were businessmen with briefcases hurrying by in the direction of the PATH station beyond Hudson Street, who looked more intent on catching a train home across the river to Jersey than stopping for any sexual dalliance, and bargaining about it to boot in the freezingly bitter twilight.

He waggled his thumbs at me as I went by and I smiled at him—it even hurt to smile in this cold—and lifted my palms up, empty, to show him I was broke. His no-nonsense eyes, erotically blunt, narrowed on me as I scurried by, his handsome face as stiff as the day.

At Bedford Street, one of the numerous crooked lanes laid out from cowpaths when the Village really was a village, I glanced down the block in the direction of Chumley's, where Poe drank in the 1840s, its door still unmarked from later speakeasy days, another old writer's watering hole where I'd tied on many a drunk. Then passed McNulty's, where the aroma of fresh ground coffee was so strong, after so many years it seemed rubbed into the very wood of the shopfront itself, even escaped through the tightly sealed windows and could be smelled out in the street in passing, even on such a nose-numbing day. It was here in this shop a young friend of one summer's affection—one of those crocus romances, open one morning, gone by evening, but lovely enough for all its brevity; he left for San Francisco in the fall—had once bought me a gift of lemon grass tea, the remembrance of it summoning forth in my nostrils its hot citrus fragrance, lessening the bite of the icy wind.

Another young hustler standing in a doorway just beyond McNulty's looked very much like he could use a cup of that same tea right then and there, or a cup of something hot. His eyes watery, his cheeks blue with cold, he slapped his hands together loudly at his crotch, for warmth, and to draw attention. His head bared, the wind raked through his short cropped hair, cut punk-rock style, a studiedly surly expression on his sallow face, as he leaned against the building, one hip canted enticingly, the cheap, vinyl-shiny jacket he was wearing, made to appear like leather, much too thin for such brutal weather. As I hurried past, the image of Rimbaud, still fresh in my mind from the Oscar Wilde, leapt before my eyes, the early daguerreotype of him, the same flat-eyed, defiant expression as that in the face of this young hustler, who I could see was visibly shivering, clenching his teeth to keep them from chattering.

Below Hudson Street, posed under the antique curving marquee of the PATH train entrance, stood a long-haired willowy figure in dance pants, a long scarf wrapped several times around a long, thin neck and trailing dramatically on the ground, its back against the cutting wind, the eyes, shaded green, languorous and inviting, the message unmistakable. Impossible to tell whether male or female, transvestite or transsexual, in the limbo light, no longer day and not quite evening, filtering down now over Christopher Street.

Block after block of the century-old brick tenements looked even sootier and more weather-begrimed in the failing day. And on either side of the darkening street, stretching toward the Hudson, the harsh white lights of the apartment house entrances and the softer, warmer lights in the windows of the boutiques and bars glowed more visibly now. At the end of the street, the slash of a winter-orange sunset was caught an instant between buildings far down by the piers, then faded rapidly.

Also framed there, beneath the elevated span of the closed and slowly disintegrating West Side Highway, the river visible beyond it, moored vivid against the sparkling, jittery lights of the far Jersey shore, was the bright hull of the training ship *S.S. John W. Brown II*, reminding me of the oceangoing cruise ships that sail out of Pier 40 just to the south of Morton Street Pier, their hulls painted brilliant white to deflect the tropical suns they steam under, the envious thought in itself enough to warm me as I finally approached West Street and my destination.

The front of the shop facing the river was painted a sunny lemon-yellow, no doubt to appease, and possibly mislead, the parents of the neighborhood who had vehemently protested that it was a source of corruption to their children—a few of whose saltier obscenities overheard back up the street were still ringing in my ears—when the bookstore opened in the vicinity of the neighborhood schools, and had long tried, unsuccessfully, to shut it down.

For all the crisp, sunshine brightness of its exterior, the place, with its boarded over windows, had a sealed, sepulchral look. If you had no notion what the place was, and what went on there, I suspect even the most adventurously curious would hesitate to enter, it had such a shut and forbidden look. The boldly lettered sign on the otherwise blank door itself, ADULT GAY BOOKSTORE NO MINORS ALLOWED, gave me a momentary sensation of puritanical queaziness on approaching the forbidden. Warily, casting my eyes right and left at absolute, and absolutely oblivious, strangers, who I was sure, nonetheless, all knew where I was heading and what I was up to, I hurriedly pushed open the door and got myself inside and out of sight as quickly as possible.

After the noise of the wind the interior of the place seemed eerily hushed, welcomely overheated, too, after the biting cold of the street. I rolled up the mask of my sock hat, not wanting to be mistaken for a possible bandit again, as at Oscar Wilde. Since the front door was unlocked here, the owners evidently felt more secure: Was there a direct alarm to the police station, I wondered, in case of robbery or harassment? Or did they pay protection money? Surely they had to, I figured, to stay in business.

I took off my gloves and stuffed them, along with my hat, in my duffel bag, then looked around cautiously, feeling my muscles stiffening in nervous apprehension, my face burning in the sudden change from extreme cold to extreme heat.

On the lefthand side of the shop, at either end of a row of glass display cases, three clerks, all looking Hispanic, sat behind the long raised counters, from the higher vantage point better able to spot pilferers, no doubt, and to keep an eye on the clientele. Huge convex mirrors, pointing down at the customers at all angles, were also spotted here and there around the ceiling, one noticeably at the opposite end above the turnstile leading into the backroom, the open entrance to the latter a smudge of shadow in the rear wall. I quickly averted my eyes from it, feeling a quiver of uncertainty.

The clerks lounged behind the counters, joking, one of them in a sly and exaggeratedly nelly voice teasing another who was amusing himself playing with a battery-powered, handheld game of some kind.

"Don't talk to me in English," complained the clerk with the game, petulantly, "you know it gives me a headache." And the other two laughed and spoke in Spanish thereafter, continuing to rib him.

There was only one other customer in the shop, a bespectacled youth bundled up in scarf and overcoat and wearing a knit cap pulled down over his eyes—since it was so hot in the shop, I wondered if, trying to conceal as much of his identity as he could, it was an unconscious mask. He stood down at the magazine section on the right, picking up one magazine after another and, holding each one close to his face, pored eagerly and carefully over the naked details of the men on the covers.

Hundreds of magazines, stacked in floor to ceiling open racks, were sealed in tightly wrapped cellophane or had clear plastic covers slipped over them to keep them smudge-free and, probably the main reason, to discourage overlong and unprofitable voyeuristic browsing. Signs along the rack warned patrons not to take the magazines out of their protective covers, adding COPIES AVAILABLE FOR SALE AT COUNTER.

Between the magazine racks was a row of tall, brightly lit glass cabinets where videotapes and 8mm films—*For the Man who likes Big Men*—were on display. These more expensive items were locked behind sliding glass doors, the stills of sucking and fucking reproduced on the lids, shot from all angles, in every imaginable position and combination, of bareskinned youths all of the same shade of tan, only to be looked at through the highly polished glass, til purchased.

I moved slowly past the magazine racks with their wide and varied titles, names like *Cowboys, Wildboys, Hot Ones, Forced Entry, The Rawhide Male,* and *Butch.* There was even one, stashed up near the ceiling out of hands reach, called *Man's Best Friend,* its cover a graphic photo in color beginning to fade, of a nude man reclining beneath the haunches of a muscular dog he was fellating.

Most of the glossy cover photos, however, were of nude young men (none appeared to be over 25, and many a good deal younger), their bodies, in faulty color reproduction, a uniform sausage-pink, their torsos smeared with shiny baby oil the better to catch and accentuate the photogenic highlights of muscular curves and bulges, which gave to their oil-slick flesh the unintended texture and gleam of overroasted pork rind.

The detailed shots vividly showed minutest purple capillaries threading along glistening shafts, many fully erect, most grotesque in size, muscular muscles of blood with straining veins. Photos titillating and yet so clinical in their details, leaving nothing to the imagination, they collectively gave off as chill and austere an emanation as that of the atmosphere permeating the air of the shop itself.

And for all their colorfulness, their vividness and technical sophistication, there was also an absence of affectionate humor, of the genially erotic, giving the photos a stiff and mechanical air. The shop itself breathed that same severe aura, a cold ambience despite its tropical heat, and this, paradoxically enough, in spite of all those countless photo reproductions in hot and flesh-warm tones, exposed in practically every inch of space, seemed to leach out of the room whatever tinge of warmth there was in a curious erasure of color.

Perhaps it was that earlier mentioned puritanical conditioning rising to the surface again, but I, too, felt drained of color, feeling as chalky and cold as the rays of the ceiling spotlights aiming their wan and agitated light down on all the paraphernalia below. A chill went through me, as if I'd suddenly stepped into a walk-in freezer, all those starkly naked bodies coldly on display like sides of meat hung up for my impersonal inspection.

Although the stock was enormous, there was an ascetic spareness in the layout of the place. Perhaps all this severity, this separation of feeling from the senses and absence of inviting, pleasurable color, was strictly and purposely designed to arouse reactions of guilt in the spectator in the awareness that, for many of us, particularly those still locked in their closets, guilt is inseparable from pleasure, and costly. In observing the expensive price tags on most of the items, I couldn't help connect with the fact, in more ways than one, that, as an inheritance from our puritan fathers, forbidden pleasures did not come cheap.

By now several other customers had entered, faces red and eyes watering from the cold, each browser concentrating intently on the merchandise in silent absorption, standing carefully apart from each other. There were no occasional friendly scraps of talk here, nor even the customary exchange of "pardon me" of bookshop etiquette when someone passed in front of you at the shelves. The clerks, from their high places behind the counters, watched wordlessly now or, perhaps to break the heavy tedium, sometimes kidded each other, but there was no bantering back and forth with the customers, no cheery or amiable conversation as with the clerks at the Oscar Wilde. After the initial surface excitement, the covers of the magazines and the films gradually made me feel more and more cut off and alone.

One glance down the center island of shelves where most of the paperbacks were lined up was enough to tell me, my eyes quickly scanning a few of the enormous number of titles available, such as *Cornhole Buddies, Rock Lance's Hotrod,* and *The Count of Monty Crisco,* their sexually direct cover drawings of scantily clad, muscle-ballooning men with baskets and buns so outrageously exaggerated they were like deformities, that my little book with its pale blue cover, which would have looked *very* pallid among the lurid, eye-snatching covers on display, was nowhere in sight.

I had to laugh at myself, for my naive foolishness in thinking it might be on sale here, realizing, sap that I was, that I should have listened to myself in the first place and gone directly on to the Three Lives instead of wasting my time coming here, making the long trip down Christopher Street in all that cold weather for nothing.

Since I *was* here and it was *warm* inside, I thought I might just as well stay a little while longer, at least til I thawed a bit, and then head out again for Seventh Avenue, rested and fortified to face the icy winds again.

Curious, not having much familiarity with such books—my preferences leaned to the pictorially erotic—I picked up one of the paperbacks, *Cocksure* by S. M. Stagg, opened it in the middle and read: " . . . Buck's long and beefy bloodred member throbbed like a dynamo of desire out of its thick, tangled bush of carroty crotch hair. Timothy, lying naked and tied spread-eagle on the bed in this cheap motel room in a sleazy honkytonk part of town, stared wide-eyed over his shoulder at that pulsing instrument of possible torture and undoubted delight. He emitted a low moan of terror and yearning. His creamy, hairless buttocks began to visibly quiver in a confused mixture of apprehension and lust as Buck advanced slowly toward the bed. Spitting in the palm of one hand and skinning the head of his cock back as tight as he could with the other, the huge empurpled crown of his manhood glistening under the naked lightbulb, his ruggedly handsome face split in a wicked grin . . ."

I shut the book, getting a slightly dizzying tingle in spite of myself, and put it back on the shelf. It was all nonsense, but you had to hand it to the author: He certainly accomplished what he set out to do, grabbing your attention and getting your glands going, all at the same time. "Jaggoff" fiction they called it—what one reviewer in an early review in the gay press accused my own book of being.

As with the magazines, I was amazed at the staggering number of titles for sale, wondering who churned it all out, a job like any other job, I guessed, the going rate $500 or so a crack as I remember some years back, when I was drunkenly contemplating the possibility of trying to earn some money at it, getting some pointers from a young writer in the Lion's Head who did just that for a living, grinding out a book or two a month to the porn publisher's specifications. But I decided it wasn't for me. Not out of any high-mindedness. I'd simply reached the point in my drinking where I could barely write anything at all, even my own name on the checks I passed over the bar to keep me going.

Still feeling the buzz of a turn-on from what I'd just read, and feeling guilty about it too since the passage I'd come on was none too subtle in equating sex with torture, I stole another uneasy glance toward the turnstile leading into the entrance to the back-room, the light framed there so shadowy it was almost opaque, the dim figure of a male flitting by, peering out like a curious ghost into the brightly lighted shop a moment before disappearing beyond the door.

I looked away, my heart giving a sudden start, realizing that although I'd been back there once before on a quick trip through out of curiosity my first time here those few years back, I surprised myself at how nervous I was at the thought of going back in there again.

The door swooshed open, blowing in a blast of frigid air along with the lilting sound of cooing soft giggles. It was the black youth in carpet drag I'd seen earlier out on Christopher Street, who now, clutching his bag in one fist up around his chest, shut the door carefully behind him and leaned against it a moment as he let out a long breath and a sigh.

The clerks exchanged glances.

Eyes and nose dripping, he looked like he'd come in just to get in out of the cold. Glancing covertly, shyly, to the left, in the direction of the clerks, as if waiting to see if they would say anything, and receiving only their silence—perhaps the bitterness of

24

the day tempered their response—seeing that he could stay, he adjusted his rags, which had been blown somewhat askew by the winds, more comfortably about his shoulders and waist, and strolled into the shop. Like it was a regular ritual, he set his sack on the floor by the pay phone, bending over it and smoothing out its plastic folds and creases, warming it with his hands, clucking quietly to it, like it was a living creature, some child or pet he carried about with him constantly.

Delicately brushing his curls aside with the tips of his fingers, he stood on one side of the island of paperbacks, diagonally across from me, and began to search the titles, but only pretending to, just as I had done a short time back at Oscar Wilde. Actually, his eyes were looking over the top row of books, that flirty light still dancing in them, glancing obliquely at me and also around at several of the other men in the shop, particularly the youth in the pulled down knit cap, who had now moved on to the film cabinets and was too intent on studying the photo-stills on the boxes behind the glass to pay any attention.

In the heat of the place his ragged garments began to thaw, and from across the island of books wafted the distinct mildewy odor of an abandoned cellar.

My own eyes sought to glimpse him covertly, trying not to be too obvious, turning myself into the invisible writer again as my mind swiftly registered further impressions of him to jot in my notebook as soon as I could, which would be difficult here, I knew. I had to restrain myself from scrabbling in my bag for pen and pad to scribble it all down. Instead, I observed the youth in carpet drag as circumspectly and minutely as possible, deciding to get it all down the first chance I got, away from all these everwatchful eyes.

I turned and walked over to the row of showcases, the glass, as was all the glass in the shop, impeccably polished, to look at the commodities displayed there, seeing that this side of the shop was devoted mainly to what are called "toys," including plastic, battery-powered vibrators in every size and shape, and dildos of mythic proportions in an equally wide variety of lengths and thicknesses, some with hard studs protruding like spikes all around the shaft or just beneath the neck of the crown, a few models having an attachment of a length of thin hose with a squeezable rubber bulb. Except for a few token chocolate- and saffron-tinted ones, this broad choice of plastic flesh, exact replicas right down to the very pores and tiniest veins, all had the color and texture of the skin of Barbie dolls.

I wondered if the dildos and vibrators were kept behind glass for sanitary reasons, to keep them away from the constant touchings of impulsive and curious hands. Then I got to laughing to myself, thinking such merchandise couldn't be behind glass to prevent their being stolen since, seeing the size of more than a few of them, it would be like trying to walk out of a bakery with a loaf of French bread concealed under your arm.

The dildos reminded me of my first visit to the shop, sometime in 1976, when one of the sales clerks, with giggling ooolalas, swapping eye-rolling smirks of delight with the other clerks, had unpacked and put on display on top of the counter an enormous redwhiteandblue dildo manufactured in honor of the nation's bicentennial. It looked, with its red cone head, white metallic shaft, and blue balls the color of jet flame, just like a space rocket poised for flight, a true replica, at least, of the not-so-hidden glandular spirit behind all the national hoopla at the time.

I thought of that time, as I continued to stroll past the showcases, eyeing each strange item with increasing curiosity, of that first time here, when the place had just opened, and I was being given a tour by that same friend who would later tutor me in my first trip to the baths and who seemed to know of the existence of all such places, even before they opened. There was no turnstile then and no admission charge to the backroom and, following close at his heels, I'd hurried nervously through what then seemed, in my naiveté, a confusing maze of passageways, remembering only men, mostly young, with pallid, expressionless faces in the murky light, who I innocently mistook for hustlers, lounging along the walls or in the doors of the viewing booths, seeming detached, yet watchful of everyone passing.

It had all been so strange and new, and I was so timid, so ignorant of the procedures there, it didn't occur to me until after we'd left that men actually had sex together in those booths, a slow realization I carefully tried to conceal from my more sophisticated friend, not wanting to show how green I was. Actually, I knew what went on behind the doors of the booths, since my friend had told me, but I found it hard to believe guys would take such risks, especially with the dangers of the vice squad, still being then very much in my 1950s head, having only recently awakened from my comatose sleep of alcohol and drugs to discover that a different, less uptight world had unfolded around me while I'd slept.

My mind was drawn back to the showcase as my eye became absorbed with a series of thick plastic cock collars and chokers, stimulators in a variety of sizes, with spikelike studs inside and out—similar to what De Sade mentions in his writings. Many of the objects, designed it seemed for every excruciating nuance of dominance and submission, including a few short-handled whips, looked like instruments of torture rather than enhancers of pleasure, and were a puzzle to me, sending shivers down my back, they appeared to have so much more to do with willful brutality and punishment than with erotic desire.

I had worked my way down to the crook in the long counter where, just above me, the clerk at the turnstile sat reading the pink classified ad pages of *The Advocate*, in between dispensing change and guarding the entrance to the backroom. A large sign behind his head warned NOT RESPONSIBLE FOR VALUABLES. I became captivated with an object lying flat beneath the glass top of this last section of the display case: an inflatable rubber man with glossily painted jet black hair, blue protuberant eyes, and a round pink mouth the size of a giant carp's, staring up at me through the glass of the bright fluorescent-lit case like a drowned fish in an aquarium. Myself, the face in the barroom glass a scant ten years before, and, shuddering in recognition, turned away.

I had now come full circle and discovered that the arousal generated by the movie stills and books and magazine covers had increased by degrees as I made the circuit, and had now skillfully guided me back to the turnstile where, for a buck-fifty—signs of inflation, but cheap enough, considering even the afternoon cut-rate bargain prices at some of the baths—I could enter the backroom and continue to heighten that arousal by watching the film loops in the viewing booths or work off some of my excitement with actual flesh and blood males behind the closed doorways of those very same plywood cubicles.

Suddenly I heard the voice, with its slight trace of a Puerto Rican accent, of the clerk sitting in his high perch behind the counter at the turnstile, petulantly scolding, "Please *do not* remove the plastic covers from the magazines!"

Looking up, startled by the abrupt sound in the heavy silence of the shop, I saw he was addressing, with flinty displeasure in his dark eyes, the youth with the sock hat pulled down over his brow.

He had evidently tried to seek a little reality beneath the plastic by dislodging one of the magazines from its protective sheath.

"This is *not* a library," the clerk admonished testily.

"I'm sorry, sorry—excuse me," mumbled the youth, tugging nervously at his glasses, his face genuinely contrite. He then fumblingly tried to insert the magazine back into its slip jacket as quick as he could, like a guilty boy caught in the act, very like the young cowboy who had dropped my book at Oscar Wilde. "Sorry," he repeated, what could be seen of his face beet-red as he finally managed to get the magazine tucked back in and up again on the shelf.

The clerk, somewhat mollified, his voice a little less harsh, said to him, "Just don't do it again."

And the youth, his shoulders hunched, his head ducked down in the collar of his overcoat, peeping uneasily left and right, continued to scrutinize the covers of the magazines, this time keeping his hands stuffed deep in his pockets.

Glimpsing him, I instantaneously, and begrudgingly, recognized a past and hidden aspect of myself when, my existence shrunk to the size of a bottle, my own faggot reality, such as it was, was also confined largely to these same glossy color photos of fantasy men who existed for me only on paper. They seemed, in their size, in their unobtainable beauty, such superior, godlike creatures who could do as they pleased and could have everything, and anyone, they wanted; spurs, in my obsessive comparison, in which I never measured up, goading me with perpetual dissatisfaction with everything I was, giving me the mentality and outlook of a slave, with all the self-mocking humor and all the hidden arrogance and burning resentment, the cynical irony.

Such glossy shadows have always been seductive reminders of my mistaken inferiorities, although I didn't know it then, manipulative signals raising my blood in feverish, and masochistic, lashings (self-abuse, in more ways than one), only slightly more powerful than the desire to draw blood. Sex, in time, became a form of revenge—the ancient male curse, a weapon, an angry fist, to beat myself and, obliquely, others with, til, twisted beyond recognition, it no longer had anything to do with sex and everything to do with my anger and envy and the struggle against the increasing shrinkage of light, my erasure in oblivion in those endless glasses, through booze, through speed and downs, in misperceived and distorted attitudes of who and what I was. Such photos, under the influence, led me astray, in directions away from myself, in directions away from the self, connected to life, I could never discover.

My fingers on all those endless ink-tacky pages of similar magazines, pages that never seemed to dry, giving back no warmth, no genuine sensation of touch, leaving smudgy fingerprints in false identity, as I tried, idiotically, to get from paper, from the cold light of blue movies, from the electric blue light of television screens, what I couldn't get, in a desert of taboos, from others, in scarcities of intimacy as harsh as any famine; my senses reaching out then in a vacuum of shadows, mocking and elusive, paper shadows, inky shadows, slipping out of my hands the moment I reached to grasp them.

No more shadows, I thought, looking back over my shoulder and surveying the racks and display cases. No more phantoms, my own or others, to stand between me and what's real. From now on I wanted to live my life blunt, unbuffered any longer by booze or drugs, to see and feel plainly what truth I could behind the phantasms surrounding me.

With each opening of the door a rush of icy air blew into the shop. A youth entered, his cropped hair cut punk-style but left in its natural mouse-brown color, not dyed pink and green or some of the other popular pastel combinations I'd seen on a few of the shorn heads of punkrockers hanging out in Washington Square. He was wearing an old maroon letter-winner's jacket with WYOMING in gold letters across the back, a bookbag slung over one shoulder, tears streaking out the corners of his eyes from the cold.

Without glancing either to right or left at any of the merchandise on display, he marched directly to the turnstile, handed his money up to the clerk, who then pushed a buzzer, releasing the bar, and the youth quickly shoved through the stile, entered the backroom, swung off to the right and was gone.

Then, barely a moment later, the door opened again, sending in another arctic blast, and two more men came in, one after the other, and just like the youth in the WYOMING jacket, headed straight for the turnstile and went right on through after paying their admission.

My heart beginning to race a little, I stared enviously after the last man as he pushed through the stile and entered that underground-seeming opening as nonchalantly as if he was entering the Sheridan Square subway station up the street. His and the others' apparent unruffledness gave me a measure of courage. Why not join them? I asked myself, hesitant, not only because of my reminiscences of a few moments before, and that old sexual uncertainty and fear of the unfamiliar, but also, more practically, because of the Saturnalia and a desire to save all my energy for that. I was reluctant to risk sapping my strength here; unwilling to wear myself out in whatever encounters I might chance upon on the other side of that glum but alluring doorway.

I glanced at my watch. Still almost two hours before I would have to leave for this evening's celebration. I *could* spend a little time back there, I told myself, only looking around, of course, not necessarily getting involved with anybody, before heading on to the Three Lives. In my head I counted the money in my wallet and the change in my pocket, just to be sure, and figured I could swing it, afford the entrance fee, if I bought a pound or two less of the fruit I planned to pick up at Village Produce on my way crosstown; or, better yet, I could go without breakfast on my way home next morning and still have just enough left for a cubicle at the baths that night. I felt a little guilty, thinking of Bambi and the other drunks out on the street I might have given the money to, but my mind was drifting more and more into the backroom, preoccupied with getting myself through that forbidding door, shy of its bleakness, shadow though I knew it to be, but still an impenetrable barrier I was timid and wary of, like a bird which will not fly into darkness.

The stills I was now gazing at sideways, and however distractedly, in the skinflick cabinets, soon began to exert the old familiar power over my senses and, as my pulse quickened and that well-known dryness tickled my throat, I started to feel the blood rush with erotic warmth through my veins. I flushed, prickling skin of my face, my neck, even the roots of my hair, tingling and burning as though I'd swallowed a massive dose of niacin.

Reaching into my pocket and counting out the exact amount in change, I hitched up my bag more snugly on my shoulder, shoved my chin forward, my pulse pounding harder with the excitement of my determination, and advanced on the turnstile, extending my money up to the clerk, who boredly turning away from the pages of *The Advocate*, and with that mystical buzz from his finger on the release button, allowed me to push through.

It actually did turn out to be as easy as going into the subway, and within an instant I had passed beyond the dark door and into the sparser light of the backroom itself which, although I'd been there before and it appeared not to have physically changed all that much, was still a totally different place altogether, as if I'd never been there at all.

I found myself in a wide, short corridor, and the first thing I saw after my eyes adjusted to the dimmer light was another large hand-printed sign on the wall: NOT RESPONSIBLE FOR VALUABLES—THE MANAGEMENT. I took my wallet out of my back pocket and zipped it up in a side pocket of my ski jacket, then feeling a little more assured, looked around.

It was like an anteroom, dimly but garishly lit by a large gaudy jukebox, a shiny chrome and plexiglass monster squatting in its dark niche just inside the entrance. Above it hung a large techni-colored poster advertising *Kansas City Trucking Co.*, a popular gay porn film. Men brushed by me, all heading in the same direc-tion—the movement here appeared to go counterclockwise, or widdershins, as we say in our Fairy Circle, contrary to the sun— toward a darker doorway beyond the jukebox, leading into the deeper, hidden areas of the backroom, passages lined with booths like inner sanctums.

In a recess, next to the jukebox, his face and body almost blacked out in shadows, a dim figure, probably just in from the cold and warming himself, lounged watchful on a low radiator against the wall, the tops of its metal ribs so smoothworn they had a polished edge in the glare from the jukebox.

Directly across the way was the partly open door of a toilet and next to it a padlocked door, a storeroom perhaps. A young man in a heavy lumberjacket leaned against it, keeping an eye on those entering through the turnstile and those going in and coming out of the urinal, keeping an eye on me, too, as I stood hesitating a few paces in from the entrance, getting my bearings.

In the dark doorway of one of the two large plywood movie booths on either side of the jukebox, the one nearest me, stood a tall young man in a down jacket, opened to reveal an unbuttoned plaid shirt beneath. He was casually leaning one shoulder against the jamb, thumbs hooked in his levi pockets, his head cocked to one side, idle and at ease, but his eyes, and the shine of his scrubbed, chiseled face in the wan glow cast from the jukebox, alert and alive to any newcomer pushing in through the turnstile. As I took a few steps into the area and passed him, he glanced sharply at me from under his lids, mechanically, briefly, and glanced away.

31

Men continued to move by me in a slow, careful walk, still funneling through the half-light of the doorway past the jukebox, faces expressionless, solemn—lust appeared grim and unsmiling here, just as at the baths—not much different from the faces I'd seen on my first visit, yet each pair of eyes having that same alert watchfulness as the eyes of the young man leaning in the booth, and the other by the jukebox, an intensity of scrutiny and swift appraisal that gleamed with an unmistakable light out of the heavy darkness.

Caught up now in the movement of traffic, I fell into step behind the others; the pattern here appeared to be you move on, you lean against a wall a while, you shift, you step into a niche, you try your luck in a different booth, you wait. Several men, like the youth in the WYOMING jacket a few paces on, I recognized from out in the shop as having pushed through the turnstile ahead of me. All were, as I said, heading for that doorway to the right, and when I passed through it myself I found it led into a narrow passage lit in a sallow powdery light from barely alive fluorescent tubes which gave everyone passing under them a chalky, shabby look. The ceiling was a dark confusion of wire and heating ducts, strings of grime, like Spanish moss, hanging from them, the dry hum of heat sounding in the dusty vents. The brick floor, worn to unevenness by the round-the-clock, years-long tread of feet, was littered with cigarette butts and popper wrappers and crumpled tissues, as if the place was never swept, perhaps there never was time for that, since the bookshop was open twenty-four hours a day, seven days a week; like the baths, it never closed its doors.

Just inside this doorway the barely visible outline of a man stood pressed in a shallow niche, silent and stiff as a mummy, only the sense of his eyes alive in the cellarlike dark. My eye was caught by flecks of whiteness down around his ankles where, for months, perhaps years—the place also looked as if it had never been painted, except by the stain of time, and nicotine and pot smoke—the scuffing heels of countless shoes and boots had chipped away the lower wall, baring the plaster beneath, incongruous spots like moths of light flitting startlingly in the pool of black shadow at his feet.

Next to this niche was a narrower viewing booth constructed of the same flimsy laminated wood, the exact same flammable-looking paneling, it occurred to me with a shudder, as the walls of the cubicles at the old Everard Baths.

In its door stood a man, his features and figure obliterated by the darkness, only the wide brim of his cowboy hat protruding beyond the opening. Opposite, on a wall worn and scarred by the continuous rub of buttocks and backs, someone had drawn, in white spray paint, a ghostly graffito of a huge erect cock with enormous balls, a zigzag of a lightninglike vein on the underside of the shaft, the whole of it glowing eerily disembodied in the dark passage like a primal stick drawing on the wall of an ancient cave.

One lad now leaned his broad shoulders and narrow hips against it as I crowded past him in the narrow space, his body slumped, the slit of his eyes, careful as lizards, observing the face under the cowboy hat in the booth across the way. Screwed to the wall next to the entrance to that booth were a pair of faded technicolor movie stills of naked young men posed in sexual acts, both photographs under heavy plastic in cheap wood frames. One still tantalizingly promised what you'd get to see if you dropped your quarter in one slot: TRUCK STOP—*Wild Action*; the other, what you'd see if you chose the other slot: THE NAIVE HITCHHIKER—*Hot Cum Shots*, all for the same price, and under each photo: *For the Man who likes Big Men.*

Above was a sign which read: ONE PERSON PER BOOTH — KEEP DOOR CLOSED WHEN IN USE, and under this, in smaller letters, *The films you are viewing can be purchased at the counter.* NO LOITERING PLEASE.

I sensed movement behind me and, turning, saw the broad-shouldered youth slip silently across the passage and, reaching a hand between the legs of the man in the cowboy hat, and receiving no rebuff, moved into the booth as the other stepped back, the two disappearing from view into the pitchblack interior.

Off to the right, a fair-sized corner nook was formed by the angle of the two corner booths. The light was even more meager here, but I made out what looked to be a youth and a somewhat older man embracing each other tightly, kissing passionately in front of a metal exit door, its dull paint chipped and scarred, even buffed in spots, like the wall behind me. I wondered what this door opened onto, perhaps the alleyway between the buildings.

The corridor made an abrupt turn to the left down a longer passageway of booths, four in all, two joined back-to-back on either side. Behind the shut door of the nearest one came the whirring hum of a projector, and the agitated light from the screen within glowed up through the perforated roof, illuminating the smoky air like firelight flickering out the top of a chimney.

Through the open doors of the other booths, barely defined in the gloom framed in each entrance, only their profiles visible, the heads of three men peeped out, each head turning, at my approach, as if attached to a single wire, quickly scanning me, then looking away, all three then turning in the opposite direction at the approach of other footsteps on the worn brick, then swiveling back again as one, as another man rounded the corner behind me, their heads constantly swinging right and left at the slightest tap of footsteps coming from either direction down this longer passageway, their heads like those of alert and everwatchful birds, their quick eyes bright in the sooty air.

I moved by them, like walking a tight gauntlet in this fissure of a corridor where you had to turn to the wall to let another pass, glancing covertly in at them, at their flat-eyed, immobile faces, eyes which again also glanced back at me, in closer inspection this time, and as swiftly looked away.

Now along the way, more nooks and crannies to stand and lounge in, to cruise and ogle and entice. To the left, in a dingy alcove at the end of the row of booths, stood a gray-faced man, his hair like ashes, head and shoulders scrunched back against the bricks, legs spread, a foot pressed against the base of either wall, his fly open, his fist so tight the flesh of his knuckles gleamed in the darkness as he pulled on his long flaccid prick. Behind his head, like a nimbus about his shoulders, another phallic graffito had been sprayed on the wall.

I wondered if that sunken space was a hangout favored by older or allegedly "unattractive" men, like the darker corners and cubicles at the baths, it was such a deep recess, so deep in shadow, it would blur the features, and years, of anyone who occupied it, more so than any spot I'd passed so far, including the booths. My nose acutely sensitive to it, a sharp and grainy whiff of alcohol wafted from the niche and trailed after me down the passage.

Just a few steps beyond, the passageway opened onto a more spacious area, the light here so bleak it was practically nonexistent. Through tiny cracks in an exit door slivers of the light still lingering out on the street shone in, but at first it seemed as though I'd stumbled into a large very dark closet. I waited a moment at the threshhold until my eyes adjusted to the almost total lack of light.

Nearer to me, with the help of the wan ceiling lamps in the passage behind, I could finally just barely make out men propped along the wall, eyeing me tentatively but carefully, observant of every movement around them, hands in pockets, fingers fiddling at crotches, lures to the eyes; or with thumbs slipped through belt loops, hands spread, fingers fanning idly over thighs, over flies, more lures, in a dance of hands, hooked fingers to attract a curious and baited pair of lips out of darkness heavy as water.

The aroma of marijuana permeated the air like burning hemp, orange coals sparking in the dark as several solitary smokers slumped along the wall, none of them, oddly enough, sharing their weed with anyone around them, as is usually customary, particularly at the baths. One man, closest to me, tall, Spanish-looking angular face with thin black beard and mustache, hungrily sucked in one toke after another.

Amidst the smoke, the chemical reek of poppers curled in the air like oil. There was the creak of boots, of leather jackets, the creak of patient waiting in the leathery darkness.

To my left, along a wall opposite this larger space, was another movie booth, apparently empty. Its open door, in this murkier air, looked like the gaping mouth of a bottomless shaft, as if once you stepped in, you dropped out of sight forever.

Now I could begin to see more splinters of light coming through around the edges of the exit door which had a tightly sealed look to it, but at its base I was surprised to observe a thin crack of waning daylight, startling, such natural light seemed so alien here in this dungeonlike atmosphere.

Equally surprising was to hear, on the other side of the door, the footsteps and voices of people hurrying by on the sidewalk outside, the twinkling shadows of their passing feet visible in the narrow slot of light; and to hear, too, the occasional swish of tires on asphalt and the squeal of brakes as cars stopped for the traffic light on the corner at West Street.

And above it all, the frequent roar of gusts of wind out on the street, and whistling in in low moans through the crannies around the door, which was the greatest surprise, the cold day seemed so distant now since I'd entered the hushed and overheated confines of this other, subterranean world.

As my eyes began to distinguish things a little more clearly in this darkest spot I'd come to so far in the backroom maze, I saw the others were intent upon watching, or what could be seen of them at least, four men, barely visible in the thick shadows, two of them standing side by side, each with his head thrown back against the door, eyes shut tight and legs spread wide, bared thighs smudges of white against the invisible blackness of their loosened clothes, which were indistinct from the dark door they leaned upon, each pair of hands cupping the skull of another man squatting before him, the hands of these two men, in turn, clasped behind their thighs for balance as they hunkered back on their heels, heads bobbing vigorously between luminously naked legs, both men bowed like ecstatic worshipers in a darkly sexual rite of supplication and adoration.

Above them, through the chinks in the door, the scratches of daylight vanished now, the reflection of passing headlights out on the street played across the cracked plaster of the ceiling, so I knew full darkness had now fallen and this longest night of the year begun.

Several of the watchers stood pressed in the corners, mute and stiff, while others leaned nonchalantly along the bricks, idly observing the little that could be seen. My erotic imagination, however, instantly lit the scene like a bonfire, so that the two standing, now bucking and rearing, and the pair hunched bowing and weaving before them, all burned with the redness of coals edged at the back of my eyes, and I could feel spreading again, as I had out in the shop, a renewed rush of desire which scorched my lungs with the rapidity of burning brush, my throat catching in sudden dryness. I wet my lips, squinting in the darkness.

Suddenly I froze, a nervous tingle of fear prickling the roots of my hair as the shrill squawking of a police horn split the silent air, sounding like it was coming from a patrol wagon pulling up just outside the emergency door.

My mind raced with images of the vice squad busting into the place through the front door, while also simultaneously breaking open this same emergency door the two men leaned against as they writhed and groaned, swarming in all the passages throughout the backroom, pounding on the doors of the booths, bullying, rounding us all up in snarling commands, the entrapments and dragnets and gay bar busts of the fifties still etched deeply in my brain; and although the unearthly staccato howling of the police horns of today in their mulelike heehawing are different from the slowly rising wails of the sirens back then, the bloodchilling effect on me was still the same.

I stood paralyzed as the horn continued to sound, louder and louder, rapidly seeking escapes in my head, realizing in an instant it would be foolish to try to use the emergency door here, for anyone breaking through it would surely plunge right into the hands of the cops waiting out on the sidewalk, covering all exits so no one escaped.

I glanced nervously, fleetingly, back over my shoulder toward the first exit door I'd come to in the corner of the passage, where I'd seen the couple embracing, wondering where it led, if it really did open out on the alley between the buildings, where I could still be trapped behind the high fence separating the backs of the apartment houses and the bookstore. I saw myself clambering up its chain links and over the barbed wire, to get away as quickly as I could, to escape being caught again as I once had years ago in San Francisco.

Tensed for flight, already in my mind's eye I was running back along the passage, yanking open the exit door, escaping behind the building, fence or no fence, at the first sign of trouble. I would pound on the first door I came to, ask to be let in so I could escape through the building, beg for sanctuary, if necessary. Would the clerks out in the shop warn us? Turn on all the lights, maybe, as a signal the cops were on the premises? I stood tensed, listening, every nerve in my body, my scalp, still tingling and tight with fear, as the sharp hootings of the siren cut the air.

Eyes darting about, I tried to see how this sudden frightening noise was affecting the others, but the men on the outer fringes stood smoking calmly, the sparks from their joints spitting in the dark as one or another inhaled deeply. They continued to hang along the wall as before, apparently deaf to it, as if they had heard nothing at all.

I began to relax a little, but was still uncertain, especially when the siren blasted off once more. I was sure it was coming from just outside. Moving crablike, my hands out before me in the tangible dark, I sidled through it, darkness slipping around me like a glove, my body a hand moving in black velvet past the others, tripping over the feet of a black man invisible against the dark wall, carefully making my way around the four men huddled at the door, they, too, like the others surrounding them, unmindful of the siren's noisy proximity, as I squeezed myself into that blackest corner and put my ear close to a chink in the door and listened.

I was puzzled, hearing nothing but the dull thud of footsteps and the swift click of heels passing on the pavement outside, amidst an occasional high whisper of freezing wind numbing my ear. The siren was still sounding, sure enough, but where it was coming from now I couldn't at all be certain. It seemed to come from within the walls of the backroom itself, but I knew that was impossible. I decided it must be some emergency vehicle stopped close by on other business and made myself relax, ignore the intrusive sound, like the others, who appeared so calm and at ease, intent on watching the four men grouped against the door.

I was now standing so close to them I could have put my hand out and touched them. They, however, were anything but calm in their heightening frenzy. I narrowed my eyes in darkness as dark as the bottom of the sea must be, and continued to try to observe what the twisting shapes beside me were doing.

What I could see was the taut, spreading fingers of the two men standing clutch close to their groins in the same instant the heads of the pair bent before them, the noise of the latter like clapping their lips in a gusto of eating; heard the quickening gasps of the pair standing, knew, from the sharp intakes of breath, the increased sharpness of their cries, they were gemini in orgasm, and with such loud hoots and abandoned groans, their buttocks slamming against the emergency door in unison, I was certain that anyone passing by on the other side would be sure to hear them, mistaking their cries for mayhem, even murder.

Just so long as no one was prompted to call the police! I thought in renewed panic, and then had to laugh at myself at the absurdity of it.

After, when the two standing had pushed in their shirttails and zippered up, each holding his leather jacket knotted in a fist clamped on his hip, they took turns slapping the shoulders of the men who had risen now to a standing position, each of the latter snorting with that choked breathlessness, rubbing at their eyes, one of them briskly running the back of a hand under his nose, symptoms they had each given strenuous pleasure.

Singular again, disentangled from each others' interlocking arms and legs, the four moved away from the exit door and as they stepped into the faint fringe of light from the passage beyond, I could see their faces were flushed with grins. Before separating and heading down the passage, presumably toward the turnstile, one of the men, poking an arm up into the sleeve of his jacket as he struggled into it, again put his other arm around the shoulder of the man who had knelt before him, his face creasing again in a wide smile as they parted. The other, his eyes and nose still red and runny-looking, lowered his eyes and you could see he was

secretly pleased as he went off to the right through another archway, probably going in the direction of the toilet to wash up.

My blood humming, I followed after, to that same wide archway,
supported, curiously enough, by two art deco posts, a step down
from which were three more of the oversized movie booths around
the walls of an irregular-shaped area lit by a single red bulb. A
huge pinball machine sandwiched in between two of the booths
threw off a nervous, glittering light that suggested a Times Square
penny arcade.

To get my bearings and check out this new space, I leaned a hip
against one of the pillars, which felt like it was made of cast-iron
and, like its mate, jutted out inexplicably from the side of the arch
like a boundary post between the blackness of the "closet" area
behind me and the slightly better lighted pinball arcade which I
now faced.

The posts were so incongruous with the rest of the drab, gim-
crack decor I figured they must have been left standing as part of
the design of the original structure or as a decorative remnant from
some past renovation. The embossed geometric patterns down the
shaft were worn smooth, like the walls along the passage, with
patches of glossy shine from the constant rub, like polishing
cloths, of numberless shoulders in cheap flannel shirts and
behinds in snug denim; worn down from so much leaning against
it, as I was now, as probably so many others had before me,
discovering what an ideal observation post it was to keep an alert
eye on the comings and goings in the closetlike space over my left
shoulder, plus partial views into the booth across the aisle, and,
over my right shoulder, glimpses into the three other booths down
in the arcade area, where there was endlessly circulating traffic.

In that booth directly across the passage I began to perceive just
within its doorway two very young lads slowly stripping each other
and starting to make love standing up, shyly, silently hugging and
kissing, the one, pale and bony, speaking quietly at times in the
ear of his partner, who was just barely visible. Several of us
watched through the open door, even though not much was to be
seen in the poor light, as their clothes dropped one by one about
their feet.

A thick-bodied, balding man with glasses, wearing a glossy tan
leather jacket, his back to me, shifted and twisted like a shadow
boxer as he hunched, mesmerized, with outstretched arms over
the glass top of the pinball machine, his stubby fingers gripping

the sides, his hips shimmying with such vitality as he wrestled to maneuver the little stainless steel ball around, it set the bunch of keys on his left hip jingling loudly. But not loud enough to drown out the high-pitched electronic blips and squeals coming from the machine itself, the glass-paneled upright box at the head of it a swirl of scattering electrical stars winking rapidly, its eerily thin outer-galactic noises contrapuntal music to Donna Summer now singing "On the Radio" on the jukebox at the other end of the corridor, as the pinball player, still manipulating his short, bulky body with amazing skill, racked up astronomical scores in astral-flashing explosions of light.

Abruptly, in the midst of all these computerized sounds of outer space, and Donna's singing, came, once more, the prolonged and penetratingly shrill scream of a police siren. My heart gave a lurch as I stiffened again, my hands tightening about the post behind me, my head snapping around toward the larger dark space in back of me. I listened carefully, holding my breath, then realized, once and for all, that the siren wasn't coming from out in the street but, in a peculiar and misleading deflection of sound, as I turned my ears back to the arcade, its piercing wail, as an additional sound-effect in mind-obliterating distraction for the player, was actually screaming from somewhere deep in the electrical innards of the pinball machine itself.

I listened in amazement, then, relaxing my grip on the cold iron of the pillar, began to laugh at myself, at how easily I'd been fooled only minutes before, hearing that same honking siren and thinking the place was about to be raided.

I hugged my chest, flooded with an immense relief and was at the same time annoyed with myself for my skittishness. I was even more annoyed at the management for installing such a nerve-wracking apparatus on the premises, with its terrifying sound and all the associations connected with it, especially in the minds of those of us old enough to remember earlier decades.

I looked into the younger faces moving around me, faces uncon-cerned, in search of their pleasure, only a slight suggestion of tension in the eyes, the tension of pursuit, and possible rejection; but all of them apparently oblivious to the fearsome noises roaring out of the pinball machine. Another generation, oblivious to my memories, too—perhaps rightly so, I thought. And yet a nagging doubt persisted that even the constricted permissiveness in back-rooms such as this, or in the baths, the bars, could be snatched away overnight, as continued to happen in other cities, regardless of how much tolerance was gained, or how much was paid in police protection.

In the doorways of the booths in the arcade below, men stood staring out, their faces and bodies, bathed in a faint ruby sheen from the red bulb overhead, a little clearer in this somewhat brighter illumination, their features stiff with minute observance, standing in patient rigidity in the half-light of the open doors.

A lone youth sat watching the action of the pinball machine, sitting in the wooden windowseat which ran flush against another set of boarded up windows. Despite the whirling, dizzying lights of the pinball, and its racket, and the raw redness of the single lightbulb, this area had, in contrast to the rest of the backroom, a tinge of warm and inviting light, even the walls of the booths giving off, for all their grubbiness, a mellow aura, the wood, stained in the light, a deep winy hue.

From behind the closed door of one of the booths, the one down below next to the pinball machine, came unmistakable cries and gasps from within, punctuated with bumps and scufflings against the inside walls, so energetic and loud they even rose above the staccato clatter of the machine.

By now I was breathing easier, began inhaling again that intense erotic odor of the place, the smell of it impregnating the splintery wood of the booths, even seeping into, it seemed, the dank brick walls themselves. As it filled my lungs, I felt again a growing headiness and excitation, and, not looking where I was going, walked through the arcade slowly, taking it all in, and finally came to the last movie booth where a hand-lettered sign tacked beside the door announced in a large scrawl, JEFF NOLL — NEW THIS WEEK. Jeff, I figured, must be one of the current stars of gay skinflicks and no doubt a favorite of the regulars. Just beyond, was a final dark and scarred niche in the wall, where a man peered out at me half-concealed in its shadow, and, after passing beneath another archway, I found myself back where I'd started, in the anteroom with its turnstile entrance. A newcomer, his mackinaw collar up about his ears, now pushed through it noisily with eager haste and hurried to the right in the direction of the bleak entrance to the maze, where I'd started my own tour around a short while back, joining that circling dance of mute cruisers where artful eye contact and silent, skilled body signals were the only language needed.

From the jukebox against the far wall, the Village People were now singing exuberantly of the unchristianlike pleasures to be found at the YMCA. As for myself, my blood continuing to rise, I was keenly interested in discovering some of those same delights right here, in this very backroom. Now that I'd seen all of it, I wanted to find an empty booth for myself and wait and see what would happen, reminding myself to be moderate, of course, what with the Saturnalia ahead and the promise I had made to myself not to get involved back here: Well, maybe not *too* involved, I thought, tempering my original decision.

I started around again and coming to the TRUCK STOP booth, almost got knocked down by the broad-shouldered man I'd earlier seen entering it, as he emerged unexpectedly through the door. Tears were in his eyes, like he'd just snorted coke, and he was sniffing back phlegm and clearing his throat, like the two men I'd seen squatting a few minutes ago by the exit door, signs and sounds that he'd also just given pleasure, without doubt to the young man in the cowboy hat, only its pearl-gray brim visible, who was standing back unseen in the doorway, adjusting his clothes.

Wiping at his eyes, coughing, having what looked like symptoms of the most virulent flu, there was yet the hint of a smile and a look of satisfaction on the face of the man with wide shoulders as he hustled past me, mumbling an apology for bumping into me, and went out toward the turnstile. His partner soon appeared, hitching up his levis and setting his hat straight as he stepped down the hall, moving toward the jukebox area.

I poked my head in the booth and after several moments of staring into darkness the color of pitch to make sure there was nobody else left inside, I gingerly took a step through the doorway and went in. Like a blind person, I ran my hands along the walls, finding the interior was little more than the width of a telephone booth and about three times the length. I figured that anything that went on in here, unless you were a contortionist, had to be strictly standup. Slick under my fingers, these inside walls, like the outer ones, were made of the same laminated wood as the cubicles at the old Everard. The booth had a dry, dusty smell mingled with a faint odor of sweat and dried semen, and that peculiar cheesy fragrance of winter clothing, perhaps from the two most recent occupants, which still hung in the close air, undoubtedly from the heavy clothing of all the others, too, who had occupied this booth throughout the day. I kept my jacket and vest on, not yet having gotten all the cold out of my bones, or perhaps not yet feeling secure enough to shed them.

If nothing else, it would be good to give my feet a rest, and I searched along the back wall til my outstretched fingers touched the seat for viewing the film loops, a single board braced between the narrow walls, its grainy surface satiny smooth, the edge rough and splintery with wear. Unslinging my bag from my shoulder, I eased myself down.

The place was silent, even the jukebox was still for the moment. Out in the brick-lined passage, instead of the sound of footsteps passing, there was the swish of polyester garments and that constant creak of leatherwear when someone went by the door. I sat quiet for a few moments, getting used to the darkness, listening to the light beat of my heart tripping rapidly in my ears in apprehension and anticipation.

I suddenly realized, from battling the wind out in the street and from the heightened excitement of this new adventure, plus seeing my book in Oscar Wilde, how tired I was, and hungry. I rooted in my bag amid my usual supply of sunflower seeds and whole grain crackers and thermos of woodpressed apple juice diluted with water (no more coffee, no more smokes, two more addictions gone since my trip to the baths), til I found an apple, then tipped my head back against the wall and munched on it in the dark, waiting to see what would happen, straining my eyes around to get an idea of what the rest of the inside of the booth was like.

There really wasn't much more to see: Painted on the plywood wall directly in front of me, just inside the door, was a small screen, a smudge of white, about one by two foot in size. I glided my right hand along the wall next to me, fumbling for the sliding door, to see if it worked okay in the event of a surprise visitor, and was pleased to see that it did, after a little nudging.

I craned my neck back and gazed up at the ceiling and saw it was perforated with tiny air holes, to prevent asphyxiation, I supposed, from too much cigarette or pot smoke, or overexcitement from either viewing the film loops or any hot and heavy activity that might ensue. The holes, though, were mostly all plugged up with accumulated dust, and only a few pinpricks of light managed to pinch their way through from the anemic fluorescent tubing out in the corridor.

Attached to the wall at my left, my hand touched the cold metal of a coin box, solid and durable, evidently made as tamper-proof as possible. Reaching a hand up behind me, I touched, near the roof, a narrow slot of glass, sticky from the smudges of other fingers, behind which was undoubtedly the projector concealed in its casement behind the booth.

When I finished my apple I tucked the core out of the way in a far corner under the seat, thinking the scent of it would help sweeten the stale air a little. Then, feeling optimistic, I reached into my bag and poked around in the bottom til I found my small round plastic container of Life, "a vitamin-enriched lip conditioner Made in Hollywood," which I'd purchased in the health food store in my hometown. "Will soften, soothe, and heal dry, cracked, irritated lips—Contains natural vitamins A, D, E, with a special sun screen to protect your lips from the sun," the latter claim being absolutely of no use in the perpetual wintery darkness of the back-room booths, but the salve really ideal in this weather, or any weather or place, I'd discovered, as a fast and convenient slick-ener of the lips for easier and deeper fellatio and for getting your vitamins at the same time. (I gave up on Chapstick when I found out I was ingesting too many petrochemicals.)

I snapped open the lid, got a good gob on my fingers and generously smeared my mouth with it. Then unzipped my jacket half way, leaned back in the seat, and waited.

Several heads popped in, and either because I sat so far back they couldn't distinguish my looks, or because they were search-ing for a booth themselves, they quickly ducked out and dis-appeared. A few others, unaware of my presence, stepped into the booth as if to make use of it, and when they sensed it was taken, or else, moving to the rear, stumbled against my knees in the dark, also backed out wordlessly and moved on.

I began to feel a little guilty, occupying the space without stick-ing any money in the slot, but others, I'd noted on my quick trip around, were doing the same thing without compunction, loung-ing in the doors or sitting back out of sight behind them, as I was doing, and I was determined not to waste a single quarter if I didn't have to.

What I wanted anyway was more possible, and preferable, here in lifesize, breathing flesh than any shadowy reflections, however visually exciting, but which would be shrunk anyway to the less exhilarating dimensions of a tiny screen in this cramped peep-show of a closetlike booth. Besides, I told myself, for whatever comfort it was, once you've seen a few such loops—and I'd seen plenty of them unreeling nonstop in the darkened little theater at the baths on First Avenue—you've seen them all: males so huge in physique and genitalia, not to mention boundless staying power, cavorting across a good-sized screen which, even so, could barely contain their strapping bodies or their exuberance, flesh glowing the color of peaches, or, as with the few black men who appeared, glistening like onyx.

And then, sooner than I expected, someone was standing diagonally against the wall opposite, peering steadily in at me, the phallic graffito behind him rearing up high above his head. In the only illumination filtering down from the ceiling lights, I could see, framed in the doorway, that he was short in height with clipped brown hair and clearly defined eyes of such lightness they appeared to glow in the shadow and could only be the brightest shade of blue. He had a slight, compact build and was wearing a brown leather jacket, with levis so snug the tight outline of an erection visibly bulged the cloth aslant one thigh. His eyes, gleaming like flecks of sky, watched me with that steadfast and serious gaze that always means business.

I leaned forward far enough on the bench to let him know I was interested and so he could get a better look at me.

He now crossed the passage and stared searchingly into the booth, one hand resting on the doorframe, those light eyes, insistent, never once leaving mine. I had a moment of fright in this first encounter, a quick surge of disquieting adrenalin, still uncertain in the place, the pinball siren over by the exit door still echoing fearfully in my ears. He had the same earnest and single-minded air, a certain uptight rigidity I'd seen in the handsome face of a certain plainclothes policeman stationed in the men's room of the George Washington Bridge bus terminal, his beat being to stand at a urinal playing with himself in order to lure unsuspecting tearoom faggots and arrest them. I was afraid the youth staring in at me might be a vice cop, foolish paranoia perhaps, but I couldn't help feeling uneasy about him.

News stories I'd read flashed through my mind of the raids on gay skin-movie houses in recent years, such as the Ramrod, with its live acts, uptown. But it instantly occurred to me, as he started to seductively fondle himself outside the door, that porn was a multi-billion dollar business and perhaps those movie houses weren't paying enough protection, whereas the bookshop, if it was part of that empire, must surely be paying off somebody, since it

45

had never been raided so far as I knew, and was therefore probably safe.

Whether or not it was speedy rationalization, speedily arrived at by my hastily increasing desire, I felt relieved at the thought and, true or not—his tension, too, I realized, might very well be caused by that quickening of appetite crossed with the uncertainty of satisfying it with a total stranger—I smiled at the youth and tilted my head back in a come-on-in gesture.

He stepped in immediately and I stood up to meet him. After a moment of awkwardness as we stood facing each other—he was at least two heads shorter than myself—I bent down and placed the palms of my hands flat on his thighs, one hand curling around the thick swelling down the side of his pantleg, felt the shiver of muscles tensing beneath the rough denim.

He was all taut and concentrated energy, the sharpened lens of his eyes, even more luminous close up inside the booth, focused on me in beaming intensities, making my face feel like a screen onto which he was projecting rapid and flickering images of desire, far more vivid and real, I was certain, in my own eyes, than any of the shadow images I could easily imagine, colorful, graphically sensual, had flashed innumerable times on the now empty screen ashen and dead on the wall just over his shoulder.

He reached between my legs and stroked me there, but I, still held by his small-featured handsomeness, and particularly the imagery in those eyes like double projectors lighting up my own with all that streamed from them, even though I was terrifically excited, all my erotic blood having rushed up first to my head, my eyes, and not yet, even by his tempting and tentative touchings, dropped down below, felt only content to look at him, to be the mirror to his yearnings.

But within moments, sympathetic to the urgency in him, I turned to business and, with fumbling fingers, unbuckled his wide leather belt and began to unzipper his fly, while he, preparing himself, spread his legs wider for better footing as best he could in the narrow space. He wasn't wearing any underwear I discovered, with that momentary surge of provocative surprise that always, for me, accompanies such discoveries, perhaps wanting to make himself all the readier for action, especially here where I imagined the action could be fast and furious; or maybe, too, it was because he was so large briefs were an irritable confinement.

Either way, as I opened his levis, like parting a curtain, it leapt out, stiff and full-blooded, in that dramatically vigorous and enormous transformation which never ceases to amaze me.

Always a renewed excitement, seeing it—so much so I forgot all about sliding the door shut—these muscles of blood, these miraculous rosy resurrections (Christ's crucifixion by the castrating Father a deadly corruption of this eternally lively magic), however dimly perceived, as here, such magnificence sprung in such poor light, so that my excitation depended largely on the odor of it, an odor of cheese, made more sharp in the tight stretch of skin from roots to crown.

As I crouched before him, my nose wrinkling mouselike, my thumb peeled back the lid, the large slit of it, a cat's eye in the dark, staring back at me. The rapid pulse of his heartbeat fluttered in a swollen vein pressed beneath my thumb, as my tongue flicked out, a frog in darkness, the taste of him salty with sweat.

My fingers reached between his legs, combed the curled hair there, brushed like wool, on a scrotum so tight, the balls within, slippery as eggs, slid under my prodding fingers and rode up the shaft in the hard pull and strain of it.

I kissed it, lovingly, my thumb pressed in pleasant discovery against the blood-hot metal of his cock ring. In a few moments I could feel his pulse in that same vein quickening against the roof of my mouth, a seismograph registering tremors deep within, when, to my surprise and disappointment, he pulled away abruptly, dropping his hands from my shoulders, which he'd been clutching so fiercely, whispering, more like an apology, the first words I heard him utter, "Not yet—I don't want to yet."

With difficulty, bending a little at the hips to do so, he gingerly stuffed his enormous erection back into his levis, zipped himself up ever so carefully, gave me a hurried squeeze on the shoulder, murmured, with a crooked, embarrassed grin, "See ya'," stepped out of the booth and was gone.

I lifted myself back onto the seat and sat there a moment, my hands hanging between my thighs, dazed a bit at the suddenness of his departure, but not too surprised: at the baths such aborted experiences were common, of men wanting to hold off til they'd investigated more of the possibilities offered in the place; I had done it myself on occasion, not wanting to spend myself too soon.

But having had a taste of it, an appetizer so to speak, only left me hungry for more. Seeing nothing wrong with smelling the other roses in the garden, I hitched the drawstrings of my duffel bag over my shoulder and, using my fingers as a brush, hastily smoothed my mustache and beard back into place as best I could, stood up in the doorway and peered out into the passage.

Several men, of indeterminate age and figure, passed by, collars pulled up, a few roly-poly in puffy jackets of down, evidently new arrivals fresh in from the cold, their faces having that drawn, stiff look as they turned to eye me, a few with lingering glances, their bundled up bodies gray as dust in the faulty light of the fluorescent lamps overhead.

As the last of them went by, I spotted him, standing in the brief angle of wall catty-corner across from my booth, in almost the same spot as the previous lad, timidly gazing in at me, a slim youth with wheat-colored hair, appearing, in light which almost obliterated all color, like he was dressed completely in beige, including his jacket and shoes; and that, along with his hair and the fine, long slenderness of him, made me think of a supple sheaf of wheat as he stood there quietly, a thin, pliant body outlined vividly against the scarred, dreary wall with its spray-paint graffito.

Sensing that he was like a wary animal, intensely curious but poised for instant flight, that if I made too sudden a move he'd be gone in a twinkling, I very slowly and carefully extended my hand beyond the door, as one would to patiently coax a wild creature, and waited.

He looked cautiously both ways along the passage, hesitating, as if about to cross a dangerous street. I could see the indecision in his eyes and stretched my hand out farther to him, rubbed my thumb in a slow circular manner over the tips of my fingers in an encouraging gesture. With one quick last look down the passage toward the jukebox area and then back at me, finally, with a soft, shy tread he stepped across the aisle and slipped his hand into mine. I squeezed it gently and pulled him in slowly beside me.

As I peered into his face, a fine-featured, boyish face glowing like a small spectral moon in the dark corner of the booth, he stared intently back into mine, searching it, it seemed, for some hint of assurance, of what I wasn't exactly certain, a lad, it appeared, surely no more than 16 or 17—I remembered the sign at the front door of the shop with its warning to minors and had a quaver of doubt about proceeding further—although it was hard to tell in the bad light just how old he, or anyone else here, was, for that matter, if it mattered at all.

Close to him, I detected even more clearly his uncertainty, his reticence. It looked to be his first trip here, too, and I reached up and stroked his hair, which was silkily sleek and had the muted gleam of platinum in the darkness, and caressed his cheek, which had the slippery sheen of a baby's skin, to quiet him. I could still sense his reserve, his inner struggle, not yet being certain of me, perhaps fearful to expose himself, to me or anyone, he seemed so bashful. Although he tried to appear calm, as I continued to caress him there was an increasing importunity in his eyes, his hands reached out for me, briefly grazed my shoulders, then as swiftly withdrew, his shyness still revealed in his gestures.

However, quickening desire began to override all his timidities, and in a sudden decisive movement, with eager, stumbling fingers, he undid his clothes, unsnapping the buttons on his jacket, the flaps parting wide, then unbuckling his trousers and opening them, next peeling down his briefs, like he was peeling a banana, this simple gesture becoming in the meager light straining in through the open door, a magical act, baring the not yet fully developed hips and belly beneath. Although I'd barely touched him, his cock, matching his long, slim physique, was, unlike the rest of him, fully grown and curving, a firmly ripening tropical fruit.

The sight of his slight, partial nudity in the partial light, the dangling blossom of him a strange and brief night-blooming orchid opening in the dark, was enough to raise the heat of my own blood to torrid temperatures.

I was caught by surprise at an unexpected smarting in my eyes, not only at the aura of emerging loveliness he emanated, but was also moved by the courage the gesture of his openness cost him. I drew in a sharp intake of breath, feeling sudden precise affection for him, keen as a blade.

Not forgetting this time, I slid the door shut as carefully and quietly as I could, so as not to startle him, and in the complete darkness, to reassure him, clasped my hands about his waist, leaned over and kissed his lips. Within the hushed silence of the narrow walls I could hear his light rapid breath.

He was so slim I could hold his buttocks in the palm of one hand, and as I lowered myself and eased him toward me, breathing him in, his skin, tinged lightly with sweat, luminescent as only youthful skin can be, had the milky odor of hedgeblossoms. I could feel the squeeze and arch of his flesh, in shivering anticipation, impatiently coltish under my bridling fingers. The dimpling cheeks of his thin behind, the skimpy muscles, stringily tight and rippling by turns, worked in my hands with increasing rapidity as he thrust himself eagerly in and out in ever longer strokes, the sharpening tip of my tongue the delicate beak of a hummingbird rooting for honey in the sensitive eye of a tubular blossom.

"I'm cumming!" he warned in a tense whisper, then, the words strained, plaintive, "Don't want to yet," but there was no stopping it, and it was over quickly, his taste singeing my mouth like the fiery juice when you bite into a spear of the first wild onions of spring. Amid his whimpers of pleasure I could hear murmurs of regret, a disgusted sound, as if annoyed with himself at having gotten off too soon. When his body ceased its tremblings, he spoke in a voice edged with soft contrition, "I do that some-times—I'm a fast cummer," and he gave a quiet, nervous little laugh.

I rose and put my arms around his shoulders, thinking of the other youth who had been in the booth with me only a few moments before, of his overexcitement, just like this lad's, like my own, on occasion; and others, too, at the baths, and certainly here no doubt, gripped with the immediacy of sexual possession, the excruciatingly sensitive hairtrigger need for release uncontroll-able, exploding beyond mind or will.

He ducked his head, like it was hard for him to admit it. "This is my first time here."

"Mine, too," I said.

He glanced up at me quickly, as if to read my face in the dark-ness, to see if I was putting him on, then, realizing that I wasn't, he became more relaxed, wanted to know what I did, where I lived—all this in hushed tones in the quiet dark of the closed booth, as if we were in a confessional.

"I'm from New Jersey," he offered with a little wistful smile, "It's kind of boring," and I empathized with him, having grown up in South Jersey myself.

I told him I lived in a little town twenty miles outside the city, that I was a teacher, telling him only that I taught English, which was true in a way, thinking it prudent to leave out the fact of my being a writer and that that's what I taught one day a week to earn a few bucks, very few, in fact. Sometimes people get nervous when they find that out, that you're a writer, especially in such intimate circumstances, and particularly in places such as this, which isn't surprising.

I asked him how he liked the place. "Cheap sex," he joked, his laughter muffled, self-deprecating. I smiled at his wisecrack, knowing what he meant, that for a buck-fifty you couldn't beat it. Now at least I knew where to go when I was in the city and horny and broke, which was pretty often, on both counts, although I didn't think it was necessary to mention this to him. But I did tell him I didn't think it was cheap with him and he was fast to say, No, he liked it, a lot, "even though it was over so quick," and that same slightly embarrassed, apologetic tone came back into his voice.

"Quit worrying," I said. "I liked it fine."

Suddenly, thinking of the evening ahead, I had an idea, and, feeling recklessly impulsive, generous, placed my hands on his shoulders. "Come to the Saturnalia!" I blurted, leaning excitedly close to him, then instantly realized how peculiar it must have sounded, but was glad I had asked him, to have hit on the idea, knowing I could explain everything to him. But before I got the chance, I could feel a slight tightening in his shoulders, could sense him peering at me strangely again, the slowly developed trust evaporating and his original hesitancy returning, suspicion, really.

He drew away from me. "What's that?" he asked, his voice careful.

I tried to temper my enthusiasm, to not sound so wild for it and maybe put him off completely, hastening to explain as briefly as I could, what little I knew, which was little enough, never before having been to one myself, sketching out for him what I'd been told at the Fairy Circle was to take place that evening in the loft over on the Lower East Side, that there would be singing and chanting and dancing, some rituals to the gods and goddesses, and something to eat and drink, and probably smoke, in celebration of the winter solstice.

"It's over on Second Street. It's a bit of a hike in the cold but we can take the crosstown bus, if you want. Please say yes!" I concluded, feeling myself babbling but enthusiastic again, slipping my hands up the sleeves of his jacket, thinking, penny-pinching be damned, I'd even spring for the bus and walk to 178th Street and the bus station tomorrow morning if I had to!

There was a moment of silence. I knew he was staring uncomprehendingly at me in the dark, felt a tensing in the slim muscles of his forearms. "I don't think so," I heard him breathe finally, as if trying not to hurt my feelings, but with that strong hint of uncertainty still. Perhaps one new experience in one day had been enough for him. Or maybe, having spent himself, he wasn't in the mood right then to think about any further possible excitement. Or maybe it was the word itself—*Saturnalia*—it had such an odd ring to it, it may have turned him off. Then, too, and perhaps the most likely reason, he might have decided that I was just a nut and was afraid to risk it.

Whatever his reasons, he pulled up his briefs and began buckling his trousers. "Thanks a lot, though," he added. "For inviting me."

He turned to the door and, as an afterthought, either remembering his manners or out of genuine impulse, the latter I think, or at least want to think it was that, he reached out and touched my hand, then leaned forward and quickly brushed my lips with his. Groping for the edge of the door, he finally managed to find it and, sliding it open, hurried away.

When I heard the last of his footsteps retreating down the hall and the squeal of the turnstile as he exited, I shoved the door shut and slumped down on the bench, a little down at not having convinced him to join me for the evening's festivities, but feeling very up at the same time, his presence still with me, the excitement of him, especially in my throat, which was pleasantly scorched, the fire of him still burning there, the same as when I eat raw garlic, I imagine it burning in my blood with a lavender flame licking through my veins.

I thought of going around to the toilet to rinse out my mouth, but it pleased me to have the taste of him with me for a little while longer, as often, after lovemaking, not wanting to shower immediately, reluctant to erase so soon from my body the kisses and fingerprints of a beloved I may have met only an hour before, and so sat there savoring the memory of him, put my hands to my nose and breathed in deeply, his odor still fresh on my fingers.

After a few moments, feeling the urge to get moving again, plus the need to breathe a little after the stifling air in the closed booth—even though I knew that out in the passages it was only a little less stuffy—I slid open the door and went out and around to the toilet.

Finding it vacant, I went in, a space not much bigger than a cubicle, and realizing I hadn't pissed since the bus terminal uptown earlier that afternoon, stood at the urinal reading the backroom bulletin board, the graffiti-marked wall with its innumerable scrawled messages and telephone numbers: HOT BUNS WITH SPICY

MUSTARD HUNGRY FOR 9″ HOTDOG CALL NATHAN 828-0211—CHAIN ME, WHIP ME, BOOTLICKER SUPREME CALL TOM 401-9623—MEAT ME HERE FOR HOT CUMMING ATTRACTIONS.

When I was finished, I went to the sink and, since there was no hot tap, gargled with cold water, drying my hands on my handkerchief, since there were no paper towels either—I supposed at these prices you were expected to bring your own—although the wastebasket overflowed and the broken tile floor was littered, curiously enough, with heaps of damp tissue.

I combed my hair and beard in the mirror and remoistened my lips with a generous smear of the Life lip conditioner.

Always on the lookout for nooks and crannies to write in, particularly here, it suddenly occurred to me the john was a good place to start getting down some notes on the backroom, especially on the two youths I'd just been with, the naked bulb glaring in the ceiling a far better light to see by than any other I'd found. I wasted no time getting out my pad and pen from my bag, but unfortunately hadn't scribbled more than a line or two when the door opened and a guy in a fat down jacket, eyeing me curiously, came in to relieve himself.

Then, almost immediately, another man stuck his head in the door, wanting to use the place, throwing me an odd look as I stood pen poised in hand. Since the toilet only had room, comfortably, for two men at a time, one at the urinal and one at the sink, and since I didn't want to arouse any suspicion, I reluctantly dropped my notepad and pen back in my bag, slung the latter over my shoulder and, squeezing past the man in the down jacket at the urinal and smiling at the other waiting at the door, left, thinking I'd try to find a more private corner later on to get down my notes while they were still fresh in my mind, difficult as I knew it would be to find such a spot in this overly dark and busy place.

I started around again, in the same direction as when I first made a tour of the place, not getting very far before coming upon, outside a booth in the bend of the passage just around the corner from the TRUCK STOP booth, three men standing out in the aisle peering in at one of the film loops unreeling on the small screen painted on the bare wooden wall just inside the doorway. The fluttering illumination from within danced on their absorbed faces in a fitful light, the occupant, whose quarter was unwittingly entertaining more than himself alone, sitting unseen behind the plywood partition at the rear of the booth.

I came up and stood behind them, peeping over their shoulders, curious to see what these films, so graphically advertised on each booth and out in the shop, were all about, to see if they were any different from those shown at the baths.

According to the come-on outside this particular booth, one film was titled, THE LURE OF JOCK STRAP [sic]—*Packed and Sweaty Jock*—NEW YORK PREMIERE, the other announced simply the brand name of a line of films on display in the glass cabinets in the shop, *Great Cum Shots!—For the Man who likes Big Men.*

I turned my attention back inside the door of the booth where, on the little screen, in a long shot, two naked young men appeared, each with terrifically sculpted muscles. One, a blond lying on his belly, faced the camera, eyes closed, mouth tensed, while the other, a brunet, lay on top of him, his slim hips pumping in slow, easy thrustings between the legs of the blond, his brow wrinkled in concentration, his handsome face solemn and serious, the same face as the one in the technicolor still on the wall outside.

Then a quick, extreme closeup on the action, detailing clearly each kink in every pubic hair, the camera panning lovingly along the lube-glistening shaft working like a piston in accelerating strokes, the lens then zeroing in at ever closer range, exposing the tiniest jagged vein; catching, too, in exact attention, the woolly fringe of fluff scattered over the plumply rounded buttocks of the blond, parted cleanly by the dark, stiff brush of the other.

In a sudden shift to a full shot, taking in the long length of his body, the movements of the brunet became spastically jerky as his hips pounded harder and harder; the blond, in a brief closeup, was shown wincing, his mouth pulled back in a grimace that could be seen as either pleasure or pain. A flashback to the body of the brunet, shoving maniacally now, a fast closeup of his brow, which was even more tensely furrowed, beaded with sweat, his glaring eyes having a fiercely angry look as he bit his lower lip and . . . .

There was a click heard in the projector casement slanting out the back of the upper part of the booth, the screen went blank, time had run out, and the interior was abruptly plunged into darkness. The men outside shuffled their feet and peered around them, not at each other, but either way down the passage.

I was about to move on, erotically agitated and yet feeling annoyed with myself—the shadows again—when I saw a pale hand inside the booth reach toward a coin box and slip in another quarter, which meant a continuation of the same film. In spite of my vague discomfort at gaping at celluloid phantoms, I stood rooted where I was, irritated at my immobility and yet as eager as the others apparently were, since none of them drifted away, to see the outcome of the scene.

There was another clicking sound from inside the projector casement, and those of us loitering out in the hall, despite all the warning signs against it, stiffened in readiness, held together in mystical fascination of watching lighted shadows moving in the dark, turning our attention again through the open doorway of the booth as a square of white light flashed on the screen and the film began rolling again, exactly at the same point it had left off: The contorted face of the brunet, still grinding away, loomed into camera range once more, his forehead now streaming with perspiration—from the exertion of genuine, or simulated, passion? I wondered, making mental notes to write down later; or from the hot camera lights? Or perhaps from desperation, needing the money and having to come through, no matter what.

There was a shot now of his hips as his body convulsed sharply, once, twice. He sucked in his muscular gut, rapidly pulling himself out from between that sloping hilly flesh, swiveling his hips about, brows knit, squinting annoyed an instant to his left as if someone off camera had spoken sharply to him. Then his eyes fastened on his groin, mouth wrenched, baring his teeth in a look of pain, and clutching the roots of his cock tight in one fist, he jerked up the thigh closest to the viewer, concealing his erection from sight, as he lunged a hand between his legs, the partially visible tendons in his forearm working vigorously, as up from between his thighs spurted what looked like globs of heavy cream in long ribbons across the tiny screen.

The thick, milky fluid gushed in such high arcs, the topmost spurts of it shot right off the top of the picture, pumping like a regular geyser, so unnatural, it appeared like it might be coming from one of those same dildo models on sale out in the shop, equipped with their syringes and lengths of thin hose, and perhaps slipped out of sight under the belly of his partner before the cameras rolled, ready to be snatched up and squirted on cue.

Then the unexpected click and the booth went dark again, and the men once more shuffled their feet uneasily, like restive animals, and looked around them down the dim passage.

The pale hand of the unseen viewer inside the booth suddenly appeared at the door, curling his fingers slowly in a come-hither gesture, directed at anyone of us standing outside in the passage. I thought of the priest in the confessional, in the late Saturday afternoon in the little hometown church when I was a child, his hand through the wine-dark curtain beckoning the next one in line to come tell him their sins.

The man nearest the door, a tall, thin youth in his midtwenties, his straw-colored hair, Clairol-bright, looking, in its cadet trim, pressed flat across his skull like it had been carefully ironed, cocked his head to one side, scratched his chin, then poked his head inside the door, peering in hesitantly, obviously undecided.

There was the sound from within of a quarter being dropped in the other slot, I noted, catching a glimpse of the hand as it moved slowly away from the coin box, so we'd be seeing the New York premiere of THE LURE OF JOCK STRAP.

Whether this made up his mind for him or not, the thin blond finally then stepped up and moved inside as the film loop flashed on the screen, his startled face, hair icily brilliant, caught briefly in the beam of the projector, becoming inadvertently part of the screen as he squinted blindly into the intense glare, the flinching features of that leanly handsome face lacily dappled for a moment with the jittering technicolor imprints of the two figures in the film, before he ducked out of its light. His body half visible, he stood in the doorway, head held to one side, facing the back of the booth, eyeing its unseen occupant, both of whose hands, lower down as from a sitting position, appeared once more, reaching out to encircle his waist.

Those of us in the passageway, joined now by a few new arrivals, which created a bottleneck in the increasingly busy flow of traffic in the close space, continued to watch, craning over each other's shoulders, our eyes fastened on the screen, as this time a black man, his fly gapingly revealing the beige elastic of a swollen jock strap, embraced a totally nude white man, both of them young and muscular, both hung, the latter youth, silvery-skinned and blond in aryan luminosity, a prime prerequisite, it seemed, to star in such films.

As the white youth on the screen snapped back the supporter and began to massage the uncut cock, which tumbled massive and black out of its confining pouch, the pair of hands in the booth were seen reaching out for the trousers of the lean young man who, legs parted wide, hands on hips, and eyes steadily fixed on those pale white hands busily opening his trousers, stood rigid in a stance of expectation.

Perhaps because the man sitting back in the booth was closely following the action on the screen over the shoulder of the lean youth standing before him, his hands, too, like the ones now in closeup in the movie, began to slowly massage the penis of the thin man in a slow, easy rhythm, matching stroke for stroke and gesture for gesture the same kneading movements as the blond in the film.

The lean man continued to stare down at these flesh and blood hands delicately fingering the skin of his cock in gradually quickening tempo, then gave a fast look over his shoulder at the hands in the film, hitching his head to one side to see better, since part of his head made a shadow on the screen. He continued to turn his attention at regular intervals, first down at those skillful hands conjuring the bud of his penis to bloom within seconds, fleshy as the head of a peony; then back at the screen to take in the equally swift flying fingers of the blond in the picture, his fingers now like they were playing nimbly over the stops of a stout flute made of teak in a piece of fast and intricate music.

My eyes, like the lean young man's, like the eyes, I noted, of the others clustered around the door, also moved back and forth, from the two men on the screen to the two men in the booth—the latter couple a man and a pair of hands, to be more accurate—as though we were watching a tennis match. Viewing this double feature of silent movie and silent mime, the one, beamed on the splintery wall of a plywood booth, the other, a pair of actual, living males aping the exact same sexual intimacies as the mute shadows they watched, my own eyes, oscillating from one scene to the other with such dizzying speed, became confused as to which was the shadow and which the substance, conditioned as I was to see the reflected thing as more real than the thing I'm actually seeing, the writing of this scene more real to me than the experience itself.

However, the excitement of my image-snapping eyes, like roving cameras panning to and fro in double vision, flashed signals to my brain in lively erotic ideograms of fantasy and actuality, impulses speeding instantaneously down the network of my nerves to snap open that nether stalk-eye, which I sensed peeling its lid and rousing itself inside the flap of my briefs.

As the blond on the screen positioned himself in front of the black, whose trousers now lay in a heap around his ankles, the straps of the supporter dangling around his knees, the hands within the booth artfully tugged down the levis and shorts of the leanly built youth, the levis, so snug a fit, dropped hanging only part way down his thighs, the hands then sliding around and cupping the scrawny buttocks, just as the white youth in the film loop was doing, in a slightly longer reach around a more solid and ample rump, flicking his tongue over his lips for moisture, puckering them as he drew nearer to the black, who was fully aroused now in a close range view that filled all of the screen in a dark mass of glistening flesh shot here and there with veins that gleamed in flame-colored highlight. As the hands in the booth pulled closer, drawing him into the darker recess at the rear at the same time, the partly nude lean youth, along with the hands, disappeared from the doorway.

Just as the petal-pink mouth on the screen was about to touch the quivering black glans, a deep purple dahlia in full frontal iris shot blossoming over the entire screen, finally obliterating the light, the click of the projector was heard once more and the screen went blank, the booth fallen in total darkness again.

There were several plaintive sighs from the men around me, and hitching of shoulders. Traffic began moving again as other late-coming rubberneckers cleared away. I waited around a few moments, along with a couple of other diehards, to see if we'd get to see the end of the loop, but no hand again extended itself to stick money in the slot. It was evidently too busy with reality at the moment, both men now hidden well back behind the doorframe, and, from the sounds coming from inside, a steady creak of wood and a scraping of feet, counterpointed by murmurous breathing and delicate licking like water lightly splashing, obviously losing no time providing a clearly audible soundtrack to a very live scenario, in contrast to their earlier silent movie-miming.

The hand of the invisible occupant did appear once more, however, only its waxen fingers actually, grasping the edge of the door as it was slid shut with quiet finality and nothing more was to be seen.

The other men began wandering off down the passage, and I did, too, doubly stimulated now from that unexpected double feature, my swelling fly abuzz with erotic humming, the nosy eye within wide awake and fully open, hornily eager, as always in such moments of blind desire, to poke itself in somebody else's business. Leading me around the darkened maze again, like an ever-watchful seeing eye dog, it wasn't long before that undercover private eye of mine sniffed out, with its sharp nose, a likely prospect.

I almost missed him, he was standing so far back from the opening of the booth, one of the darkest, on the other side of the niche from the TRUCK STOP booth, located in the angle of a busy corner in the narrowest part of the short hall. He looked like he was wearing an old army fatigue jacket and appeared to be leaning back into the interior, his jet black beard, his eyes, a match for the darkness framed in the doorway, darkness so thick it seemed to have the solidity of anthracite. It was his eyes which caught my own, fixing on me with such an eager, imploring look, I found it hard to ignore, or resist, them, like the appeal in the eyes of a stricken animal.

I walked by slowly, scrutinizing him, trying to make out what the rest of him looked like, which was impossible in shadows that blotted out most of the details of his body, and a few paces on turned around and went back and stood near the entry staring in at him. His eyes caught mine again, held me fast.

I stepped in with him and he immediately drew the door shut, fumbled for me in blind blackness, his slightly damp hands moving hurriedly over my face, my shoulders, down around my belly. His breath, close in my ear, was hoarse, his manner all instant and agitated excitement. I was put off balance, not only by the crush of his weight leaning heavily against me in the abrupt and total absence of any light whatsoever, but also by so immediate and huge a hunger, which caught me by surprise. I grasped his arms as he fondled me, to steady us both.

He hunched forward, his mouth searching for mine, brushing my cheek and nose, large moist lips hungrily trying to kiss me. I touched between his thighs, the cloth of the khakilike material there already tugged tight. I stroked him evenly, trying to calm him, much as a jockey would the withers of a skittish horse, to lessen a bit that overexcited energy which streamed everywhere around him, bombarding the booth with an invisible strength that seemed to strain at the walls, too large a force for such a crimped and stifling enclosure.

As he unbuttoned himself, awkwardly, hastily, with one hand, he stretched the other out against the wall, as if suddenly dizzy, his breath coming sharper and quicker. As I crouched down, letting my duffel bag slip to the floor, I could smell the odor of him rising up into my nostrils, a rank and pent-up odor, goatlike in its acrid sexuality. He was all such impatient avidity and haste, I wasted no time, clutching his tightening buttocks to balance myself as he bucked into my face, at first stabbing blindly at my chin, my Adams apple, both hands fastened firmly on my neck as if my throat were reins, his back rearing in such a way it made me think of broncobusters in rodeo movies where the spine of the horse becomes a perfect exclamation mark in its rearing, its hoofs joined in a sharp point of focused yet untamed energy, trying to throw the rider.

I held on, squeezing his hairy haunches tight in my fists, feeling the booth swaying as he rocked my body back and forth, in his keening breath imagining high-pitched whinnying in my ears, the booth a stall sharp with horse-musk in sprays like ammonia, stinging my eyes.

It was his peppery taste, actually, that made my eyes water, and when it was over, my back shoved up against the wall, there was no neighing, only me hacking and clearing my throat, the smell of strong sexual sweat like singed rubber in the small enclosure and a sense of embarrassed silence on his part as his clenched fingers dug out of my shoulders and he pulled himself fully erect. I could hear his hand swipe against the partition as his arm shot out again to support himself against it. With his free hand he immediately shoved open the door and stepped aside clumsily with a hesitant, sheepish smile I could just barely see in the skimpy light now coming in through the opening. He was allowing me to leave first, but I wanted to adjust myself a bit before stepping out into the passage, make myself a little more presentable. I tucked in my clothes and even managed to give a quick comb to my hair and beard in the close confines of the booth, my elbows scraping the walls, even once or twice poking him accidentally in the chest, for which I quickly apologized. But he stood silent, pushed back against the rear of the booth, not bothering as yet to button himself up or adjust his clothing, waiting, impatiently it seemed, for me to clear out.

It had entered my mind that he might want to leave first, now that his needs had been taken care of, letting me have the booth to myself so I could have a little rest on the viewing bench before going around to the toilet to rinse my mouth and wash my hands, but it was obvious he wanted to stay on, to maybe have a rest himself after his arduous exercise—or, perhaps, given the size of his appetite, even to try his luck again.

I could sense him glancing at me nervously from the shadows, and then, perhaps feeling self-conscious, he began poking into what appeared to be a bulky knapsack stashed out of the way on the board seat, slowly, deliberately taking his time, and, from what I could hear, doing it all with some awkwardness. Then he stopped. I could feel him peering at me through the palpable dark, certain that imploring look was again in his eyes, although this time I sensed it to mean something else, which I couldn't pick up on.

His behavior was peculiar, puzzling to me, but I put it down to some personal quirk, or perhaps even to that slight embarrassment now that he was calmer, his embarrassment at the intensity of his unbridled passion only a few moments before.

Whatever it was, I got the message, hoisted my bag up from the floor and slid the drawstrings up one arm and over my shoulder, and turned to go out. He stumbled forward a step or two, one hand sliding along the wall while the other grasped my arm. He began to thank me profusely, and looking at him, unable to see his eyes clearly, his voice sounded sincere enough, but it had such eagerness in it, a certain undercurrent of relief, I wasn't too certain what he was thanking me for: the gratification I'd just given him or the fact that I was getting out of the booth at last.

I gave his arm an affectionate squeeze in return and mumbled something like "That's okay," and got out the door and walked a few steps down the passage, past the jukebox, where the Supremes were singing "Baby Love" from the Golden Oldies selections, and went around to the toilet, the tune instantly rolling in my head my own old tapes of the drunken sixties.

Opening the door, I saw one man standing at the urinal looking back over his shoulder at another man who was at the opposite end at the sink combing his hair in the mirror and at the same time staring back in an interested way at the reflection in the glass of the one pissing.

I closed the door and waited, figuring the two of them, from the exchange of looks, would probably be a little while longer, contentedly watching the other customers cruise by, making the rounds of the backroom circle again and again, vigilant, the naked hunger in the eyes of most shaded with wariness, a caution in the uncertainty of being refused, but the immediacy of desire so

61

urgent here, sexual snobbery appeared to be held to a bare minimum. Several times I saw the most handsome and well-built of Christopher Street clones disappearing into booths with men beautiful in their own unstylish way but who I would imagine anywhere else they would all but ignore.

A youth leaned with arms spread over the plexiglass top of the jukebox, feeding it coins, punching the buttons, his face gleaming like an iris in its purple glow. The Village People burst out through the loudspeakers with "Macho Man."

A very tall lad with a small head and the incongruously pretty features of a very little boy, peeped out at me now and again from the doorway of the booth directly across from the john. I smiled in return but felt no urge to pursue it further, satisfied for the moment, and a little worn out, too, from my first couple of encounters, my throat still scorched from the most recent one, like I'd swallowed a monstrous gulp of seawater. My main thought was to get to the sink inside the toilet and gargle with cold water, for a little relief, plus crude, and probably illusory, sanitary precaution.

I was standing in a direct line with the turnstile and could see who was entering and leaving, having a clear view in either direction in this larger vestibulelike space, another good vantage point, as the youth standing here when I'd first entered must have known, just like the spot over by the art deco posts.

Pushing through the turnstile now was an extremely tall, big-limbed, heavy-bellied youth in a fawn-colored cowboy hat, ragged sheepskin jacket with leather vest beneath, and blunt-toed wrangler boots, looking like he'd just ponied in from the freezing plains of Wyoming, but more than likely had just stepped out of the boozy coziness of Boots & Saddle up the block, probably like so many of the other cowpokes moseying around the passageways.

He paused a moment just beyond the entrance, blowing first on one, then the other, of his cold hands, looking left and right, getting a sense of where he was, then ambled languidly along, peering down carefully into all the faces that approached him. He pulled up short at the first booth beyond the turnstile where the young man with the babyface leaned out, and stood there deliberating a short while, then stepped in to check him out, and had to stoop considerably since he was quite a bit taller than its occupant. Once in the door, he had to take off his hat to fit inside and even with his hat off the back of his head was pressed flat against the roof and his neck was bent double, which must have given him quite a crick, I imagine, if he was the kind who took his time about things, and from the size of him he looked like he might be. He must have found the babyfaced youth agreeable because, within seconds, the door was slid shut and stayed that way for as long as I stood there.

Most of the men parading by wore, like unofficial uniforms, regular leather jackets, and motorcyclist's jackets with stainless steel rivet designs, and wide belts with big buckles in elaborate metallic patterns; black, stiff-crowned military hats on a few heads; and bombardier's brown leather jackets, and cheap plaid shirts and heavy wool lumberjacket shirts, and levis and Lee's Wranglers and Frisko Jeens, and jackboots and thick-laced construction worker's boots; most of them also sported bushy mustaches.

Several guys had stripped down to their T-shirts, leather jackets slung over their broad, muscle-knotted shoulders, or clamped in a fist on their hips, to better reveal the bulging biceps of their bare arms, the cotton fabric stretched tight across each chest clearly outlining overdeveloped pecs like buckled plates of steel beneath, muscles lovingly developed, not for strenuous lifting, or for working, but to be simply beautiful to other men, to attract them; a body like a poem, or sculpture—the weightlifter the sculptor of himself, the body as art.

All of them looked pretty much alike, however, as they strutted past in their jackboots, wide shoulders grazing the booths they sauntered by, and into, getting it on, tight-lipped, solemn, with whoever they wanted with a confident, unhurried directness, which was often, and only with guys who looked very much like themselves, right down to the bunches of keys hanging on belt loops.

Others, like myself, in my ragged ski jacket and down vest and patched levis, not to mention my shaggy hair and beard, were dressed somewhat differently, some even quite a bit differently.

There was, for instance, a pallidly handsome youth circling by with short black hair neatly combed, his beardless cheeks having the sheen of fresh, warm milk. He was dressed in conservative dark suit and tie, his light-colored topcoat folded carefully over his arm, an apparition, in the ghostly light of the area, of a flashback to an Ivy League preppie-type of the 1950s, but perhaps in actuality a student from a nearby school, older looking than his years, come into the place seeking to broaden his knowledge, and maybe also to research a little after-class satisfaction.

His eyes, thickly lashed and piercingly beautiful—I could see their beauty in spite of the glum light—glanced shyly, fleetingly, at me as he passed, his step swift and nervous, like a shy, careful animal, a lamblike anomaly amidst all the older, more ruggedly dressed men roving around him.

So many of us, I observed, array ourselves in the approved masculinist fashions, the clothes we wear the enslavement we unconsciously accept, projecting, like the images on the peep-show screens, the faulty and diaphanous shadows of an alleged virility, our fantasy costumes, from three-piece suits to full-dress leathers, an accurate reflection of the carefully concealed dark side of the male in society's mirror. This hidden away backroom the dark side of that larger mirror beyond the locked and unmarked exit door, a sealed little world kept invisible in the wide-angle reflection of panoramic Manhattan, the prick-shaped island itself stippled with concrete and steel skyscraper-erections, stiff and unyielding monuments to that glorified virility (the penin-sular cities of New York and San Francisco genital appendages on the continent faggots have instinctively migrated to for decades and decades).

Looking from inside out was like peeping through a scratch in a blackened looking glass wall through which I spied, in sharply focused miniature, a reality beyond it not much different in its impulsions from what was going on back here, however much in paradoxical play, in connected identity, in tacit and unrecognized approval of all that outside brutality, out on those streets, behind those skyscraper walls where lives are daily decided; any extreme taken, in ultra masculine drag, in stiffly posturing attitudes of apathy betraying the circular and receptive spirit, the curvaceous earth itself, *to not be like women*, at any cost, to be free of the abhorred taint of women's blood, erasing the mothers in mur-derous denial, erasing the prints of their hands on us, the incred-ible gift of their breath and blood.

"The face of the monster is nothing but our own face in the mirror."

While I was standing there, several men had come up, opened the toilet door and started to go in, then stopped abruptly, seeing it was occupied, and went off around the passages to try again later. But one burly man my age, once he'd flung open the door and gawked at what he saw going on inside—I caught a quick glimpse over my shoulder of one man leaning against the sink, a look of bliss on his face, as the other, the one who'd been at the urinal, knelt in front of him—this burly guy, with an impish grin, stepped in to join the pair, pulling the door shut firmly after him—so now there were three in there to wait on! I slumped back against the wall again, folding my arms over my chest, and tried for patience.

"I WANT TO BE A MACHO MAN!" sang the Village People lustily, as from across the way the booth rattled and shook with the strains of rambunctious fucking within, so much so that at any moment I expected the head of the tall cowboy to come punching through the roof.

Then I saw him, the man I'd just left moments before in the dark booth, swinging around the corner not more than a few yards from where I stood, recognized him by his beard and especially those eyes which, as they darted stealthily from side to side at those passing around him, still had a harried, imploring look.

He had his knapsack slung over one shoulder of his fatigue jacket and walked with a lurching but surprisingly swift gait as if eager to get out of the place, surprising, because half his body was leaning heavily on an aluminum crutch braced under one armpit. In the skillful way he handled himself, in the agility of his maneuvering, a stumbly walk, yet hurtling himself forward on his crutch deftly and sure-footed enough, it looked to be the limp of one who has been "crippled" for a very long time, perhaps since childhood.

I was also surprised to see, in this clearer light, that he was younger than I thought.

He didn't see me but I stepped back anyway against the wall, knowing his secret now and not wanting to embarrass him in case he recognized me, thinking how carefully beforehand he must have concealed his crutch in the farthest, blackest corner of the booth, so that I, or anyone else who happened in, wouldn't come upon it.

As he limped toward the turnstile, heads turned, following his lurching progress, watching with apprehensive glances and a certain curiosity, those passing around him giving him a wide berth even in this larger space, a look in a few of the faces like they were wondering if he'd somehow gotten into the place by mistake.

I watched him go, admiring how he got himself nimbly through the turnstile, turning his body sideways, then dragging the crutch through after him, all in one neat, economical movement. His motions were as hurrying and eager as his actions in the booth had been, only now he appeared anxious only to get away, as if he didn't want to be seen as he was, not only by myself or anyone else who might have been with him, but by anyone at all; as if his very visible lameness, particularly here, where every fantasy, where every inch of space from floor to ceiling in image after image screamed physical perfection, was something to be deeply ashamed of. Hastily, shamefacedly, he scuttled off alone out into the cold anonymity of the streets.

Then the toilet door opened and the burly man emerged first, followed closely by the other original occupant, his cheeks now flushed, an uncommon brightness in his eye, as he made a beeline for the turnstile and exited. At last, I breathed quietly to myself, and ducked inside before anyone got in ahead of me, shutting the door and waiting til the third man, now standing at the sink hacking over the basin and spitting out water, finished, and, giving me a sideways look as he wiped at his mouth with a handkerchief, his eyes red and wet, drew himself up to get past me and left.

I took his place at the sink and turned on the faucet, ran cold water over my hands, splashed some on my lips and around my mouth, and cupped my hands and filled them with water and took a sip, tipped back my head and gargled, then spewed it out and took another handful of water and rinsed out my mouth.

As I combed my beard, which was mainly salt and pepper in color with glints of red in it from all the raw carrots I eat, I got to thinking that another "advantage" of the backroom was that bodily contact was reduced considerably, the pesky nuisance of catching crabs, as in the more total nudity of the baths, reduced here practically to zero—unless, of course, you had a beard.

I stared suspiciously at my own. Parting a few strands with the comb, I leaned forward for a close inspection in the glass.

Nothing.

Still, even though I kept it clipped, I imagined, with some anxiety, crabs, Tarzan-like, swinging from hair to hair from the pubic jungles of those men I'd so far been close to right into my bush of a beard, and decided that when I got home next morning, I would douse, as I always do when I return from a trip to the baths, not only my lower areas with A-200, but my beard and mustache as well this time, just to be on the safe side.

As I raked the comb through the longer locks on my head, I thought of dousing them, too, but considered that an unnecessary worriment for now and put off thinking about it til tomorrow.

Peering cautiously at the door, which had remained closed for some time now, I quickly decided to take advantage of the empti-

ness of the place to try again to jot down some more notes, especially on my last encounter with the youth with the crutch, and
seeing his departure.

I propped myself against the wall, and started to write, manag-
ing to fill up two or three pages, including a few lines on the lad
with wheat-colored hair, when, just as before, the door swung
open and two men entered, one on the heels of the other.

That prompted me to give it up, for the time being at least, but
reluctantly, since the light was so good. Just at the moment I
stepped out of the toilet, I heard a commotion of raised voices in
the bookstore. Had the vice squad really busted in this time? I
stood still and listened, my scalp prickling again as it had earlier
at the pinball siren.

One of the clerks was shouting, "You're always coming in here
causing trouble!"

"Oh, darling, *please*," cooed a quieter but no less insistent
voice which I recognized immediately as that of the black man in
rag drag. "I *never* do!"

"You smell up the place and you annoy the customers!" yelled
the clerk. "You make trouble every time!"

"*I do not!*" responded the other flatly, and then, still in firmly
insistent tones, "Let me go in."

There was a sudden eruption of Spanish as the clerks began
chattering heatedly among themselves, with a phrase here and
there from a voice that seemed a little more lenient, citing the
weather and saying that the black youth could come into the backroom so long as he behaved himself, whatever that meant. Soon
the voices grew quieter and I moved away, starting down the short
passage towards my lucky TRUCK STOP booth. As I went, I heard
behind me the metallic whir of the turnstile and looked back to
see if it was the black youth, if they had finally let him in. Although
I waited several long moments I didn't see him enter the passage
and figured, if he had come in at all, he probably had gone around
the other way, toward the pinball section.

As I continued on down the aisle, I narrowly passed one of those
men with shoulders so wide they brushed the walls on either side,
a slow and stiffly muscled youth with a face like Dane Clark. He
was one of the several weightlifter types I'd seen plodding heavily,
solemnly through the aisles, and lumbering past me by the toilet
door a short time ago, their sturdy muscles like armatures of flesh,
with shoulders that filled the passage so you had to hug the wall,

as I did now, to let this youth pass. His biceps and pectorals were really straining the sleeves and chest of his T-shirt and, pressed so close to him I could have easily leaned forward and kissed his cheek, I smelled strong wisps of booze trailing from his set, firm mouth, his large, handsome eyes, somewhat bovine, like Dane's, having the moist, bleary look of the chronic drunk.

As he shouldered his way past me, clutching his leather jacket flung over one shoulder, the black hide of an arm band straining around his upper arm, stout black leather gloves riding up out of the back pocket of his heavy-duty levis, I was both attracted— what would it be like, I wondered, to get it on with the ghost of a movie star you once had a crush on in your early teens in the secret Saturday afternoon dark of the Embassy Theater in West-ville, New Jersey?—and repelled, too, by the reek of the alcohol, and those sad, dissolving, liquid eyes set in a rigidly handsome face.

But I dismissed it from my mind, seeing, as I've said, that such men appeared attractive only to each other, and making the turn in the passage, decided to try a different booth this time, discovering that the last one on the right in the corridor leading into the black, closetlike area beyond was empty. I slipped inside and leaned a shoulder against the door, propping one foot in front of the other and hooking my thumbs in my belt loops as I'd seen cowboys do in Grade B movies when I was a kid, the same way many of the men stood around here in other doorways and against the walls. I tried to imitate their easy nonchalance, even imagined a hay straw clenched between my teeth, attempted to freeze my features, like so many of the expressions around me, into an adolescent's pas-sive, invulnerable face, registering no more than a keen but hidden alertness to everything going on around it, a hawk in my watchfulness, totally patient, totally still, revealing nothing.

A bulky gray blur swept suddenly down the middle of the pas-sage, paused for a fraction of an instant at the closed door of the booth just across the way—from inside of which came the grap-plings of energetic activity, hoarse yelping sounds as from a ken-nel—and rapping sharply on the door, sang out in a lilting fal-setto, "*Avon calling!*" before streaking off like a dusty whirlwind into the deep shadow by the exit door at the end of the corridor.

Before this speedy apparition disappeared, I had only a split second to recognize that it was the black youth in rag drag, that he had made it in after all, and chuckled to myself, thinking that if what I'd just witnessed was an example of his fey playfulness, it was no wonder the clerks out in the shop were unhappy with his business.

After the unexpected knocking, there was a moment's deathlike silence in the yipping, frisky action in the booth across the aisle, but the puppyish sounds soon started up again, even more vigorously than before.

Now outside my booth stood a slight, small-boned Puerto Rican youth, wearing a bright red athlete's jacket, his tight curly hair glistening with oil. I invited him in and discovered, after his nimble fingers snapped open his fly like a pod, that, just as in proportion to his build, he was small, uncut, the foreskin, hanging curled from the end like a leaf of flesh, an unsprung fern as long, surprisingly, as the stem itself. I swirled my tongue around inside, flicking the tip lightly, a moist bud protected in its hooded sheath. He squeezed his small thumbs against my throat and hissed with pleasure, sharper and sharper sibilant whispers. *"Dios!"* he cried, in a hushed voice, his neck stretched back, and *"Gracias a Dios!"* although he was barely up at all.

Then, with a spastic jerk of his hips, he pulled out quickly, clutching himself. I could smell the cold of the streets still fresh on his jacket, so I knew he had just arrived, that I was perhaps his first encounter, and that he probably wanted to wait, not spend himself so quickly, hair-trigger sensitive, like so many uncut men.

He closed up his trousers in one deft sweep of his fine-boned fingers and departing swiftly without a word, slipped out into the passage and scampered away.

I saw him several times later, circling with a quick, light step in the corridors, where a few times in passing, eyes lowered, he glanced sideways at me through his heavily lashed lids. Once, I saw him standing silently waiting in a hidden corner off the aisles, the bright red of his jacket signaling his presence like a flare in the darkness.

I straightened up and, standing again in the doorway, the hors d'oeuvre I'd just tasted giving me an appetite for more, I groomed my mustache, brushing at it with both hands, stuck my head out and stared, birdlike, both ways down the passage, my head turning in unison, I noted, with my two neighbors in the booths next to mine, just as I'd observed those other heads turning along this part of the maze when I'd first entered the backroom.

Stepping briskly into the passage and moving energetically from booth to booth was a slim, wiry man, looking to be in his sixties, dressed in an old navy peacoat and black turtleneck, the high rolled brim of a sock cap slouched flat over his sloping skull, a fringe of gray hair about his ears. Not at all timid about sticking his head into each doorway and reaching a hand inside to grope its unseen tenant, in no way deterred by refusal—if his hand was shoved away, as it was by both my neighbors along the aisle, he simply moved on in his springy step to the next open booth to try his luck again, which happened to be the one I was leaning in.

He squinted in at me with a bright, inquiring look, then slipped his hand out and touched my crotch, murmuring slyly, with a little smile both impish and cocky, "Whaddaya' say, kid? Want me to sharpen your pencil?" his fingers persistent, sure and skilled, like an old pro, stroking me into instant arousal, so that I was just on the verge of inviting him in when I remembered the long night ahead of me.

Not knowing what to expect there or how much energy I might need for it, I clasped his hand affectionately, leaned out of the booth and whispered in his ear, "Listen, thanks a lot, but I can't right now," and then added, without thinking, more perhaps because I didn't want to hurt his feelings, "Would you like to come to a Saturnalia?"

He cocked his head back and to one side, like a rooster listening, and stared at me curiously. "A *what?*" he finally asked, screwing up his features as if he'd just smelled something rather unpleasant. I attempted to explain to him as rapidly as possible, as I had with the lad with wheat-colored hair, but even before I was halfway finished he dropped my hand and started backing away, muttering in staccato out the side of his mouth, "Sorry, buddy, thanks but no thanks. I got other things to do tonight."

He hurried away in his brisk, lean gait, almost a trot, shaking his head and glancing back dubiously at me, then made off directly around the corner, no doubt to poke his head into the first open cubicle he came to there.

As I watched him go, I could've bitten my tongue, thinking how foolish it was of me to spout on about the Fairy Circle and its Saturnalia celebration, extending invitations to utter strangers, idiotically trying to share my own excited anticipation, here, of all places, where interests focused chiefly on one thing only, and much of it fast and not too choosy either. It was as preposterous as if I popped into the McDonald's over on First Avenue on my way to the East 2nd Street loft tonight and went randomly among the male customers munching on their Big Macs and fries, inviting any and all to join me in the evening's festivities. I really vowed this time not to mention another word about the Saturnalia to anyone again here in the backroom, a vow which, once more in my overwhelming enthusiasm, was later to be broken.

The muscle-bound man who looked like Dane Clark ambled by on another of his turns around, riveting his eyes on me an instant before continuing on his way. When I stuck my head out the door a little to gaze after him, I noticed that he had stopped a few strides on in the niche diagonally across the passage, the one where the grayhaired man had stood masturbating. He was staring back at me, his tipsy eyes narrowed to slits, his leather jacket now draped casually over his wide shoulders. Even in the dim recess I could see he had dull beige hair clipped short about the ears, and despite his massive build was boyishly appealing, with one of those broad-featured, open faces you feel you can trust, the kind of face that's likely to get away with anything, even murder.

He was probably in his mid-twenties and as he widened those large, innocuous eyes I could see they had a hint of a smile in them as he slapped his gloves idly in the palm of his hand while he continued to observe me with his level gaze, his body swaying slightly from side to side, whether from tipsiness or an idle, unconscious rocking motion, I wasn't certain.

I stared back at him, uneasy, excited by the reawakened ghost of my silly adolescent crush on a creature in grainy, celluloid shadows, his flesh and blood counterpart appearing equally shadowy in the movie-dark niche across the aisle with its spray-painted graffito gleaming phosphorescent all around him.

I was put off, too, as I've said, by the memory of his booze-strong breath, and wanted to look away but found that I couldn't, that I was fascinated by those eyes, which once again narrowed on me, that I was taken by the whole look of him, fascinated against my will.

He now started posing, flexing his heavy muscles for me in a rippling show of pride. Watching him, I felt myself unexpectedly bitten by that mischievous imp which reminds us not to take ourselves too seriously, was stung with a sudden giggly longing to be a totally lovely sissy, the nelliest of queens, the airiest fairy with see-through rainbow wings, free of all that stiff and solemn testicular heaviness, that masculinist strut in boots and leathers, always reminding me of the goose-stepping Nazis in the newsreels of my childhood, boots always stomping someone or something beneath them, fists in leather gloves always slapping somebody around.

In the face of his pumped up stiffness, I yearned to grow even more supple and willowy, with pliant, uncalcified hips swivelly enough to undulate in dancing circles around all the unyielding tetherposts I'd ever been tied to, those hobbles of cock-worship in fearful appeasement, from my father on out, of power and threats which had nothing at all to do with the playfulness of butterfly delights and everything to do with bullying and maiming and death.

I thought of our little Fairy Circle, of all our past gatherings, and our gathering again this night in the Saturnalia ahead, of our raised energies moving sunwise from joined hand to joined hand, as in all the previous circles I'd been to, and suddenly had a sharp physical hunger to be there, right that very moment, to feel that clear strength and unity again, that indefinable glow of affection, the bubbling excitement and levity that lifted me out of myself into airy regions of inner and outer space and awareness I'd never dreamed existed before.

I wished with all my heart it was quarter to eight and I was there, in the loft on 2nd Street. If anyone needed our Fairy Circle, I thought, starting to feel calm again, it was the man in leather across the aisle who, perhaps having sensed the mockery of my irreverent silent laughter, gave me a lazy, superior smile and, his jacket having slid off to one side during his muscular preenings, hitched it up over his shoulders, stepped haughtily out of the niche and, thrusting his head back, strolled grandly away in his rocking gait down the corridor.

I drew nearer to the door and peeked out, watching him move along the darkened wall of the open area near the emergency door as he eyed the men leaning there quietly smoking, each of them shrinking back closer to the wall as his shoulders swung past, until he melted into the shadows in that darkest corner and I could see him no longer.

I held my wrist up to the ghostly fluorescent light to read my watch: just after six. Too late to go to the Three Lives and the other bookstores for they all must be closed by now, so I calculated I still had an hour to spend before starting across town for the Saturnalia. Since it was far too cold to wander the streets, or stand under a streetlamp or outside a well-lighted shop window trying to write with frozen fingers as I had on the way down Christopher Street, and to go into a cafeteria like Bagel And, with its fancy prices, for warmth and note-taking, would mean buying something at least, I decided it was more practical to stay where I was and spend the little remaining time here the best way I could, perhaps even at last finding some hidden away place to comfortably write in. Perhaps, too, I would have another amiable adventure in one of the dark booths before departing. My spirits perked up at the prospect.

First things first, however. Even though my intimacies with the Puerto Rican in the red jacket hadn't amounted to much—no size-queen pun intended—I still figured it was prudent to get myself around to the toilet for a quick rinse out.

On the way, as I rounded the corner of the passage, I noted that the dark area by the exit door was now curiously empty, except for a lone, indistinguishable figure standing back in the deepest corner. I stopped, bewildered, seeing what I at first took to be the voluminous shape of a woman dressed in a long-sleeved gown, gray as dawn, puffy around the waist and tapering in descending layers of coarse-looking fabric to a narrow hem around the calves, standing very still and straight, almost prim, like a statue, but the corner was so dark I couldn't make out features or form. The enigmatic figure had a smokily archaic appearance, like a recently unearthed fertility goddess propped up mysteriously in this dingiest recess of the backroom. Flashes of passing auto lights through clefts around the edges of the door swept occasionally across its face, giving it a strobelike illumination, the strong, blunt features seemed like the carved ebony head of a god or goddess under deep jungle foliage, speckled with dancing sunlight leaking down through dense liana leaves from high above.

My curiosity overcoming my apprehension, I moved a step or two closer, peering intently and then soon scented a familiar odor: the moldering, cellar-damp smell of rags. And of course it was he, I perceived now, standing quite stiff and dignified in his mildewy scraps. Close to him now, I could also detect the sweet, heavy odor of Dixie Peach Pomade on his greasy curls.

"Yazz, yazz," crooned the black youth, beginning to sway, leaning closer and closer to me, the hairs on the back of my neck bristling as he swayed nearer, finally whispering confidentially, in a hushed, breathless voice directly into my ear: "Walk careful on the grass, honey, you might crush a violet," then swinging away and rocking back and forth on his heels, humming to himself.

It flitted through my mind, after that remark, that he'd be a distinct asset at the Saturnalia, but I hesitated to mention it to him, worried the others might be put off by his malodorous scent and resent it if I brought him along.

Now, along with the shrill thin music of the wind pushing in through the cracks in the door, came the assaultive beat of cock-rock blaring at full volume, evidently coming from one of those Loud Mouth transistor radios carried on the shoulder, speaker clamped against the ear, the volume increasing as its owner approached, the aggressive sound blasting directly through the door as it passed, then fading as it moved on down the street.

"Yazz, yazz," hummed the black youth over and over, shimmying his hips to the rhythms on the radio, shaking loose with renewed pungency at the same time the odor of his rags, the strains of the beat growing fainter and fainter as whoever was carrying the radio moved across West Street in the direction of the river.

Before I left, I touched his hand, and he stopped rocking and singing to himself, seemed to wait. I kissed him quickly on the cheek, whispering thanks to him, for what he'd said about a violet in this empty, blind corner with its wintery drafts blowing in all around us, telling him I knew just what he meant, that his words reminded me of days in early spring when the new grass is so painfully green you hate to walk on it for fear of hurting it.

Then I hurried away, and slipped around the corner, careful going down the step this time, getting to know the place, and moved into the cheerier-lighted arcade area, feeling a springiness bounce back into my step again.

I had the toilet all to myself this time, so I was able to finish my business in peace. Then, wanting to take advantage of this unexpected privacy, knowing it wouldn't last long—I'd given up all thoughts of trying to scribble in here—I leaned my shoulders against the wall, sticking my legs straight out in front of me, closed my eyes, and luxuriated in the solitude, even finding the glare of the naked bulb burning red against my shut lids a relief after so much heavy darkness out in the booths and passageways. My arms dangling behind me, I felt so relaxed I began to go off into a very light doze, standing on my feet, my eyes snapping open, after only a few seconds it seemed, as the door scraped open and a man in tie and business suit revealed through his unbuttoned overcoat, peeped timidly in and, seeing me, started to back out, perhaps because I must have looked like a junky on the nod.

"That's okay," I said, waving at him to come on in, "I'm finished."

I shoved myself away from the wall and moved past him and went out into the anteroom area, actually feeling rested and more wide awake after those few moments of being alone and my very brief nap.

Now I began to feel that old growing excitement, like a pod about to burst, not from increasing erotic stimulation, always running in me anyway like the blood itself, but from the accumulation of details and impressions I'd been picking up here and there since the Oscar Wilde Bookshop and my walk down Christopher Street, and particularly here, in the backroom, where my mind, in storing it all up, was now becoming so really saturated I desperately needed to find a quiet place somewhere to sit down and begin to unload some of it on paper.

It suddenly struck me that I could go into one of the booths, thinking immediately of the booth where I'd had so much previous luck, stick in one of my precious quarters—hard to part with, but I could think of no other way at the moment—and by the light from the screen be able to see well enough, I hoped, to get down the most pressing and important observations, no matter how brief the illumination from the inexorably timed projector, if I wrote fast enough.

The need taking on the proportions of uncontrollable urgency, I turned quickly into the passage at the right and headed down it to good old TRUCK STOP.

When I got there I was disappointed to see a dim shape hovering in the doorway, a slim young man, his fringe of a sandy beard jutting out the door. I decided to wait and not look for another since I knew this booth had a door which could be shut for privacy, and a bench for sitting, and easier writing, all necessary requirements, I felt, for my few valuable moments of twenty-five cents worth of light to write by.

While waiting, I stationed myself at the corner and my impatience to get into the booth momentarily subsided as I became absorbed with the many types of men milling past me, and listened as I overheard a breathless amazed voice through the wall of the booth opposite exclaim, "You're so *skinny* and it's such a *big* one!" and a softer voice responding slyly, "The closer to the bone, the sweeter the meat," and the first voice answering, "In that case, I think I'll have seconds," and lapsed into silence.

From the jukebox down the aisle to my left, Donna Summer was singing again, ingenious at hitting just the right notes to set vibrating a luxurious self-pitying loneliness in the listener. I tuned her out, resistant, unlike less sober days when I slobbered alone over the bar at such music, thinking instead of the plastic JESUS FIRST sign she carried around in her grab-all clutch bag and held up to a TV audience one night, her flawlessly unspontaneous performance when she sang appearing as carefully calculated, right down to the swing of her arms, as her recorded voice, a voice so technically perfect it sounded studio-manufactured in meticulously selected acetate bits and snippets.

A big-boned youth with thinning hair and childish good looks, in long-sleeved red and white striped polo shirt, swayed, with disco hips, to Donna's tune in the doorway of a nearby booth, singing along in a voice you could tell, from the lift of his brows, he thought was pretty snazzy, singing to anyone wandering by who would listen and maybe be enticed to enter his booth to make different music.

A few black men were circling around in outfits just about as ragtag as my own, ripped and faded fatigue pants and sweatshirts and long, colorless, nondescript jackets and coats; a few dressed like laborers in dull heavy-duty workclothes and knit GI caps; and others in streetcorner-casual outfits, varied, unmatched, loose, like what people hanging out on the street might wear; one hefty man the exception in business suit and porkpie hat; none of it looking like the self-conscious attire of the cowboys without horses and the motorcyclists without motorcycles posturing everywhere in the aisles.

Serious black faces, all but shadows themselves staring out from the shadowy booths, yellowish whites of the eyes showing guarded suspicion as they look at you like they are not looking at you, a sense of their being there, yet not being there, that self-preserving desensitivity in white surroundings, aliens even here, among all the other aliens.

Far down the longer aisle, just before the obliteration of all light in the yawning darkness of the small orgy area beyond, I spotted a youth, one elbow propped shoulder high against the wall outside the niche with the smaller version of the spray-painted phallic graffito. His mousy hair was shorn close in punkrock style, giving his puffy, sallow face the strangely attractive look of a surly boy, very much like the facial expression in the daguerreotype, taken just around the time he'd met Verlaine, of the seventeen year old Rimbaud in *A Lover's Cock*, the book I'd used as a screen at Oscar Wilde.

Except this youth, instead of wearing a crooked, clumsily tied bow tie and heavy woolen jacket, was squeezed into a cheap imitation leather jacket, one of those tan colored vinyl jobs, already cracked and flaking from wear and cold weather, his wrists poking out the too short sleeves—"Wet weeds slapping at my wrists in the mornings," sang in my head, from one of Rimbaud's on-the-road poems—the jacket, unless it was a hand-me-down, probably chosen a few sizes smaller on purpose since its tightness nicely pointed up his well-formed chest and arms.

He looked familiar to me, and as I screwed up my eyes to get a better look, I realized he was the same young hustler I'd seen earlier standing by McNulty's near Bedford Street on my way down here. Couldn't blame him for coming in out of the weather, the cold so severe, and business way off no doubt because of it.

He looked to be no more than twenty, and was speaking earnestly to the man wearing the pea jacket and navy blue sock hat I'd seen earlier darting from booth to booth and who had turned down my invitation to the Saturnalia. He was leaning forward, listening attentively to the hustler, head tipped to one side. After a few moments, he flatly shook his head and stepped impatiently around the youth, moving into the black shadow at the far end of the passage, disappearing immediately as if he'd dropped into a deep pit.

Shrugging his shoulders, the youth pushed away from the wall and advanced a few steps down the aisle to the first of the booths, moving closer to where I stood. Buttonholing another, also somewhat older man, he again leaned his elbow up on the nearest wall and began to talk to him in the same earnest and confidential manner. He seemed high on something, was agitated and quick in his movements and speech, speeding, like he was on amphetamines, maybe on those same Black Beauties hawked on the street, speaking in that same hushed babbling.

When this man, his mouth set firmly, also shook his head and walked away, the young hustler hurried on to stop and corner yet another middle-aged man, catching this one as he peered curiously in at the doorway of the next booth, swinging around to face him with a slightly startled expression, the youth repeating his hustle all over again, precisely as before.

Eventually he worked his way around to me, his face breaking into a charmingly affable grin as he approached. Seeing that smile, a little too open, a little too friendly, I instantly stiffened with resistance, my nose quivering with caution. Remembering the sign by the turnstile and the one just inside the entrance to the back-room, I touched my wallet in the side pocket of my ski jacket, making sure the pocket was zipped shut.

"How's it goin'?" he asked, immediately palsy, a pleasant, easy-going tenor in his voice, that seductive register I used to hear in my own mouth, like an attractive stranger speaking, when I was high on benzedrine, the same drug-eeriness out of his own lips. He suddenly lurched to one side, like a drunk, catching himself just in time, his grin now becoming an apologetically foolish you-know-how-it-is grin. Since I couldn't smell any alcohol on him, I figured he must be on drugs for sure, though what, exactly, I couldn't tell. Beside his right eye, so swollen it was all but closed, was an ugly black and blue welt.

In spite of that, his smiling eyes, at least the good one, crinkled with geniality, looking directly into mine, artfully, nakedly flirta-tious, in swift foxy glances suggesting glimpses of untold and undreamable pleasures.

I thawed a little, but was careful.

"I'm fine," I ventured.

He put his hand on my shoulder, his eyes never once leaving mine, eyes all sincerity. I shifted my feet, uncomfortable, knowing I was about to be worked over, yet having to admire his talent, his ability to charm, instantly conveying that feeling that you are the most important person in the world at that moment.

"Look, I'll level with you," he began, in that tone of voice I had heard countless times before, even in my own ears since, as I said, it had issued often enough out of my own mouth, which tipped me off that I was in for a walloping snow job. But again, his looks and manner were so irresistible I simply had to hear the rest of it, and so ignored my suspicions and listened politely.

Leaning his arm over my shoulder against the corner of the booth, in effect pinning me there, his face intimately close, drop-ping his voice to that attractive pitch which told me he was taking me into his confidence, he spoke in the same skimmingly quiet tones I'd heard him use with the others, telling me the same old story: When his parents found out he was gay, they kicked him out of the house, another youthful throwaway, which was certainly sad enough, if it was true. Ever since, he'd had to make his living by his wits and cunning alone, up and down Christopher Street and on the streets of the Village, in good weather and bad, taking what he could get, ending with, "I'll be honest with ya': yeah, I'm a hustler, but I give you your money's worth," and here he jerked his head in the direction of the booth he was leaning against, "Whaddaya' say? Maybe the two of us can work something out. Let's tell that bozo in there we wanna use the place," meaning the sandy bearded youth still standing in the doorway of TRUCK STOP, and he gave me a winningly lascivious smile, adding, "You won't be sorry, buddy, I'll *guarantee* you that."

That smile of his, and his Rimbaud looks (did he also write street-poetry?) and the cant of his sinuous hips, told me I was certain I wouldn't be, except for the matter of his being so strung out, so spacy. I couldn't blame him for seeking the warmth of the backroom to hustle in, futile as it might be, and I shifted my feet again, uneasy at being hemmed in, trying to duck out from under his elbow, but he stood unmoving, ignoring my attempt to move away. Then, not knowing what else to say, I said simply, "But nobody pays here."

He eyed me briefly, his face deadpan now, drained of its affability, a cross expression, fleetingly visible, quivering across his bloodless features. But not giving up that easily, his adolescently attractive face broke into that amenable smile once more.

"Take a look at what you get!" he grinned, his hand slipping from the wall, freeing me, as he doubled over from the hips in the aisle, blocking the way, so that several men wanting to get by had to stop and wait.

Snug and shapely in trousers made of a loose but clinging fabric, he stretched out his behind as far as it would go and, pointing it up in the air, began to waggle it vigorously and provocatively back and forth. Gyrating it in slow, enticing circles, his jacket gradually riding up, the flesh of his hips became exposed, the cleavage of his buttocks, bunched and bulging in the tight waist of the low-slung trousers, squeezing in and out, the dimples over his kidneys winking in the ashen light; an increasingly spastic, unerotic wiggling, so speeded up and grotesquely violent finally, I stepped back a pace into the shadowy area between the booths, unnerved by his desperation, and saddened, too.

At length, he pulled himself up and, out of breath, staggered again and had to grip the edge of the booth for support. He was still smiling at me, hopeful, the smile a bit forced now, tiny points of color, like dabs of rouge, glowing in each pallid cheek.

"Whaddaya' say?"

I shook my head, extended my palms out, empty. "I'm broke. I tried to tell you."

A tiny grimace of displeasure pursed his lips for the fraction of a second, then, like he'd pressed a button somewhere within him, that automatic grin broke over his face once more.

"Right!" he cried, agreeably enough, all confidence again, slapping my shoulder, then leaning close, his good eye, genuinely serious for the first time, glancing sharply either side of him, as if he might be overheard, before whispering, "Listen, even any spare change'll do, babe, if you got it. I really need it."

I blushed for him, seeing the edge of shame in his eye, what it cost his pride to ask me that.

I fingered the lone quarter in my pocket, the two-bits I planned to insert in the coinbox in the booth to buy myself a little light as soon as the booth was vacant. The hustler had tried so hard with his little spontaneous act, the show alone had certainly earned him something. I was sorely tempted to part with my measly twenty-five cents but, since I really needed to write down as much as I could of what had happened during the afternoon so far, and since I could've used a handout myself, I had to pretend to ignore his request and asked him instead, "How'd you get the black eye?"

He glanced at me quizzically, the question obviously catching him off guard, but he replied without a moment's hesitation, "Got it falling down the stairs when my folks kicked me out. My old man booted me square in the ass, yelling he didn't want no fag of a son living under his roof."

I saw his one clear eye gleam in the dusty light, as if the idea had just occurred to him and that he might use this latest bit of information, true or imagined, to work me over some more, to finally loosen the strings of my heart along with my purse strings.

All I said was, "Does it hurt?"

"Yeah," he said, touching it gingerly, "it hurts plenty," with a note of self-pity, wincing and making a shushing noise between puckered lips. Watching intently for my response but seeing nothing encouraging, he suddenly snapped out, "Gotta split! Catch ya' later, babe," and lurched away down the passage, swaying from side to side, his shoulders bumping the walls as he went.

I watched him as he stopped and spoke to another man, also around my age, who had just turned into the far end of the corridor. The young hustler again leaned his arm against the wall in front of this new prospect, all but blocking his way, holding him captive just as he had done with me and the others, tilting his head close, delivering his spiel in that same intimate, confiding manner.

You had to hand it to him, I thought, watching him admiringly. He was an artful con, if not a successful one, at least not here. But no sooner had the thought gone through my mind when, after only a few moments of listening, the older man, who was weaving a little like he was a bit tipsy, nodded understandingly, and patting the youth's shoulder, gave a toss of his head to one side, indicating the booth they were standing next to, the very same one I'd been in with the young man with the crutch, and, even in that dark stretch of the passage, I could see the flash of the hustler's seductive smile, a smile now of mingled gratitude and triumph, as he swaggered into the booth with the older man and the low rumble of the door was heard as it briskly slid shut after them.

I'd been so preoccupied watching the hustler proposition this last prospect, I'd neglected to keep a steady eye on my lucky booth, and was relieved to see that that thinly bearded chin was no longer sticking out the doorway, its slender occupant evidently having vacated it while I'd been absorbed in the little scenario farther down the passage. I quickly stepped in, feeling a bit like a criminal, stealing space and a few minutes time for purposes other than what men came back here for. But I realized how out-of-place it would look, unnerving to the other customers, and risky, too, if I just casually leaned against a wall and openly began scribbling things down, looking like a reporter. What a stir it might cause, and might get me kicked out in the street as well!

With the door shut tight it was too black in the booth to see anything, never mind trying to write down notes. I wished now I carried in my bag one of those tiny penlights, as I'd also wished at the baths when I was first searching for the number of my cubicle, the kind kids flicked on to read by under the blankets when they're supposed to be asleep. That would've been a great convenience, and moneysaver, at a time like this.

Having glimpsed them earlier through the open door of the booth across the way, where the two men mimed the actions of the pair performing on the screen, a peeping tom watching a peep show, I knew how quick, like premature ejaculations, these briefly timed film loops came to a climax, so to speak, and so made everything ready: got out my ballpoint pen, clicked out the point, ready to write, clutched my notepad in the same hand, while with the other I grudgingly fished the quarter from my jeans and stuck it in Slot A—TRUCK STOP, which promised "Wild Action," but the only action I really looked forward to in the next few moments was moving my pen over those small sheets of paper once the screen lit up.

As I heard the projector snap on above my head, instantly lighting the screen in that cold white light, I had barely put the point of my pen on the paper, preparing to write down a few particulars on my encounter with the youth with wheat-colored hair, when there appeared, snatching at my attention, a closeup shot in listless technicolor of an aryan-blond teenager, fuzzy at first, fading in and out of focus, a black trucker's cap perched rakishly aslant his gleaming curls, skin tanned buttery gold—one of Hitler's dream-children, except that these glacially Nordic eyes, the blueness of fjords, were closed in dreamy ecstasy, the moist lips, pink as sockeye salmon, parted in eager anticipation, as into the lefthand corner of the picture, aiming directly toward that glistening rouge-red aperture like a fish drawn to a flickering lure, swam the ceramically glossy glans of a black and husky penis.

Slapping my head, fiercely reminding myself what I'd put my money in the slot for in the first place, I tore my eyes away, forcing myself to concentrate on writing about the real, living blond I'd been intimate with only a short while back in this very same space, determined not to waste one more second of light, nor one more penny of my equally precious quarter either, and dutifully scratched away at my pad.

But the illumination from the screen was disappointingly weak so that I had to scrunch closer to the picture to get any light thrown on my note paper at all. Just then a shadow fell across the page and, looking up, I saw, to my dismay, and also with a sudden start of erotic excitement, that the scene had changed and the black man himself had now appeared, in fullshot, also wearing nothing but a trucker's cap set squarely on his head, visibly and hulkingly muscular in every part of his anatomy, which was a treat for the eyes but a disappointment as far as the light in the booth went, since the darkness of his skin, despite the glistening highlights of his well-oiled muscles, darkened the interior considerably. What little light there was in the first place now became so diminished that even though I stood pressed as close as I could to the miniature screen, I was unable to see what I was writing.

Next, I tried holding the pad up directly into the lightbeam from the projector, but found that was no good either since, not only was it awkward, but my head and either shoulder, no matter how I turned, blocked a good deal of the light.

Luckily at that moment the bright blond youth beamed out at me amidst the celluloid shadows, his mouth opening so wide it revealed not only two rows of perfect, very white, light-giving teeth, but even the pink glittering flap at the very back of the throat, which was quivering noticeably, his image brightening the inside of the booth again, making it possible once more to write.

I held the point of my pen frozen suspended above the notepad, however, as I watched, saucer-eyed, what I at first took to be a humpback whale arching and slicing its way across the waveringly spumy light of the screen, but which turned out to be the enormous genitalia of the black man still swimming in its teasingly slow journey up from the bottom of the frame toward the beckoning lips of the blond adolescent, lips which undulated in the watery light now rising up to the top of the picture, like the rosy flukes of some enormous albino sea creature.

As the camera zoomed in on that dark leviathan, lovingly detailing every glistening barnaclelike pore along its humped and lengthy surface, the face of the blond, my main source of light, was once more completely blotted out, and it was again impossible to see the small square of paper in front of me.

I clicked shut the point of my pen and, admitting defeat, slumped back on the scarred wooden bench, deciding, at a less eye-straining distance, to at least get my money's worth and observe the rest of what remained of the loop, which now depicted the blond youth slowly beginning to hunker down in front of the black, a sun-bronzed worshiper bowing before some darker monumental phallic idol, when I heard the abrupt snap of the projector from within the wall above my head and saw the screen go blank, the booth plunged in total darkness again, the coin box hungry for another two-bit fix.

I sat glumly for a few moments in total blackness, realizing it had been a goofy idea in the first place, thinking I might just as well have given the money wasted here to the young hustler, for all the good it did. I refused to put another coin in that insatiable slot, feeling cheated, not only of light to write by, but even of the small satisfaction of seeing the outcome of the film (although I knew very well how it would end, I still felt a crotchety disappointment). All the loops were evidently timed to shut off precisely at such enticing high points, interrupted deliberately to lure another quarter from your pocket, and then another.

As I sat there I got to wondering about these young men, who they were and why they did it, literally exposing themselves to the world with innocent, open faces—or at least the ability to project that—aware, as women have always been forced to be aware, of their salability. Many of them no more than boys, really, with negligent beauty who are never so beautiful again, and who maybe attempt to cash in on it while they can. A lot of them doing it I supposed because they had to, needing a buck; and others maybe doing it just for the plain hell of it, proud of their bodies and their apparatus, vaingloriously eager to show it all off. Nervy kids, with fine sturdy physiques they're simply just born with, who just love fucking and love sharing what they got, especially when there's a camera around, with anybody, anytime, for money or, more often than not, for nothing.

Was part of it also an unconscious, inarticulate need, in fear of death, to freeze that quickly aging body in time, in frozen frames of acetate? In years to come, as the looks fade and the buns sag, the once proud cock shriveling, was there the desperate need for the still-gratifying realization of the immortal male self (since immortality seems so much a male preoccupation), young and alive and as potently and profitably beautiful in its nakedness as ever, spinning, in one's old age and even long after one's death, somewhere out in the dark night on the movie screens of skinflick theaters in Times Square or on Eighth Avenue, or on the walls of steambath orgy rooms, or in any number of private rooms with curtains tightly drawn, or here in these same shoddy peepshow booths, arousing the blood, still, of those in secret, hidden watching, living on in the enlivened blood of other men, capable still of rousing their hungers, the eternal youthful self animate forever in grainily flickering electronic shadows?

I wanted to write all this down right then and there, but resigned myself at last to the fact that my hope of finding a bit of illumination here in the backroom for note-taking was hopelessly doomed. For the remaining short time I had I might as well relax and look out for pleasure. So resolved, I scanned the passageway in both directions and, feeling optimistic, reached into my bag again for my little container of Life and touched up my lips with a generous daub, then peeked out into the corridor once more. I didn't have far to look, or long to wait.

He had a full head of curly hair and a neatly trimmed beard, so red, hair and beard seemed to gleam with a fire of their own in the dark air. A man of medium size, he looked in as he went by, a cursory glance, took a few more steps, paused, then circled back again, his shoes catching my eye—he had surprisingly small feet—they were so polished they almost twinkled in the slate-gray light. He was wearing a smartly tailored knee-length overcoat, a slim attaché case gripped in one hand, and looked very much like one of the business commuters I'd seen hurrying down Christopher Street to the PATH trains at the beginning of the rush hour.

He paced by the booth again, once more gazing in at me, this time with a more lingering, penetrating glance. On the next turn around he stepped up close to the doorway and I could see concealed in that dense bush of fiery beard a fine pair of eyes and well-shaped nose. Although he was obviously fair-skinned, his face appeared lightly tanned.

I nodded to him and stepped back a pace, and he, accepting the gesture of welcome, moved in beside me with such alacrity I stumbled backwards against the wall. He mumbled an apology and, no nonsense about him, set his attaché case on the floor, spread his legs apart for better footing (an almost universal gesture back here), unbuttoned his overcoat and, parting the flaps wide like he was opening a stage curtain, held them bunched back in his fists as he breathed softly to me in a raspy voice, "I just got off work and I'm horny as hell."

I reached a hand between his open coat, my fingers spreading, caressing the woolly darkness of his trousers, traced the outline of his penis as it swelled down his left pantleg, stretching the wool tighter and tighter, felt the flesh beneath the cloth throbbing as my fingers strummed up and down it; could smell the cold from the street still hidden in the deep folds of his coat, and closed my eyes and breathed it in deeply, tiny pockets of fresh air in the stale, overheated atmosphere of the booth.

The flaps of his coat held jammed on his hips formed black wings that blocked out even what meager light there was from the corridor, but, with the deft fingers of the blind, getting used to seeing with my hands in the dark, I quickly undid his belt and loosened his clothing, tucking aside his shirttails and skinning down his briefs, then sank back on the seat and pulled him close to me.

Even with the door open, it was too dark to see, and I hadn't the sensitivity of the blind to feel color, but I imagined his pubic hair to be as red as the hair of his beard. I did, however, clearly perceive a band of very white skin around his hips the precise size of a pair of bikini swim trunks, the flesh on his belly and thighs a deeper olive shade, a suntan no doubt gotten on a recent winter vacation. I hungrily pressed my nose close to his belly to smell the color of sunlight there, dreaming cabanas and royal palms and tropical waters like jade, the scent of a promise, in this shortest day when the light shut down so early, of the sun returning.

I wasn't prepared for the fatness of it, nor the length, which suddenly sprang up an inch or two above his navel. As I took him into my mouth, he began pulling and rubbing my hair, rolling my head gently between his palms, like he was loosening the skin of an orange, and tweaking my ears playfully, then reaching down my shirt and pinching my tits with a light, teasing pressure. None of it painful, was just this side of it, was, in fact, extremely stimulating, especially when he rubbed and massaged my scalp with his hard, blunt fingers.

Once, to catch my breath, I peeped up and saw that he stood with his head thrust back, the tip of his beard pointed in the air, the half-moon of exposed throat amazingly white beneath, while his strenuous hands continued to work over my hair and down my chest, a lively tingling that sent me back to my work with a will.

As with most men that size, it took a while, but finally, with a raucous cry, he slammed hard against me with his hips, in his eagerness trying to get his entire tool down my throat, a clear impossibility, so that it was painful, gagging me, but I pressed my hands firmly against his thighs, holding him at a reasonable distance, which he didn't try to break, circled one hand around the base of his cock, shortening his strokes and allowing me space to breathe, as he shuddered against me in wave after wave of such dizzying force I felt for sure, like my earlier experience with the broncobuster youth with the crutch, he would set the whole booth rocking.

When he quieted down at last, he pulled me up by the shoulders and kissed me. "You really know how to do it," he murmured, in such a way that it made me feel good. We talked for a few moments as he straightened his clothes and I took out my handkerchief and swiped at my eyes and nose; spoke, I noted once more, in those hushed tones used here, as though we were in a confessional or a funeral parlor.

I asked him where he'd gotten such fine color and he told me he'd just flown back the day before from Aruba—the image of the white-hulled training ship that looked like a cruise liner moored at the foot of Christopher Street, the one I'd seen on my way down here, loomed in my mind.

"Spent two weeks on the beach."

I felt a pang of resentment at the casual way he said it, plain jealous, I guess, not that I ever wanted to go to Aruba, but that he had the gay bucks to just take off and do something like that.

"In fact, just this same time yesterday I was having sex on the sand under the sun," he said, putting a final hitch in his belt. "Thought I'd worn myself out. Surprised I haven't."

I could see him grinning slyly in the dark. He reached out and caressed the side of my neck. "But there's no sex like good old sex in the Big Apple," he added in a whisper. "I *love* gay New York."

He picked up his attaché case, saying cheerily, "Maybe I'll meet you here again sometime," gripped my hand in parting and stepped down into the passage.

I leaned out and watched him head around at a brisk walk to the turnstile, listened for the metallic whir of the crossbar as he shoved through it, feeling rejuvenated after the workout he gave me, my scalp and chest still vibrating, my ears feeling as red as a blush, my throat feeling slightly scorched, not too unpleasantly, like I'd swallowed another gulp of seawater. I thought of going around to the toilet to once more perform my ritual mouthwashing with water, but as with the wheat-haired youth, I wanted to keep the taste of him with me a little while longer.

I lifted my wrist again to try to read my watch in the sparse light. Squinting close to the dial, the hands appeared to read a quarter to seven, and since we'd been told to be at the loft by quarter to eight sharp, and it would be a bit of a hike over to the Lower East Side (I'd save the fifty cent bus fare by walking), and since the address where we were to meet was in a neighborhood I hadn't been in for years—a friend from Black Mountain days having once put me up at his fifth floor walkup on East 5th Street when I was down and out and had no place to go and was in a bad way, drugging and drinking—and wasn't any longer too familiar with, I realized I'd better get started soon.

Even though it was well after five o'clock, the workday over for some time now, the aisles were getting more crowded with a scattering of slightly older, and paunchier, men dressed in business suits and carrying briefcases, like the red bearded man I'd just parted from; cruising tidy and cleanshaven among the bearded and rougher dressed cowboys and stevedores. A number of them smelled of afterwork cocktails as I brushed close by them in the narrow, busier spaces between the booths, several of them giving me the eye in between nervously looking at their watches, anxious perhaps to get to the PATH station back up the block to catch a train and make it under the river to their suburban split-levels in Jersey, in time for supper with the wife and kids, the backroom booths way stations of momentary relief after a harrying day on the job. From the jukebox, sultry women's voices belting out "GIVE ME SOME HOTSTUFF!" reverberated in the passage.

In the meantime, I decided I should get out and take another, perhaps one last turn around the maze, stretch my legs a little. But as I stood up, I saw a man standing in the doorway, gripping the jambs in his fists and giving me the once-over. He had a round, wide-featured face, heavy-lidded, full-lipped, suggesting, with its short black beard, an enticing sensual coarseness, tempered by dark eyes which, though solemnly intent, had a hint of the playful puppy in them. In his black sock hat, plaid lumber jacket, sturdy dungarees and boots, he had the look of a habitué of the place, and all he needed was a longshoreman's hook stuck in his belt to complete the image of a dockworker.

He stepped in and embraced me with such warmth, tiny feathers escaping from my leaky down vest flew up and tickled my nose, then scattered down about us like snowflakes on a winter's night in the black air of the cubicle. Unbuckling me without a moment's delay, he yanked down my frayed briefs with such abruptness the exposed elastic in the legs snagged a few of my thigh hairs and gave me a pinch that really smarted, but I was soon distracted from this irritation when he lay the flat of his broad tongue under my stem, the point of it skating along it, drawing looping figure eights all up and down, then curled his tongue round the shaft in a delicious squeeze that had me clenching my jaws and straining my neck back from the unbearable pleasure of it.

But instantly thinking of the Saturnalia and not wanting to let myself get too carried away, my fingers, dug into the bones of his shoulders, gradually eased him back, his tongue too tasty and early a treat. He looked up at me, baffled, and I took both his hands and pulled him to his feet, and holding his hands against his wide-boned hips, whispered, without even thinking, I was so jangled, "I'm saving myself for tonight," only realizing, once the words were out, how strange they must have sounded to him.

"It's the Saturnalia!" I burbled, embarrassed, knowing I was doing it again but unable to shut up, suddenly enthusiastic, eager to share it. "I'm going tonight."

But before I could say another word he gave me a peculiar look and reached for my ass. I could see right then it would be no use even trying to explain what the Saturnalia would be like, or inviting him, and a good thing, too, remembering my vow and seeing he was so single-minded in his purpose, his large, blunt hands caressing my rump with such firm insistence, the callouses on his palms an exacerbating and increasing excitement as he continued to rub them in widening circles over my shivering skin. I began to believe, much to my surprise, because of his work-toughened hands, that, unlike so many of the men strutting around the aisles in their various male disguises, he really was what he was dressed up to be.

To divert him, I kissed him on the mouth while at the same time unloosening his dungarees, no easy job since the buttons were stiff, and began to fondle him, soon hunching down before him, clasping, for balance, his solid, athletic thighs, hairless and so starkly white in the dim shadows, I discovered, centering myself between his widespread legs, that I had the uncontrollable urge to bite one of them, and did, and since he didn't protest—sighed voluptuously, in fact—I went and bit the other one, too, which made him sigh all the more. It was gratifying to think that the bruises from these lovebites I gave him tonight would make him remember me in the morning.

Drawing closer to him, over the aroma of Lifeguard soap, I breathed in his more heady, intimate odor as I shucked down his shorts, sperm-musk more alluring than an entire case of Rush, the lip of it flared like a bell, the whole of it as proportionately generous in girth as his barrel-chested physique, the feel of it like chamois to my fingertips as it stretched. I stuck out my tongue, curling the tip of it under, as he had with me, thinking of deer in winter, their bent heads at a saltlick, the tangle of hair beneath his scrotum having the bite of salt grass, and soon encouraged him to grow with such ardent single-mindedness of my own, he quickly forgot all but his own enjoyment.

A short while later he became suddenly still, the momentary stillness that comes over most men in such instants, like the hush before a cloudburst, his body concentrating itself inward, the pull of his muscles, his blood, squeezing together, right up from the toes, his entire flesh, it seemed, being sucked out in rippling implosions through the eye of the cock itself, his body turning inside out in an agonizingly sensitive convulsion no words can convey.

I wondered if at that instant, having seen it happen to my own, and those of others, in more totally nude and barefoot situations, if his toes were curling deliciously in his boots.

When my longshoreman had gone, I checked the time again, and decided to make one last turn around the passageways to check out any further details and impressions before leaving. But first, I'd attend to some crude hygienic business.

As I stepped out of the booth, I saw a number of men crowded into the small space by the exit door, all intently watching something going on behind the rear wall of the booth. I walked over and stood on tiptoe at the edge of the crowd, peering over heads and shoulders to see what was up.

There, his back against the brick wall, his heavy jacket slung over the shoulder, his cropped hair matching a brown BOYSTOWN T-shirt fitting snug across his squat muscular chest, something Mediterranean in his face and stature, stood a very short lad, clutching his lowered cream-colored trousers in one hand and gripping in his other fist a cock, with no exaggeration, the size, at the very least, of a Shetland pony's.

Before him crouched a wiry-haired, thin-hipped youth in worn levis and levi jacket who, his hands tensely gripping the short lad's hips, was trying to get the head of it into his mouth, with no luck, and had to content himself with eager kissings over the enormous crown of it and all up and down and around its perfectly shaped and incredibly thick and meaty stem.

Looking down at the top of the swiveling head bent before him, the short youth's otherwise deadpan face revealed a subtle and almost secret smile, aware of the stir, not to mention envy, his hugeness caused in those jammed around him, a hint in his dark eyes that he was inwardly enjoying the spectacle he was creating, that it was something he was used to.

90

Others now were flocking around behind me, as if the news had spread by some invisible scent throughout the backroom, attracting so many that this kink in the passageway was totally blocked with the newly arrived curious, men watching silent, fascinated, they, too, craning their necks and stretching on their toes to see over the heads of the others. With such gigantic attention focused, not so much on him as on what was standing between his legs, there came into the T-shirted youth's face a haughty expression, and with a slight lift of his shoulders, he gave the impression that in his own mind at least he had grown a couple of feet taller.

Since no one paid the slightest attention to any other part of his anatomy, including his face, he was able to watch, unobserved, all the faces looking down between his legs, and seemed very well aware of the fact that here, in the simple gesture of dropping his trousers, he was transformed magically into a worshiped and lordly giant.

The youth in the levi jacket, looking frustrated and tired, moved away finally, straightening up and wiping at his mouth with the back of his hand, while another man, anxious to take his place, shoved in and got down on his knees, he, too, having no better luck, having to be satisfied with darting his tongue along the lengthy shaft, while the object of all this attention stood perfectly still with his back against the wall, his features frozen, as if he wasn't experiencing any sensation at all.

While the men packed around him stared down dazzled, unable to take their eyes away, pushing and squeezing against each other, jockeying for better positions to move in closer and get a good look, for a chance, maybe, to touch it, even have a turn themselves, the short youth, like an aloof but benevolent god, now holding his jacket knotted in his fist clamped on one hip, allowed each his few moments kneeling in adoration before him, granting to each the pleasure of making ecstatic obeisance to his fleshly scepter, until, with a barely concealed expression in his eyes of ennui and contempt, he shoved away the last hungry mouth, permitting another to jostle in to take his place.

On and on it went, one kneeling man replacing another, until finally, looking utterly bored now, he snatched his prick from between the lips of the newest acolyte and, to the dismay of those impatiently waiting their turn, inserted that enormous apparatus, with great difficulty and care, back into the gaping fly of his creamy trousers, where, once safely inside, it bulged across his thigh as if it would burst through the cloth. He then elbowed his way through the throng of men, who obediently parted for him like he was a young deity, a sacred creature, and strolled off in a casual, unhurried walk toward the streetside exit area, more than a few of the men following close on his heels, like male dogs slavishly tracking a bitch in heat.

I trailed along at a distance, following the pack more out of continuing curiosity to see what would happen and note the reactions of the others, than real desire, not being into size myself, although such hugely hung men, like the ones on the magazine covers out in the store, are interesting to look at and exciting to get next to on occasion.

At the end of the passage, in the alcove to the right, stood a rotund, heavy-bearded man in bulging sweatshirt and levis, a thick scarf around his neck, his leather flight jacket with fur collar hooked on his thumb over one shoulder. He was trying to give away a paperback, which, from the quick glimpse I got of the cover, looked like one he'd purchased out in the shop—*Cocksure*, by S. M. Stagg, in fact—and had maybe read a good deal of, at least the juicy passages anyway about Timothy and Buck, under the better light of the spotlights out there before coming back in here.

"Wanna book? I'm through with it," he'd say, in a softly husky voice, thrusting the book out to each man passing by, including myself. No takers, though, since most of those sidling around him would just mutter something or shake their head and keep on going. Someone like myself might come back here to try to take notes on writing a book about the place, but who in their right mind would want to come back here to *read* one?

I edged past him and moved into the dark area by the streetside exit door. I could see it was busy again, so I imagined the black youth in rag drag must have departed. I squinted hard in the darkness to make sure, then sniffed the air for the scent of mold and, smelling none, realized he must have left at last, gone back on the streets, now that he'd warmed himself up a little. I suspected most of the customers back here were relieved, not to mention the clerks out in the store.

I watched as what looked to be a very young man, swinging the moons of his naked haunches in the darkness, the most clearly visible part of him, leaned bent over double, an outstretched arm supporting himself against either brick wall forming the corner, while another dark-shaped man, older looking, stood behind and entered him doggy-style, a third man, all but invisible in the black triangular space, was pressed back in the corner itself, between those wide-stretched arms, the mouth of the youth being buggered buried deep in his groin, head whipping in small, frenzied circles.

I squinted my eyes and searched around for the short youth in the BOYSTOWN T-shirt, finally spotting what looked like him in the opposite corner by the drafty exit door, completely swallowed up, not only by the darkness itself but by his pack of admirers who had followed and cornered him here and now stood crowding once more around him in a compact little circle, still elbowing each other to get in closer. Sounding distantly over the tops of the booths, Grace Jones on the jukebox was campily wailing "On Your Knees."

Inches away, in less bleak light this side of the area, I saw him again, a youth I'd noticed several times before stalking around the aisles or standing alone along the walls, usually in this darkest place by the emergency door. Once, I got a good look at him as he stood by the booth under the red bulb in the arcade, a stringbean of a youth, long-waisted, barely out of his teens, his dirty blond hair in stiff curls, traces of adolescent pimples on his narrow, pockmarked face. His clothes had a disheveled, ragbag look, like he didn't much care about what he had on, which was unusual here, and which was not only refreshing but made him somehow appealing.

I noticed, too, he spent a lot of time in this corner, gazing dull-eyed and emotionless at others as they engaged in various sexual couplings, as now, idly stroking the length of the seam of his fly with the tips of his fingers. Or sometimes pausing, he held the swelling there delicately, through the fabric, pinched between thumb and forefinger, like the most fragile and precious of orchids.

I never saw him approach anyone, or anyone approach him. Perhaps the men here were put off by his malnourished look, or his bad complexion, maybe even by his drab, wrinkled clothes which appeared even drearier in the light of the backroom.

Anyhow, there he was again, standing back against the wall, looking on as the nearby threesome, not more than a foot or two away, continued to twist and turn and thrust, their breaths and groans rising in volume and intensity.

I approached him, he had such a forlorn and friendless look, the look of a ghost from my own growing up, which suddenly filled me, especially here, with that uncomfortable and always questionable mixture of commiseration and desire, a confusion of empathy with lust.

I reached out and touched the back of his hand, the one still moving lightly up and down his trousers, in what I hoped was a combined gesture of amiable erotic invitation. But he, without once even glancing at me, brushed my hand away as if it were a pesky fly, and continued to peer through the dense shadows at the moaning trio writhing even more ardently now in their corner, again caressing the seam of his trousers.

My feathers ruffling, I snatched up his hand and seized it firmly in mine, increased the pressure for a moment, trying to convey to him by the grip of my hand alone, my irritation with his cold abruptness. Still without looking at me, I sensed him stiffen against the wall, and I cooled down a little, realizing I'd asked for it with my arrogantly pitying assumptions.

I moved away, still smarting a bit, more from awareness of my silly vanity than anything the youth had done, understanding again how I guard my heart, tough muscle not always as tender as my easily bruised pride. Smoothing my peacock feathers back in place, I resolved to keep close watch on all future benevolent impulses, and particularly on my ego which, though contained in a body as skinny as the youth's I'd just touched, was, I blushingly recognized, still considerably overweight.

I glanced hurriedly at my watch and seeing I had a few more minutes, decided to duck into one of the booths, since I was still too shy to eat out in the open here, and have myself a snack from my bag, to give me energy for the walk over to the East Village.

Seeing men standing in the doorways of all the booths in this area, I doubled back to the booth near the exit door. Sticking my head in and gingerly touching around its black interior to make sure it was empty, I stepped inside and sat down on the bench in the rear. I hungrily munched an apple, interspersing bites with gulps of sunflower seeds washed down with juice from my bike thermos, my appetite having acquired a knife-sharp edge as keen as the wintery day itself.

After I'd eaten, and as I was putting the sack of seeds and the thermos back into my bag, my eyes were drawn to the door where I was surprised to see, gazing in at me intently, a dark, slender figure standing a few paces back from the opening. He was tall and stringy, a tensely muscled, angular leanness, his clothes close-fitting, like old army fatigues.

Hoping to arouse his curiosity more, I got up off the bench to look out at him, but held back a pace or two from the entry, purposely keeping myself in deeper shadow. Even so, I felt defensive and, feigning indifference because I desired him so much and feared his rejection, made no move to show I had any real interest and stood still in the doorway, the booth momentarily becoming my old closet, that cumbersome carapace I had gradually shed. But I did return his gaze, and then I noted, as my eyes grew accustomed to the shape of him, that he had the sort of wavy hair which the red glow of the bulb seeping in from the arcade gave a crisp, fiery tint, exciting my interest all the more. I braced myself against the doorjamb, trying not to betray myself, attempting to maintain a receptive but noncommital expression.

Still he stared determinedly and didn't go away, making me feel that I was being captivated against my will by the cool, unflinching persistence of his gaze, so that several times I turned away, unable to look into his eyes anymore, but my attention always returned, fastening on him again.

He advanced a step closer, stood rooted there in the passage, his entire body held in that torsion of tight energy as tensed and still as my own, his blurred face fixed on mine, each of us staring at the other like two animals meeting in the dark, frozen with circumspection, eyeing one another warily, trying to sniff the intent of the other.

He must have instinctively detected an amiable air because without another moment's hesitation he darted into the booth and immediately pressed himself against me, the beardy rasp of his cheek scraping mine in his eagerness. Ducking his head, he began nuzzling and smelling my neck, the ends of my hair. I heard the hiss of his zipper, felt his hips, bony and sharp as my own, pushing against me, his quickening breath, bitterly scented with nicotine, in sharp and instantaneous hunger; felt my own breath sharpen in my lungs like a sudden intake of fiery cold, as pointed as pain, as burning as catching my breath had been in the near-zero wind out in Christopher Street.

With eyes closed, he stretched his neck back, showing the point of his chin, while at the same time unsnapping the tops of his trousers and shoving them down with the heels of his hands, as I curled my arms around him and kissed both sides of his throat. He placed a hand on my belt buckle and moved to undo it, but I took his hand and placed it carefully at his side, not wanting that, just yet, and let my hand stray over his thighs and through the sparse entanglement of pubic hair which, remembering the faint blush of his wavy hair in the ruby light was burning red to my playful fingers. Out of it the fibrous long stalk of him, a thickening at the base of its supple trunk tapering up to an arrow-shaped head, flat and triangular as a copperhead's, was lifting in swift degrees like a suddenly startled snake rearing through a grassy fringe of coppery dark leaves.

I could feel my own patient, sleeping reptile stirring as he reached across and stroked its head through the denim of my levis, blood slithering there in a rush of stiffening inquiry, rousing it bright-eyed with alert desire.

I humped my body down, kneeling before him, head bowed, snake worshiper in the dark to awaken the snakiness in my own limbs, pressing my thumb gently against the moist eye of it, a tiny pearl of dew already glistening there, and anointed the sharpening tine of my tongue with its acrid taste, a taste of earth, saltily venomous sap to inoculate and empower me; then ran my thumb and forefinger down its bulging shaft, the length of the sheath of skin as slippery dry as the skin of a snake; felt the increasing heat of it, the ferment of blood gushing within, my thumb squeezed now on a swollen vein along the spine, resonating with the frenzied beat of his pulse beneath.

I bent my head below, placed my face close, could smell bleachy sperm-scent through the tight, thickening skin of his scrotum, an increased and hurrying excitement in my nostrils, since he was still carrying all of his odors, like the other males I'd been close to here, all of them fresh off the street; unlike the baths, where the showers and steam room, the hot tub, left one odorless, left a bland and sterile taste in the mouth, the naturally aromatic body scrubbed of even the slightest trace of heady erotic allurement.

He leaned his shoulders back against the shadowy corner, away from the open doorway, his head once more tossed back, his thrust up chin the triangular underside of a snake's throat. I brushed the hair on his flat belly with the side of my hand, slid my fingers between his legs, the tips spiraling up in the finespun hairs whorled in the cleft, like a tiny bird's nest. He arched his hips forward, stretching the skin of his stomach as tight as the skin of his cock, a lively scepter I held in my other hand now, its serpentine energy rippling up my arm and coiling snakily radiant throughout my body, my charmed limbs weaving in a dance of cobras before the pulsing, unheard music piping from his hypnotic flute of blood.

He strained forward, revolving his hips in a slow, serpentine rhythm. Kissing the glittering eye, my lips closed over it, taking into my mouth the head of the snake he had become, which now coiled sinuously down the snake-hole of my throat as his hips turned and turned, looping themselves in wider and wider twisting undulations, the enclosure of the booth an underground cave hissing with darkness, my throat a black fissure red with the root of his blood.

Still arching back, his hips tucked forward and continuing to writhe in easy circling, turning my head with them in their slow gyrations, he slid his shoulders along the wall toward the door, pulling me along with him, and leaned one shoulder in the corner by the jamb where, even though the frail light there scarcely brushed that side of his face and torso, it was still enough to make him faintly visible to anyone passing by in the corridor, making myself visible, too.

I waddled after, crouching, both of us exposed now to anyone going by or idling outside the door, and I suspected this pleased him, that he enjoyed being on display. But it made me uncomfortable, though why at first I wasn't certain, since at the baths, on that very first visit, I had lost my shyness of having sex before others.

In the next moment I knew what it was, though: His deliberate move to display himself by the door dissolved the spell; I felt energy drain away, that I was rapidly losing the power generated between us in our ritual-like entwining.

His need to show himself broke the mood and the mystical cistern darkness the booth had become, darkness fertile in fantasy, was once again only a shabby coop smelling of stale bodies and sweat, littered with crumpled tissues and cigarette butts; and the ruddy-haired body which had been transformed in sexual magic into a snaking underground river of sinuous blood, a river I'd flowed with, had held and embraced between the changing shores of my arms, and at the blood-root spring of which, spouting on its surface out of the dark cave of his groin, I had drunk thirstily, was now just another indistinct body, just another unseen face in the dark, eager only to get off, maybe only able to do so with others watching, myself no more than a handy gullet now, just one more warm, disembodied mouth in the anonymous dark, our snakelike circle broken.

I took him by the hips and tried to guide him back into the more private shadows at the rear of the booth, but I could feel his spine stiffen as he clung by the door, posed now for all to see, lifting his shirttails higher and shoving his trousers down to the ankles, so that he was even more nakedly on display.

My energy sagged, I became bored with his theatrical, mechanical pumping, his sensual self shrunk to no more than the tiny pinpoint nerve at the tip of his glans, mouth pulled back, the tendons in his neck stretched tight, his body straining in the dark.

So much so, he was beginning to hurt me, grasping the back of my head and shoving me down on him, forcing himself deeper down my throat, his movements, having lost completely their earlier reptilian smoothness, becoming jerky, spasmodic. The cold sheen of an anxious sweat coated his buttocks as they pumped with increasing desperation beneath my hands, tensed hands I slipped around to his thighs, pressing them there to try to hold him back a little, shorten his strokes, the pain in my throat intensifying as he rammed harder and harder, my head so locked in his tightening grip, a surprisingly tight and wiry strength, I couldn't slip free of it, squirm and wrench my neck as I would.

I reached my hand up to circle his cock at the roots, to try once more to shorten his thrusts, but he knocked my hand away with a rap that stung my knuckles. He seemed frightened he wouldn't cum, would lose face before the onlookers hovering around the door if he didn't, and whipped himself into a greater frenzy.

Something in me gave way, I staggered inside myself, in a sudden rush remembering the rage of other men, their sex, twisted in cruelty, as now, his cock a boot kicking in my throat, like all the wounded cocks, gored stumps, my own once, too, remembering, in a flash of memory, as he plunged and plunged, a long ago dream of my prick swathed in bandages, another "bleeding stump," a bloodied battering ram, to prove you can do it, straining, empty of pleasure; that sad, desperate need to prove the self a worthy son, again and again, sweating, through gritting teeth, mechanically pumping. ·

In one powerful, spastic convulsion, his body a bent bow, his nails digging deep in my scalp, he came, the pumping taste of him a bitter spitting like a shot of poison scorching the lining of my throat. One last clenched cry of agonized relief escaped him, and it was over. The palms of my hands were slippery on his sweat-soaked thighs; I could feel his legs trembling beneath my fingers, like someone weak with fever.

What effort it must have cost him, I thought, despite my grogginess, this tribute—perhaps his second or third in this same afternoon—to whatever relentless obsessions impelled him.

He struggled hurriedly to pull his clothes together and got out quickly, which I was glad for, and without a word or parting gesture, which I certainly didn't expect. When he was gone, I slumped back on the seat and put my head in my hands. A face appeared in the door, alert, curious, perhaps one of those who had been clustered outside in the passage, looking on. I waved it away. "Not now," I whispered, surprised at the rawness in my voice, a burning hoarseness, his seed burning my throat. I wanted water to put it out, wash it out, but needed to rest first before going around to the sink. Feeling inert, paralyzed, my energies drained, as if my spirit had left me momentarily, I leaned back against the wall and closed my eyes.

I wondered about this apathetic use of another, wondered if it got reinforced in the stark and diminishing cockcentered atmosphere of the place, like an explosive charge of negative energy. Why was sex in this place like something imprisoned? Why was this magic hidden away, compartmentalized, fragmented, sneaked in bleak, smelly corners in grungy backrooms such as this? And even these few hidden away corners endangered, in jeopardy of always being raided, of being shut down, despite protection paid.

Open today or closed tomorrow, to whose benefit was this? Whose profit?

And what of my own complicity, my own lust? Was I deluding myself, no better or worse than the others? Worse perhaps, transforming my stark appetites into mythical and archetypical prettinesses, a spinner of airy adornments out of very real air, a puffer on invisible coals in the grimy darkness of these tawdry peepshow booths, attempting to breathe liveliness into tacky, upended coffins, shaping the place and those I touched into something they were not—all inflamed poetry, insubstantial, useless.

Like the two men I'd seen earlier sexually mimicking the pair of disembodied figures on the tiny screen in the booth, I was confused again as to which was the substance and which the shadow.

I reached up and pinched my nose til it hurt.

"That's what's real, dummy," I said aloud, the sound of my voice startling in my ears, and yet it helped to bring me around. I suddenly had the urge to get out, to leave this place, fearful that I was in danger, that I would lose something valuable, irreplaceable, if I didn't get out that very instant.

And what about the Saturnalia, which I'd been looking forward to all week with such high anticipation? Would it only turn out to be more of the same? I didn't want to believe it would; it couldn't, I told myself firmly, since, even though there would be strangers among us tonight, I knew most of the men who would be there, having been with them in all the excitement of the first Fairy Circles, and forced the question out of my mind.

I thought instead of the inflicting of pain, what the "bookshop" traded in, all those studded instruments for sale out there, lust leeched of humaneness, what pornography is at root, dehumanization, and enforcing control and topman power, "sensation without feeling."

And yet . . . and yet . . . I argued with myself, it wasn't always the same for us as with other men, our equal and consensual pleasures; fantasies in print and photos out there in the shop and in all such shops validating for us an imperiled existence forever denied everywhere around us.

But here, in these last minutes, I had felt reduced only to my mouth, a hole; the rest of me, and all that I might be, obliterated, of no interest, of no value or consequence, the object, the "cunt," only, that women have been made to be for centuries.

Imperative that I leave, yet I sat heavy, immobile, fallen back on the bench in the booth, morosely thinking of the infliction of pain and what a barrenness of the heart it is, having everything to do with dominance, the body reduced to its apertures, to its nervous system, the cock then no more than an adjunct of weaponry, a gun, an arrow.

Internally, so many of us bleeding to death, each day, unknowingly. Eyes inured, myself so conditioned in pain I'm often blind in my senses, don't always see what I'm seeing, don't always accurately feel, and, long desensitized in order to survive, ignore or passively accept the daily assault on body and spirit.

So many buried, unacknowledged shames running like a deep subterranean sewer through the land. Must learn to tread the balance on threads spun fine, and intricately whole, as spider webs.

The truth is, when the chips off the old block are down, we are all our father's sons, all our father's daughters.

The secret is, the fathers do not love you, love only their power, will destroy you for it; do not love you except sentimentally, with taps, with crocodile tears, in your obedient death, for there's profit in your dying, there's profit in your death.

100

Betray the fathers. Faggots, get up off your knees and learn sedition. Learn treason. Learn the reawakening of the heart, of affection and merriment and playfulness in service to the dark hags of ancient earthly wisdoms, bow down and listen, kiss their warts and leathery faces, kiss them on your knees and love them, and the frozen spirit will crack and the meadow of the heart will be miraculously carpeted with violets and snowdrops and the first silver spears of the grasses of spring, when we are all made new daughters again.

Surrender to the spirit of the daughter and be healed, and you will be new in the world and every day a miracle in the simplest pleasures in delight with each other.

Be truly dangerous and love one another.

And no harm done to anyone again, as sons of the crones of the cosmos again, the buried mothers, the burned and buried hag-mothers of healing nurturance and renewal, the daughter in you, burning.

Surrender to the spirit of the daughter and be healed.

I began to feel a little better, a little more energy stirring within me. I rubbed at my throat, really feeling the soreness now, and hoped it wouldn't interfere with my singing and chanting tonight.

With great effort, I pulled myself up at last, made it to the door and leaned there a moment looking out into the bleary light of the passageway.

What deserts we make of ourselves, I thought, watching the dim figures circling in the corridor, what aridities of flesh and spirit, the gods and goddesses dead in these desolate worlds, dead to women, to men, to all of all ages—dead, worst of all, to children; this darkened booth in a darkened backroom of a porn shop in lower Manhattan, a desolation, a desert of desire, an illusory oasis and mirage of sensual wellsprings, a poor substitute for the forest and fields we played in in other days, in the fragrant nights of trees and grasses, still remembered and revered in the dangerous Rambles and bushes, the dark places in parks we commandeer in service to eros, as guardians of eros; and womanmind and womanspirit absent from center, daughter-renewal absent, too; and the dry, inflexible hands of the fathers gripping us all; myself held too, forever thirsty, forever unsatisfied, and always told, the hand on my throat, the boot, the foot, it's myself to blame if I cannot breathe.

Time to bust out of the waste places, these monolithic slab cities, these upthrust glorifications to the cold and distant fathers murdering with impunity from the skies—leave them to the mummified kings of the fabulous dead.

Time for me to bust out of this backroom, too, I thought, a surge of hope and the old enthusiasm arising in me as I remembered with sudden and renewed excitement the coming Saturnalia.

I grabbed up my duffel bag and slung it over my shoulder and, for the last time, hurried around to the toilet to try to make myself as presentable as I could for the festivities ahead. As I reached the toilet door, I could see that newly arriving men were pushing through the turnstile at a faster clip, their eyes strained with cold, a few, once inside, rubbing their hands together to get them warm, mostly younger men now, in still more of the cowboy getups and motorcycle gear, the professional and business types, the undisguised ones at least, apparently finished for the day.

A man in black leather chaps was standing dreamily at the urinal when I went in, swinging his head up to take a look at me as I turned sideways to get past him and move back to the sink where I gargled noisily and longer this time, which eased my throat a little. Then I splashed some cold water on my face and dried it as best I could with my still damp handkerchief. In the glass I saw the guy at the urinal, with a look of stoned rapture, shake it and zip himself up and sway out the door.

After combing my hair and beard, I smeared on some more Life, this time to protect against chapped lips out in the street, and reached in my bag and brought out my ski hat and gloves and put them on, deciding to wait til I got outside before pulling the face mask down.

I gave myself the once-over in the mirror and, seeing there wasn't much more I could do in the way of improvements, slipped the bag up over my shoulder and pushed open the door and went out, taking a quick last look around the entrance area, which was just about the same as when I'd entered it a couple of hours before, with guys still lounging in the shadows on either side of the jukebox—over which "Come to Me" was spinning in silky and syrupy tones—and more men hanging out, lynx-eyed, in the even more shadowy doorways of the booths.

I hit the turnstile with an exhilarating sense of relief, glad to be going at last, to be moving out and away from the place. A different clerk was on duty above the turnstile now, a light-skinned black youth, looking rather scholarly in his steel-rimmed glasses, his nose buried in a copy of *Mandate*, his mild eyes lifting now and again from its pages to peer out at the customers.

102

The shop was more crowded now with men of varying ages and costumes, circulating slowly and singly from display case to magazine rack to book shelves and back again, a few apprehensively eyeing the door to the backroom as I had done, eyeing me as I came through it, two new clerks at the front standing easy and silent behind their raised counter, but watching everything and everyone with the alertness of hawks.

I opened the door and stepped outside, my lungs immediately burningly dry in the arid cold, and paused a moment to slip down my ski mask and catch my breath in the abrupt drop in temperature.

On the corner stood a slightly built youth, shoulders hunched against the wind, bouncing from one foot to the other, hands jammed deep in the pockets of his jeans, large, limpid eyes looking at the entrance of the bookshop, then at me, then looking away with a slightly embarrassed, uncertain air down West Street, shivering noticeably, like he'd been standing there a long time, trying to maybe work up enough nerve to go into the place.

Billowing plumes of steam rising from the exhaust pipes of passing autos evaporated rapidly in the very dry air. My eyes, feeling like they'd been instantly freeze-dried, were dazzled by the headlights and taillights of the cars rumbling beneath the empty and rusting West Side Highway, the changing traffic lights at the crossing itself, as they gave off sharper, more brilliant refracted gleamings in the diamond-hard cold. The night having become more unbearably bitter, there were now only a very few people hurrying by on the sidewalk. Over the buildings I could hear the rush of wind off the river like a distant bull-roarer whirled high over the city.

As I moved out onto the pavement, two policemen swung around the corner of the building and marched past me up to the entrance of the bookshop. I stood paralyzed a moment in the middle of the sidewalk, my heart doing a rapid turnover, the first thought flying through my mind, *I got out just in time.*

All shiny chrome and silver, looking heavier bundled up in their thicker winterwear, with possibly the new bulletproof vests beneath their dark blue hip-length coats, bodies made even bulkier with all the excess hardware they lugged around, guns and bullets and nightsticks and handcuffs and chattering walky-talkies hanging all over them.

With the unexpected appearance of the cops, the youth standing at the corner, suddenly round-eyed with fear, turned on his heel and took off, quickstep, up West Street.

I followed his example, but went in the opposite direction, back up Christopher. Half way up the block, though, bothered by the sudden presence of the police and determined to see if there was to be any trouble, a raid, perhaps, with patrol cars screeching up to the door like in the old entrapment days—I knew I'd never be able to go back to the place if there was danger of that—I turned around and returned to the corner and, cold as it was, swinging my arms to keep the blood going, hung around for a few minutes longer, just to see if anything would happen, keeping my eye on the entrance, my curiosity overcoming my discomfort and fear.

After a short time, which seemed much longer given the aching cold and my impatience to be off, the door of the bookshop swung open and the two cops came out, making a sharp right back around the corner again, moving east on Christopher, one of them with his head bent close to the ear of the other, while the latter listened, his mouth curled in a tight-lipped grin.

Gay cops? I wondered, my teeth beginning to chatter. Had they merely stopped in off their not very busy beat on this cold night to warm themselves up for a moment before going out into the street again? Maybe they were even friendly cops, just checking to see if everything was okay, practicing a little "community relations." I hated to think they had stopped in for a payoff, like the cops in the gay bars in other days.

I tailed the pair as close as I dared, trying to hear what they were saying, but they were too far ahead and, hearing only the faint squawks of their radios, probably wouldn't have been able to catch anything anyway in the noise of the wind, no matter how close I got. They turned right into Washington Street and were gone.

I leapt back startled as a drunken woman, her frizzed gray hair blown out in points by the wind, staggered up out of the garbage cans by the entrance to a tenement, her face, running with tears from the cold, staring stupidly, blearily, at me, her bare, scabby legs buckling beneath her as she lifted her arms to me.

"What? What?" she asked thickly, drunkenly, over and over, like someone suddenly awakened, or maybe she had scuttled behind the trash cans to avoid the two cops. With her coarse and heavy-woven Mexican shawl, spotted with stains, slipping off her bony shoulders, and her ripped and soiled peasant blouse and strings of cracked, multicolored beads tangled beneath, a large turquoise ring on one of her dirt-shiny fingers (I was surprised she hadn't been mugged for it yet), she looked like an old Village bohemian survivor of the early fifties, now evidently one of the tens of thousands of stray people who live on the streets of New York.

I put my hand on her arm to steady her. "Get out of the cold!" I warned her, raising my voice as if to a deaf person and pulling at her arm at the same time to make sure I had her attention. "Get in where it's warm!"

"What? What?" she repeated in her hoarse, groggy voice.

Looking into her face was like looking into another mirror of my own, on these same streets ten years before.

I ran to the corner of Washington Street to see if I could catch up with the cops and call them back to help her, have them call an ambulance on their walky-talkies and maybe get her taken to the Women's Shelter down on Lafayette Street for the night. But when I got to the corner they were nowhere to be seen.

Checking my watch quickly and seeing it was getting very late and knowing I'd have to get moving if I was going to get to the Saturnalia on time, I raced back to where I'd left the drunken woman, only to find that she was gone. Looking about wildly, I spotted her staggering across Christopher Street against the light, clutching her shawl about her shoulders, and making it safe, with the luck of the drunk, to the other curb, amid screechings of brakes and loud horn blowing, where she weaved on, aiming herself toward the lights of the leather bars across from the piers.

I cupped my hands to my mouth and shouted after her as loud as I could over the roar of the wind, "Get off the streets tonight! You'll freeze to death!" A lone passerby struggling against the stiff gusts looked at me oddly, and realizing the uselessness of my shouting the moment the last words were out of my mouth, breathed, in their place, a silent prayer for her, asking Diana in the moon, even though I knew she was shining far below the city now, to watch over her in this long dark night, to watch over all the drunks, and turned and started trotting up Christopher Street, really anxious to make time now.

Running, a generous tailwind pushing behind me from the Hudson speeding me along the almost deserted street, the severer cold even finally having driven the dope peddlers off the sidewalks, I reminded myself to make a quick stop, as planned, at Village Produce on Greenwich to buy a bag of fruit as my share of the food for tonight; and then decided that after that, if I alternated jogging for one of the long crosstown blocks and walked briskly the next, then jogging again, and so on, block after block, I'd not only make good time, but would help keep myself warm getting over to the East Side and would just about make it in time for the start of the Saturnalia.

Far over the dark roofs of the tenements, looking up as I ran, spiky stars were brilliant thistles stuck in the immense black field of the cold night sky.

An icy blast of wind almost stopped me in my tracks as I turned the corner off Second Avenue, surprised, as always, when there's wind at night, for I still have the childish notion that the wind dies down when the sun sets.

Jogging into East 2nd Street at an energetic clip, clutching the bag of fruit tighter against my chest, my duffel bag slapping against my hip, I slowed down as I passed under the protective scaffolding of a building being demolished on the corner and found myself in a street of old apartment houses and boarded up buildings, painted over storefronts, a few garages and warehouses with grim, heavy steel doors rolled inexorably shut, and one or two restored facades, with their freshly pointed bricks, evidence of increasing gentrification of the area.

At my left, stood the institutional yellow brick of La Salle Academy, and next to it the old Marble Cemetery where the icy wind was blowing dead leaves and gritty litter around the headstones and family vaults of long-dead mayors and prominent merchants of the city and against the black palings of the iron fence fronting it. Directly across the street the patriarchal cross of the gray Russian Orthodox Cathedral of the Protection of the Holy Virgin sputtered white neon high above, a light as cold and fitful as the night itself.

I slowed down to a brisk walk, hurrying past rows of tenement houses with their battered garbage cans knocked over by the wind, searching for Number 67, anxious once more to get in out of the biting cold. Yet, in a way, I didn't resent the bitter weather, for it helped keep my mind off the uncertainty of what I might be getting into at my first Saturnalia, which, frankly, was making me nervous since I didn't know what to expect.

And there it was, on the south side of the street across from the cemetery, the number barely visible over a high, dark blue painted entryway in a six-story gray brick tenement, which my eyes quickly swept from roof to cellar as I hurried across the street.

Bathed in strawberry blond light from a tall sodium vapor street lamp, its ornate facade, through black fire escapes slashing obliquely across it, was adorned with the stone faces of women, dark streaked and weatherworn, like busts of ancient goddesses jutting out above the lighted windows of the upper floors. To these the architect's fancy had added the heads of fierce-looking hairy-faced animals, mythical beasts perched between the window sills, and further down, set in the walls under the first floor windows, curled tendrils of stone vines and flowers, looking more like gray mushrooms coldly sprouting from the gloomy dark of the basement area below. A perfect facade for a Saturnalia site, I observed with satisfaction, as I picked my way among the dozen garbage cans upended on the sidewalk.

In the little vestibule, there were at least fifty buttons squeezed on the small buzzer panel, and, in the light of the single fluorescent tube above, I eagerly scanned the names—Rodriguez, Martinez, Yestrebsky, Horowitz, Remejka, Valdez—searching for the right button to push. My heart, already racing from the exertion of my brisk walking and jogging, suddenly shifted into a more rapid flutter as I noticed a small card inserted at the top of the board which read: "Saturnalia, Push #20, 3rd Floor," printed neatly with a bright Magic Marker pen.

I wasted no time pushing the button, and while waiting for the buzz that would release the lock, shoved back the cuff of my jacket to see the time: five minutes to eight. Not bad, I thought, taking a deep breath. Considering all. Only ten minutes late, and what with the weather, I figured they might not have started on time anyway.

Peering through the grease-filmy glass of the inner door, I saw a long narrow hall, tiled with the same bits of white ceramic as out here in the entry, and just as mottled with grimy footprints, the same Prussian blue paint on the lower half of the walls, the upper half painted a stale mustard color, the identical, chillingly sterile white light of short fluorescent tubes in the ceiling, much brighter than those in the backroom, but no less depressing.

Down the metal staircase, at the far end of the corridor, came a young man trotting with brisk agility and swinging into the hallway at a fast pace. He pulled open the door and, all wrapped up with yards of scarf tied around his neck and obviously on his way out, gave me a bright smile while gallantly holding the door open for me, and exclaimed, in a voice lilting with an unmistakable gay ring, "Coming in? You better, before you freeze your kididdilies off!"

I slipped past him, thanking him as he trotted rapidly down the front steps, thinking he was heading in the wrong direction, grateful to be in out of the weather again, thinking, too, in a reflex of exaggerated paranoia, how trusting he was, in this neighborhood, what if, with my sinister face mask, he was blithely and innocently letting in a robber or a murderer?

As the door closed after me and I headed down the hall toward the stairs, I heard the buzzer squawking faintly behind me in the lock, so I knew my ringing had been answered by somebody upstairs in Number 20. I climbed the flights of worn marble steps, hearing muffled Hispanic voices behind the dark blue doors, loud music, and singing in Spanish, on dozens of radios or tape cassettes, quick, lively laughter, spicy smells of food cooking, and arrived at the third floor, finding myself in a warren of more dark blue doors down even narrower, shorter hallways off the fluorescent-lit main one at the rear of the building.

Confused which way to go, I stood scanning the maze of possible choices til, down one of them, I heard a door open, then a soft, languorous voice drawl out, tentative, "I think this might be the place you're looking for?"

I turned and saw a pale narrow face, patches of faint acne on his cheeks like so many young faces on the streets of the Lower East Side, bad complexions from poverty and poor diet, looking to be no more than twenty, a shock of black hair tumbling over his brow, the rest, trimmed close about the ears, styled in a punk cut, a face I hadn't seen before at any of our circles, smiling out at me questioningly through the crack in the door.

"The Saturnalia?" I asked in a low, conspiratorial voice, and felt foolish, a little embarrassed, saying it aloud, however softly, it seemed such an odd question, here in this dismal tenement hallway; probably would sound odd any place in this day and age, just as it had when I'd heard myself speak the word earlier in the darkened booths of the backroom.

"You got it," said the youth in a distinctly Southern accent, smiling even more broadly. "Come on in and make yourself ta' home."

As I approached, he swung open the door, fully revealing himself now, slim-bodied, wearing an old torn T-shirt that exposed patches of a hairless chest beneath, as palely white as the shirt, and baggy, loose-fitting lime-green dance pants with a white stripe down the side, and heavy, thigh-high, gray woolen leg-warmers that covered only half his feet to just below the instep so that his long bare toes stuck out.

Seeing his outfit reminded me we'd been told to wear comfortable clothing, "the looser the better, so you can move around easy," Ed, who had started the Circle shortly after arriving from San Francisco, and who would be one of our "guides" for this evening's rituals, had suggested.

He turned to go in, then sensing my hesitation, turned back, beckoning me into the room with the easy and languishing movements, the silken ease, of a dancer.

My eyes still glazed from the cold, blurring my vision, I could at first only perceive that I'd stepped into a large, bare, white space lit solely by candlelight, with perhaps a half dozen men already arrived, talking quietly among themselves, in socks or barefoot, while lounging comfortably on the floor on pillows punched up against the walls, a few sitting on the rolled up blankets and sleeping bags we'd been asked to bring, leaving the center of the floor, which looked freshly painted, empty. In the dim candlelight, the floor appeared to be a warm and attractive salmon hue, quite polished, "hot pink," as the youth who had let me in later called it.

The others, several of whom I began to recognize as my eyes defrosted, were silent, and at first I thought they had all been involved in some form of meditation disrupted by my entrance, but then I realized they were simply waiting for the rest of the Circle, and those newcomers who were invited, to show up, waiting patiently, perhaps as uneasy as myself, since this was the first Saturnalia for all of them as well, waiting for the beginning of whatever was to happen in this loft tonight.

"I brought some fruit," I said, thrusting out the bag, my voice strained and dry in the abrupt change from the freezing night and cold halls of the building to the intense heat of the place, strained from a sudden attack of nerves, too.

There was a faint cloud of marijuana smoke hanging in the air, mingled with the peppery, sweet-scented perfume of burning joss sticks.

110

"Just put it back there, with the rest of the victuals," murmured the youth in the lime-green dance pants, pointing to a table at the narrower front part of the loft, "And you can throw your things on the pile there," he added, indicating a dark mound of coats and caps already heaped on what looked like an old, rickety desk across from the table of food. He stuck out a hand. "My name's Keith. I'm the proprietor of this joint," he joshed, in that manner, very Southern, which is immediately, winningly, personal, cozily intimate, and slightly contemptuous, all at the same time.

I pulled off a glove and offered my hand in return, introducing myself.

"I think you know most of these hombres," he drawled, gesticulating lazily around the room. "Except for Danny. Danny, stand up and take a bow."

But Danny, a fair-skinned plumpish youth with a pale sensuous face, also wearing dance pants, hips and thighs very snugly tight in shiny metallic blue, sat right where he was, crosslegged on the floor, and barely took notice of me. Never once, however, did he take his magnificent gray eyes off Keith, eyes magnetized to even the slightest movement or gesture he made, or word he uttered, his wide-featured Slavic face wearing a genial and blissful smile, whether from cannabis or hopeless infatuation, or both.

As the tears evaporated from my eyes in the heat of the room I could see the others more clearly, and smiled and nodded to those I already knew from past circles: Ian, a former public television producer in the Midwest, five years divorced and five years out, now living in the East Sixties and selling expensive specialty jewelry and curios in a tiny shop up on Lexington Avenue near Bloomingdale's, a soft-spoken, quick-witted man, scarecrow-thin, a little older than myself, with crinkly gray hair and beard, wearing steel-rimmed, tinted glasses and, "especially in honor of the occasion and the cold," as he later explained to me, a pair of sleek, bunclinging cherry-red flared trousers. Ian was the only one in the Circle, so far as I knew, who'd read my new book, discovering it on his own at the Oscar Wilde Bookshop, and, from his unstinted praise of it, I secretly called him, self-admitted book-junkie that he was, The Ideal Reader.

As I bent down to kiss him, he looked slightly tense, his eyes, as always, indistinct behind his glasses, still revealing a strained and preoccupied air, his face serious even as he gave me a little smile in greeting, probably as apprehensive as I was about what was to come.

111

Reclining next to him on a coarse brown blanket was Nick, a stocky young man with a full head of curly brown hair, and beard to match, who, having just moved to New York from Wilkes-Barre, was a factory worker by day and a political science student at night, and whose face, as I leaned down to kiss his cheek, was already flushed, his genial dark eyes a bit out-of-focus and glassy from marijuana.

Slumped against the wall across the room was Bert, a lawyer working for the city, a poker-faced, heavy-limbed, large-bellied man who, for all his phlegmatic movements, looked ruggedly athletic, and was in fact a long-distance biker on the weekends. Generously hirsute, with thick black hair and beard, a thatch of it peeping out from the open collar of his rough wool plaid shirt, he was sitting wide-hipped in levis, and, like Ian, was also wearing wirerimmed glasses, his cheeks apple-red and glistening in the heat, his mouth looking small and pink through his dark beard as he tipped his head up to grin at me when I stooped over to brush his lips with my own.

On Bert's right, hugging his knees and crinkling and uncrinkling his bare toes against the floor, sat Petey, small-boned and puckishly agile, with sparse, silky blond hair and clear milky skin, his large, bright-blue, sharply delineated eyes full of impish humor, the smile he gave me as I approached him outshining all the candles in the room put together.

An actor, he was at present performing in a revival of a medieval Passion play up at the Cloisters on weekends, playing the role of Jesus Christ, "in simple but *very* flowing robes," as he had told us at the last Fairy Circle, for which he received much teasing and about which there were many ribald and campy crucifixion jokes tossed around, heavy on Christian S/M: "Do you mind crossing your feet, JC? I've only got one spike left," and so forth.

It was, as always, a delight to see him, his busy tongue playfully flicking around my inner lips, a bee in a puckered bud, very much unlike the asexual Christ.

Really feeling the high temperature of the loft now, particularly after Petey's welcoming kiss, beginning to feel suffocated, actually, and drowsy, too, from the heavy combination of heat and smoke, I went to the front of the loft and placed the bag of fruit on the table Keith had indicated, eager to get my hat and coat off. Already on the table were a couple of plates containing what looked to be loaves of whole grained breads and cakes, and wicker baskets of nuts and raisins and pumpkin and sunflower seeds, and a plate heaped with long slices of raw carrots, undoubtedly brought by Bert, who always supplied the carrots at other gatherings, and next to it a board piled with cheeses, as well as bowls of oranges and tangerines and bunches of grapes, all of it gleaming in the light of several tall tapers burning at the rear of the table. No animal flesh present, though, none ever eaten at any of our potluck suppers in the past, none of the fairies in our Circle, including myself, meateaters, apparently.

No apples either, I noted, and was glad I had brought some, as I emptied the bag, arranging the plump tangerines and Delicious reds and yellows—the hugest and firmest I could find in the bins at Village Produce—around the already overspilling bowls of other fruit.

All this time, I half listened, now tucking my duffel bag out of the way beneath the well of the desk and beginning to take off my outer layers of clothing, as disconnected snatches of several conversations, all going at once, drifted out from the loft:

" . . . can't stand people who talk to animals and babies as though they were idiots . . . ."

" . . . have the kind of respect for nature where we can learn to walk through a landscape again without disturbing anything . . ."

" . . . men lie to keep power; women lie to survive . . ."

" . . . So I said to this stuckup clone on Christopher, I says, 'Listen, honey, this fairy's got beauties people like *you* are blind to,' and that shut *him* up . . . ."

" . . . Oh, Descartes' 'I think, therefore I am,' " I heard Keith's voice slur out, "And what doesn't think, is not, like animals and flowers and trees and earth and whole, usually *dark* populations of the planet, whatever sweats, perspires, pisses, shits, smells, fucks, etc., etc.—Well, it's all alive and no different or better or worse than myself, or any of us sitting here. I *stink*, therefore I am . . . ."

" . . . With sugar in everything, including *salt*, of all things, American food is like one long dessert . . . we're a nation of sugarcrazies . . . Junkies in the supermarket . . ."

" . . . So I spread my cheeks and wished him 'bun *appétit*' . . . He was the kind of guy who'll do that, but won't let you kiss him on the mouth . . . ."

" . . . That's queer," somebody said, and there was laughter.

" . . . All males are gay, all females are lesbian . . ." I heard Bert say. " . . . Compulsory heterosexuality's the perversion . . . ."

113

I recognized Petey's voice saying, "... How could I possibly be accepted in a society where to take another man's cock into my mouth is considered more horrible than if I put a gun into his and blew his brains out? ..."

"... Well, all I got to say is, speaking as a radical fairy feminist, a *sissy*, that is, men need women more than women need men, if only women knew that, how much men stand in their way ...."

"... Show me a man who doesn't know his cock from a gun and I'll show you a man who doesn't know his ass from his elbow ...." somebody chimed in.

"... A lot of guys still don't understand their cocks are essentially for pissing and pleasure, not for hurting anybody, or be made to stand for something they aren't ...." I heard Bert say in a mildly amused tone.

And Keith drawled out, "... I tend to agree with Sally Gearhart, the number of males born needs to be limited for at least a couple of centuries until the earth has a chance to heal herself from his craziness ...."

Petey said, "... Males are only good for one thing anyhow: spitting the spark on the egg ...."

"... Well," Keith continued, "I say give all the ones that won't learn bats and balls and let 'em play out their lives in green fields, preferably on Madagascar, and leave the business of living, as it was in the beginning, to women and magical faggots and shamans ...."

"... Hear, hear ..." several voices murmured in agreement.

The door buzzer sounded and I heard someone get up and run across the floor.

"... I wonder if the goddess realizes now," Petey went on, "that her biggest and maybe *only* mistake was the creation of us males, particularly straight males with attitude, and maybe plans to do something to correct it—phase us out slowly and gradually return things to the early days of parthenogenesis ...."

I listened intently, an electric charge of heresy in the air that both thrilled me and scared me more than a little, hearing again this dangerous language of treachery spoken so plainly and, despite the air of amusement, with such conviction.

"... Petey! How can you even think that?" snapped Keith's voice, now somewhere over near the door. "... All those beautiful men—all us beautiful men! Gone forever! ..."

"... I hope she'll let a couple of faggots survive! ..." quipped someone.

"... I bet she will! ..." Petey cried with quick assurance, and everybody laughed, including myself, at the way he said it.

By now I had slipped out of my jacket and vest and laid them on top of the other garments piled on the desk, feeling instant relief from the oppressive heat. Then I unlaced my desert boots and kicked them off, nudging them under the desk beside my bag and the other shoes and boots lined up there. Looking down, as I did so, I was annoyed to catch sight of my toes sticking embarrassingly out the tips of my holey wool socks and I quickly removed them too and stuffed them in the tops of my boots, then turned and went out to rejoin the others.

I sat down quietly against the wall on a cushion next to Nick. Two more members of the Circle had arrived while I'd been taking off my things, and I smiled and waved across the room to each as he slipped off his garments. Tim, a short-order cook in the snack bar of one of the baths in the East Village, dropped a sleeping bag from his shoulders onto the floor. His mild, prettily lashed Irish eyes were almost hidden under the bill of a too-large baseball cap, which he'd clipped with a big safety pin at the back to make it fit, his jet black hair trimmed short except for a tuft left long to hang down his nape, a little like a matador's pigtail. Jonathan, the other new arrival, was wearing a large orange button proclaiming "Witches Heal" on his jacket lapel. He unfurled a saffron-colored blanket he'd brought along. An off-off-Broadway actor and director of gay plays, he was a friend of Keith's and had arranged the use of his loft for our Saturnalia, his freckles and milky blue skin those of a redhead, even his eyebrows a light, carroty red, but the crimped waves of his hair were deep chestnut, his slender body, like his long fingers, agile and swift, as he now unbuttoned his coat, his light-lashed eyes gleaming with that teasing, mercurial and slightly superior expression which always unnerved us a little, as he grinned back at me.

"Well, personally," breathed Keith, pronouncing it "pus-onally" in his long, drawnout drawl, and speaking as if carrying on a conversation interrupted momentarily by the new arrivals, "I don't think the cosmos sounds like Bach *at all*—I hear it as more like Meredith Monk—now *there's* somebody *really* intense—or bebop maybe, *that's* hot, or even chattering sparrows"—and here his eyes widened and his eyebrows lifted in an amazed and crafty grin—"Or *even* the hum of bee's wings! Now that's *really* hot!"

There were soft, appreciative chuckles around the room. I felt a warm flush stealing through my limbs, felt, after my hard run getting here, and now with the fierce steam heat in the room, a pleasant, inattentive drowsiness, as silkily indolent as Keith's lazy Southern speech. From a phonograph somewhere at the front of the loft, Keith Jarrett pounded away in his heavy-handed style, his muted, monotonous piano sound just bordering on improvised cocktail lounge music.

I saw more clearly now that we were in a long, broad room with a high, white, tin-embossed ceiling, its exposed brick walls also painted white, the area we were in, toward the rear, emptied, as I said, of all furniture, except for the pillows scattered about the floor and against the walls, and the blankets and sleeping bags rolled up beside them (since I was traveling a bit of a distance by bus and subway and it would've been a cumbersome nuisance lugging along a bulky blanket—I owned no sleeping bag—I depended on the others bringing enough bedding to share, trusting to their generosity).

At the back end of the room were two tall windows covered with sheets of plastic to keep out the cold; the loose plastic snapped constantly as the freezing wind seeped in through cracks. Despite this, the loft, as I've mentioned, stayed surprisingly warm from the heat of two antique radiators, one beneath each window, their escape valves hissing and whistling steadily by turns.

The yellow-lighted windows of other apartments at the rear of the tenement across the air shaft were visible through the clear plastic sheeting, the cold blue light of television screens glowing in a few darkened ones, and what looked like an old wooden water tower could be seen on a nearby roof, while just beyond the roof's crookedly leaning chimneys, in a sky lit from below by the reflected lights of Manhattan in an artificially arctic neon shimmer, were the silhouetted tips of skyscrapers, several of their highest upper floors alight, cresting above them all the last dozen or so of the 110 stories of the double-monolithic Twin Towers to the south, at the narrow foot of the island in the Wall Street district.

Between the windows a little low altar had been set up on a small table where joss sticks burned in wisps of curling smoke, and more votive lights and tall thin candles illuminated propped-up pictures of many-armed Kali with points of fire burning out her multiple fingertips, and a black and white blowup of a large, huge-breasted, broad-hipped woman with long stringy black hair sitting naked and smiling among exposed tree roots like a generous,

116

genial and very much at home earthgoddess, as well as a depiction of the ancient underworld Celtic god of maleness and revivifying death, Cernunnos, The Horned One, with hairy animal legs (who we'd had discussions on in the Circle after reading Arthur Evans' *Witchcraft and the Gay Counterculture,* along with talks on the craft from Margot Adler's *Drawing Down the Moon,* plus *The Book of Pagan Rituals*—Jonathan's contribution—and dogeared xeroxes of Mitch Walker's then unpublished *Visionary Love,* with, on one occasion, taking turns in a hilarious reading aloud of Larry Mitchell's *The Faggots & Their Friends Between Revolutions*).

At the center of the table, between the candles, was a Lava Lamp, one of those glass contraptions one used to see in bars and now can occasionally find in head shops, where, magnified in the glass and lifting and falling heavy and slow in the heat of the bulb hidden in its base, globs of a red glutinous substance, starting out big and bright as tomatoes at the bottom, then diminishing, as they rose bubbling slowly to the top, to the size and color of maraschino cherries, floated continuously, hypnotically, up and down in the soft light of the lamp's oil-filled cylindrical base, the only electric light on in the entire loft.

Up on the brick wall, suspended at an angle between the windows, was a rough-handled besom, handmade of willow switches like a bundle of faggots bound with thick cord around the base. Above it hung a neatly hand-lettered sign which read: AND YOU HARM NONE, DO WHAT YOU WILL.

The newly painted floor, its resinous odor pungent in my nostrils, shone with a warm glimmer in the flickering light of the candles.

" . . . I figure every time I go down on a guy it's a blow against patriarchy . . ." someone was saying, my attention pulled back for the moment as I looked about the group, searching for the speaker and knowing by the mischievous glint in his eye and the wicked smile still lingering on his lips, it was surely Petey.

" . . . There's no doubt about it . . ." Ian was saying as my ears picked up on his quiet but incisive voice coming from my right, " . . . The white male of the species has been nuts for quite a long time. You only have to think of the witch-burnings and faggot-burnings in the Middle Ages, and then Wounded Knee and Little Big Horn, and the gas ovens of Nazi Germany, to see it plain."

"Holocaust isn't rooted in human nature but in male supremacy. bullying, in short!" Jonathan, overhearing, called out from the narrow passage as he unwound a scarf from about his neck and began taking off his outer coat and an old, faded Norfolk jacket he'd evidently picked up in a rummage sale.

"Right!" Ian hollered back, and in a lower voice, "Frightened monomaniacal males wanting everything monochromatic, safe and controllable, a brutal, boring, gray living death. And Hitler was the naked face of that, of patriarchy at last, its logical outcome. The other big papas finally got on his ass, in the name of 'democracy,' of 'freedom,' only because he got too piggish, too out about it, taking off the benevolent paternal mask to reveal the true monster underneath. A dangerous man, hated because he did what the others only dreamed of doing, and who could expose all of them for what they were, what they itched to do in more subtle and sophisticated and devious ways, and so he had to go."

"Those Nazi flicks on late-night TV give me the creeps!" Nick, lying on his side a few feet from me, interjected quietly.

"His real target anyhow wasn't Jews, gypsies, faggots—at least the straight-appearing ones or the topmen," Ian went on in his calm, steady voice. "It was 'all that was soft and womanish,' all women, and all men who were 'like' women, the woman in himself, really—all of it had to be destroyed, purified, himself purified of the taint of woman, of 'inferiority' and 'weakness,' of humanity, finally—all boiled down in the end, like the millions of Jews and faggots and dykes and gypsies and other 'inferiors,' to a cake of soap."

"Pure products of capitalist patriarchy!" Petey shouted.

"Gone crazy!" added another, so quickly I didn't know where it came from or who said it.

"He really only wanted a world of males, with females as his breeding slaves, wanted them only to produce those blond, blue-eyed, aryan-skinned, muscular Hitler youth, SA men, SS men . . . ."

The faces of the Nordic-blond lads I'd seen in the porno loops that afternoon flashed across my mind.

"You talk *real* nice," Jonathan teased, in the mockingly flattering tones of Butterfly McQueen, as he entered the room again in barefeet, followed by Tim, also barefoot and still wearing his baseball cap.

"Hitler," Ian continued, as if he hadn't heard Jonathan, "like J. Edgar Hoover, was the sickest kind of queer, who couldn't admit his love for other men, steeped in the Western prohibition against it, and millions died, and still do, at the hands of such men, whether they're a pope or a president or premier or just an ordinary garden variety papa, all poisoned in antiqueer, antiwoman patriarchal venom, the end result of thousands of years of a tragic and imbecilic taboo."

"The big daddies always want the boys for themselves," Keith drawled.

"Liberate Eros!" Petey cried, jumping up with clenched fist, "Eros humanizes! Eroticize the nation!" and everybody laughed, he had a way of saying things, the mood in the room immediately lightening. Even Ian was smiling.

I leaned back on my elbows and continued to look around the place as the others went on talking softly among themselves. Draped on the wall opposite was a banner of delicately brushed Japanese ideograms trailing like long tendrils of hanging flowers down its silken surface. Around the other walls, barely visible in the wan light, hung a series of small collages, juxtaposed cutouts of punk rock musicians, pop female vocalists, and movie stars, such as Elvis Costello, Liza Minelli and Marlene Dietrich, the work, it turned out, of an artist friend of Keith's.

"He's very *intense*, don'tcha' think?" he asked, seeing me eye the work, then announced to the room in general, "The opening's tomorrow night and you're all invited, a very *hot* artist." The loft apparently served not only as living quarters and dance studio, but as a gallery as well, evidently a private one for his friends. And then, without a pause, Keith continued right on with a talk he was having with several others, as though there had been no interruption, exclaiming, "I was at the backroom bar over on Eleventh Avenue, *once*. Oh, those bathtubs that just *drain* right onto the floor, all that *muck* you just slosh right on through, whether you want to or not; have to wear *goo*loshes or waterproof sneakers! And *lots* of sharp metal things sticking out you can cut yourself on in the dark, get tetanus, and think of what *lockjaw* would do to your lovelife! Oh, but all that shame in the darkness, that humiliation made to seem sexually exciting. What really got to me was seeing this hot, humpy guy leaning over a counter chatting casually with friends, sipping his drink, while at the same time getting fucked frantically by somebody from behind—like it wasn't happening at all! Oh, too much! Or *not* enough! Not *intense* enough!"

Just inside the door, at my elbow, against the bricks, leaned a large branch of evergreen which had a dry, broken-limb, stepped-on look, as though Keith, or whoever had placed it there for adornment, had found it in the gutter where it had perhaps snapped off some full-bodied tree being carried home by its purchaser through the streets of the Lower East Side to be decorated for the Christmas holidays, its piney odor filling the space around me, reminding me, as I closed my eyes and breathed it in, of the pine woods of the Presidio years ago above Baker Beach in San Francisco and the cold Pacific Ocean stretching beyond.

Next to it, jutting out of the floor and disappearing farther up into the wall, was a heavy piece of plumbing, a thick, angular waste pipe which, for decoration and to hide its ugliness, was draped and swathed in yards and yards of a necklace of cut-glass orange beads.

Farther on was a small kitchen, the music coming from there out of loud speakers I could now distinguish on a shelf above the refrigerator, on top of it the lighted dial of the phonograph itself, from which Patti Smith, emulating the flat throb of cockrock in a change of pace from the blandness of Jarrett, now blared hoarse-voiced, singing "GLORIA-AH!" at the top of her lungs.

Across from the tiny kitchen, and a little beyond it, was an open toilet with a long flush chain attached to the water closet high up near the ceiling, the ancient porcelain commode below fully visible to everyone, except for a long, thin mirror propped, strategically, genital-high on pipes beside the bowl, giving at least a modicum of privacy on the side exposed to the open area of the loft.

In this lengthy, corridorlike space, a second low table had been placed, for a cluster of thin-stemmed goblets and an odd assortment of glasses that looked like jelly jars, and bottles of wine and jugs of apple juice, all of it lit with several blue votive lights, their reflections glinting here and there among the glassware.

Keith's hand was evident everywhere, the space had such a fey and homemade charm in contrast to the dreariness and sterility of most modern boxlike enclosures and other man-made spaces, like the emptiness of shopping malls or urban "renewal" areas. It is the special quality of fairiness (call it artistry) which longs to bring liveliness and magic to these dead places.

"Romance, for me," Petey was saying, the conversation having moved on to other topics while my eyes had been wandering around the room, "is like flowers in a garden. It lasts as long as its season, as long as it's meant to, so that about one lover I can say, he was a daffodil, a tulip, or about another, he was a June rose, or, he was impatiens, or that one was a mum, the briefest blossom as lovely and satisfying as the longest-blooming one in all my beds of flowers," and he gave a delighted laugh, in which several of the others joined, pleased with the audacity of his conceit.

I had to smile to myself in agreement, remembering, among many, the "crocus romance" of the lad who had bought me the gift of lemon grass tea in McNulty's a summer ago.

"Egoistic romantic love, like personal salvation," said Ian quietly, "is as addictive as alcohol or any other drug."

"All I know is it's a good idea to keep yourself reasonably clean," drawled Keith, "because you never know anytime throughout the day or night when some nice man's gonna' do you a favor. If I wear clean underwear it's only in case I have one of those unexpected but pleasant accidents my mammy never breathed a word about."

"What part of North Carolina are you from?" I asked him.

His eyebrows shot up, his eyes darting about the room to see who had spoken, then alighted on me.

"How'd'ja' know Ahm from Nawth Carolin-uh?" he smiled, exaggerating his drawl.

"I spent three years there."

"Really? What part of the state?"

"Black Mountain."

"The college? No kidding! A lot of really *intense, hot* people went *there!*"

"Intense" was his favorite word, along with "hot," it seemed, at least for that night, since he used both repeatedly and with emphasis throughout the evening, the words slurred out lazily, like so much of his speech, apparently from the hash he'd been smoking.

"I'm from Raleigh m'self," he confessed, with a faint tone of apology in his voice as though it were the hickest of towns. You could see, under all his attempts at sophisticated insouciance, that he really was impressed with Black Mountain.

Just then the buzzer rang and Keith leapt up in an entrechat and glided swiftly across the floor to push a button on the wall above my head. Then he jetéed prancingly to the loft door, kicked aside the pokerlike police lock, opened the door a crack—a wave of chilly air blowing in from the hall made me shiver—stuck his head out and, while waiting to see whoever it was was arriving, began arching his back in a series of exquisite ripplings, sticking his tail up pertly in the air, in between bending his knees and turning his long feet out in perfect pliés, the ultimate dancer, never wasting a moment's opportunity to practice, or perform.

Presently, from outside in the hall, came voices and the tramping of feet up the stairs.

"I think this might be the place you're looking for," came Keith's voice back through the door, the same soft, silky welcome he had given me when I first arrived. There was an inaudible question, then someone laughing, and Keith's head popped back in as he swung the door open wide in a grandly welcoming gesture, his rubbery torso dropping in an abrupt bow from the hips like a marionette.

"Come on in and make yourself ta' home."

The first two through the door I recognized from our past circles: Daryl, his ears pink with cold, a tall, slender, darkly handsome lad with black curly hair and beautifully curved Mediterranean eyes, slipping a worn, greasy knapsack off the shoulders of his heavy mackinaw as he entered, and after that the jacket itself, revealing a gray sweatshirt beneath, slender wrists pushing out the sleeves, slim hips fitting nicely into old navy-blue sailor bell-bottoms with a thirteen-button flap; an actor, auditioning, as he'd told us at our last meeting, for a part in an off-Broadway play. And Bob, his thick beard a different shade, a reddish flaxen color, from the thinning red hair on his large, square head, with a high-shouldered, chunky build, stiff, solid, his blunt, plain features always screwed into a slightly worried look, particularly tonight.

"Ed not here yet?" Daryl asked, in that hushed, shy voice of his, which always made me wonder how he was ever going to make it as an actor, as he peered quickly about the room, smiling timidly at those of us he knew.

"Is Ed *ever* on time?" Petey asked in a loud voice.

"I only met him here last Wednesday for the first time and he was late even then," Keith said in a buttery murmur as greetings and introductions were exchanged all around.

Daryl and Bob were closely followed through the door by a third man who had apparently arrived at the same time and now introduced himself as Hal when Keith smilingly offered his hand. He was a small-figured youth, bundled up in a bulky coachman's coat which trailed almost to his ankles, the high, rounded collar rising well above his narrow balding head with its deepset, light blue eyes and a strong chin bordered in a short, neatly clipped sandy beard, his lean Semitic features both sensitive and sensuous at once, a friend, as it turned out, of Petey's, who leapt up to embrace him

122

when he came in, and who had duly invited him to our Saturnalia when Hal had arrived from San Francisco only a few days before. Amidst the continuing flurry of introductions and Jonathan exclaiming from the kitchen, where he had gone to arrange some of the food, *"Where is Ed?"* and coats being taken off, and Keith telling the newcomers where to put their things and any food or drink they might have brought with them, everybody talking at once, the room suddenly filled with a hum of excited and nervous jollity, the buzzer sounded again and Keith flew once more to the button above my head and pressed it with a light touch of his delicately extended forefinger, winking down at me as he did so, murmuring, "This better be Ed."

Within moments, barely audible above all the chattering gaiety and laughter, through the still partially open door, I heard footsteps running lightly up the stairs and presently a tall blond youth around twenty, wearing a snow-white ski jacket with red and green markings and a smart ski cap to match, burst in breathlessly, his fair-skinned face blushing with cold, fearful evidently, as I had been, that he would be late, his thick, hornrimmed glasses immediately steaming up as he hurried into the room, so that he slipped them off, revealing myopically darting, finely lashed eyes, blind to Keith's extended hand and hospitable smile as he whipped a handkerchief out of his pocket and began energetically polishing each lens with a corner of cloth.

Barely in the room, and still all out of breath, he didn't wait for introductions but immediately went quickly from one to the other of us sitting around the floor and, stooping and in a hushed, extremely polite voice, which I found instantly endearing, introduced himself personally as "Ken" to everyone, making it seem, as he took a moment and peered, however nearsightedly close into our eyes, that he really was sincerely glad to meet each and everyone of us, even Ian, whom he obviously already knew and who had brightened up considerably when Ken walked in the door, the strain for the moment leaving his eyes, and who brightened even more when Ken bent down and kissed him affectionately, the pair having been roommates for a time, as Ian once told me, when Ken first arrived from Denver two years ago.

As he peeled off his ski jacket there were "ooohs" and "ahhhs" of admiration for the bright orange jumpsuit he was wearing, undoubtedly purchased at the chic and trendy clothing store where he worked in the East Fifties, dealing in what Ian termed "*the* hottest" in gay male fashions.

The doorbell rang again, Keith springing up once more to push the button, cocking his head out the door to listen intently, shouting, "Well, it's about time!" as in a minute or so there was a rapid trudging up the stairs followed by the sound of footsteps trotting almost at a run down the short corridor and then Ed came scooting in the door right into Keith's arms, just as late as he had been to each of the circles I'd attended previously, grinning and mumbling apologies as he disengaged himself from Keith's embrace, his bulging dark green shoulder bag swinging, his face, above a stubbly, grain-colored beard kept so closely trimmed it always looked like it was just sprouting, ruddy from cold and from running up the stairs. There were cries of energetic welcome and laughter, and some vigorous teasing from all around the room, a tone in it all of relief, too, that the guide who had founded our Fairy Circle a few months back and would lead it off tonight, had arrived at last, which meant we really could get started with the Saturnalia now.

Keith kicked the police lock back into place with a clank of finality, all of us now having arrived, all now safely locked inside, protected against any unwelcome intruders in the night, save the cold wintery wind blowing in around the windows.

Ed quickly leaned down and embraced and kissed several of those closest to the door, including myself, then hastily slung his bag to the floor and unzipped his padded jacket, its nylon belly and pockets rubbed patchy with dark grease worn into the slippery fabric from long age and wear, a man in his late twenties perhaps, of medium stature, his receding auburn hair, tousled by the wind, sticking out all about his head in a wild disorder of frizzy curls, his hidden eyes, like shy animals, equally playful, sharply observant, as always, beneath thick, winged eyebrows, very dark brown eyes that shielded a subtle merriment and a tinge of mockery, an air of not taking himself or anybody else too seriously, as he now went around the rest of the room from one to another of us, putting his arms about each in a strenuous bear hug.

Except for his straight nose with its slight pudge and a high fine forehead with a tiny knit of tension where the eyebrows joined, everything about him was a fuzziness, like fur, not only lashes, cropped beard, hair, even the rest of his body hair, as would soon be revealed, having the wooly auburn fuzziness of a small animal, but his speech and manner had the same soft and furry downiness, a somewhat distracted and disordered air about him, his voice low and rasping as he explained, by way of apology, that he had spotted some handcrafted tapestries on sale, "for a song," in the windows of the Bashful Bear on East 10th Street on his way over and couldn't resist, even though he knew he was late, running in and buying several. He reached in his bag and, with a snap, unrolled one in each hand for us to see, tapestries splotched with bright, Matisse-like flowers and animals, one on a beige background, the other on a midnight blue.

Everyone instantly agreed they were so attractive, and so amazingly cheap, he would've been a fool not to have taken the few minutes to stop off and buy them, even if it meant not getting to the Saturnalia on time, his lateness, therefore, excusable in the eyes of all.

"And I *did* run all the way here," he added for good measure, with an ingratiating twinkle in his eye, and there were murmurs of approval all around.

Rolling up the tapestries and stuffing them back in the bag, Ed booted it across the floor into a corner and flung his coat after it, unbuttoned his red flannel shirt and unsnapped his fire engine red suspenders, sending his shirt flying after his coat. Bare to the waist now, exposing a chest and back coated in tiny curlings of reddish brown hair, and suddenly all business, he faced us, rubbing his hands together briskly, and announced in that raw, raspy voice of his, that the first part of the Saturnalia would now begin, the ritual of the massage.

He told us to spread the blankets and sleeping bags on the floor and to take off our shirts and undershirts, and when all that was done, with a minimum of fuss and confusion but a lot of goosey laughter, he said to choose the person nearest us as a partner, "To rub each other down and get us started off real loose and relaxed."

Except for one or two, particularly Daryl, who appeared hesitant, most of us had undressed halfway, and I felt immeasurably cooler, getting out of my flannel shirt and T-shirt, but experienced, as I gazed about the room and around at those closest to me, a feverish uncertainty about who to ask to be my partner, a little annoyed with Ed that he didn't follow the procedure at our other gatherings where we immediately formed a circle to raise energy, and the person sitting to your left, whoever it happened to be, automatically became your sidekick in whatever games or rituals followed.

But that was one of the things I liked about the Fairy Circle: its spontaneity and flexibility, its often wacky air of improvisation, just about bordering on free-form anarchy. There were no rules, except "And you harm none," as the words, borrowed from wicca, on the sign above the broom hanging on the wall stated, and no leaders—difficult in a circle anyway where everyone on any point of its circumference is a "leader"—only temporary guides, as Ed and several others would be tonight, and everybody had a say. And I recalled now, there had been a planning session for this evening, held in this very loft, in fact, last Wednesday night, which Keith had alluded to earlier, a meeting I hadn't been able to get to because I couldn't afford the busfare down to the city both then and tonight, where everything had been talked about.

Smoothing back my ruffled hair and beard to stall for time, hoping one of the men squatting or lounging close by would ask me to be his partner to save my having to ask someone, timid about it, mistaking it, from long habit and undoubtedly from the still-lingering influence of my afternoon in the backroom booths, with the chanciness of sexual acceptance, and wrongly but helplessly projecting that intrusion into this moment, I was, as always, afraid of rejection, fearful that nobody would want to team up with me.

Most of the others, I noted with growing anxiety, like the panic I vividly remembered in a gay bar at closing time when you hadn't found a bedpartner yet, had stripped now to the waist and were already paired off, while those remaining scrambled about to join up with one another, in each case one partner lying face down on the floor on a spread out blanket or sleeping bag while the other straddled his thighs and, there being no signal to begin, Ed joining in handily with the rest choosing Tim as partner, all over the room many pairs of hands began to knead themselves all up and down and over just as many backs and shoulders.

I began to feel foolish, out of it, when I had wanted so much to start out a part of things, to jump in right off and lose my unsureness. Only a few feet from me, Nick, his bushy hair and beard standing out about his head, his cheeks still flushed from the combination, no doubt, of heat and pot, his dark eyes, even through slits, glittering with a lively brightness, one of the last, like myself, without a partner, lay slumped on his side, smiling, relaxed, watching the others as though he had no desire to participate, enjoying some inner blissful images visible only to himself.

I screwed up my nerve and crawled over to him.

"Like a massage?"

He eyed me dreamily, a foolish, somewhat embarrassed grin

parting his lips, then presently stirred himself, as if from sleep, and finally nodded with an alacrity that pleased and surprised me, he appeared so laid back and indifferent to all that was going on around him. Perhaps he, too, had been timorous, had been lying there waiting for someone to ask him, undecided who to ask himself and, like me, had waited much too long, even to getting himself undressed. As he unbuttoned his shirt and lifted his T-shirt over his head, I pulled a corner of the large brown blanket, covered with nubs of coarse wool, closer for him to lie full-length on. He lay down on his stomach with a grunt, resting his head on his folded arms, eyes drooping shut, spreading his legs wide for me to kneel between them.

Awkward at first, and shy, because of my lack of experience, not to mention expertise, even though I'd massaged a few men before when asked, or as spur of the moment jobs on my part in the midst of lovemaking, I had only the skills of instinct to go on, the inner awareness from the knowledge of my hands on my own body and, thus, in extension from that, roughly knew what pleased and relaxed the body of another, tense muscles and nerves relaxing, as mine always did, under the pleasurable whisper of fingers in intimate places. I closed my eyes, imagining Nick's body my body, and blindly trusted those fingers to do their work, delighted to find them taking as naturally to the contours of his physique as wind slithering over a terrain of hills and valleys; my fingers in the hairs at the small of his back fingers of a breeze parting grasses; my fingers rubbing in the bushy hair of his head sending up to my nostrils the musky odorous oils of his scalp, akin to the shimmering odors of fields in noonday heat.

I breathed in his body as I rubbed his skin, my hands, like feelers, careful explorers in this new terrain, moving first in gentle circular motions down his back, the acrid salty smell of his torso a sudden sharp whiff of sea as I savored, with the sharpened nose of a dolphin, other scents of him like a familiar yet unknown seascape.

In firmer, deeper probings, I moved back up again to his shoulders, felt a small hard knot of tension in his neck at the base of the skull, which surprised me, he appeared so relaxed. Pressing with arched fingers there, I massaged it carefully til the bunched and tightened muscles gradually loosened, the tips of my fingers, like sensors, suddenly feeling an accompanying flush of warm blood flowing under them, blood released beneath his skin like water rushing through a dam or a floodgate slowly lifted; traced it, making my fingers spread fans, as the suffusing blood coursed down now in a crimson glow over his sturdy shoulders, giving his back a brighter ruddiness than before; pleased to hear, the instant this occurred, a sigh of deep satisfaction escape his lips, satisfied myself to discover my fingers knew more than I knew they did.

Pressed my hands flat beneath his armpits, the thatchlike hair damp and hot, and on my joined fingers, curious, lifted the scent of him to my nose and breathed him in, the pungent saline odor of him a hotter gust of sea this time; slipped my hands under his chest, my palms rubbing his tits around and around in cupping circles, then making tweezers of my fingers and taking the tips of his breasts between them, milked the nubs, and there was another long sigh and shudder of pleasure as his chest muscles shivered beneath the heels of my hands as they worked his ribcage in and out, like bellows, squeezing out one more voluptuous sigh from deep in his lungs.

I looked up to either side of me, searching for pointers, seeing a roomful of half-naked men, arms and backs in scissoring ripples of tendons and muscles as they knelt over the bodies of their partners, kneading their flesh with tensed hands, faces lost in concentration, each watching in dreamy reflection the consistently rhythmical flexing of hooked fingers moving down flesh, our body heat, as we bent to our work, adding considerably to the heat of the room, the aroused odors of sweat and secret body musks filling the air with the tang of a locker room; farts, too, as belly-flesh was vigorously manipulated, peals of laughter here and there at their unexpected ripping sound; pleasant, I thought, as I rubbed away, on a cold night such as this, the sensation of warmth of a fart fanning over the buttocks.

Taking hints from these other, more practiced masseurs around me, who appeared to lean to their task with more skill at it, I massaged his heavy arms, and then rubbed at his legs through his trousers, wondering what the direct touch of his muscular thighs and calves would be like without the barrier of heavy twilled cloth.

All the others still had their trousers on, Ed not having mentioned removing them at the outset, just our shirts, so I assumed it was part of this initial ritual, that we would no doubt, as the evening wore on, peel our clothes off by degrees.

And then Ed's voice, low and hoarse, announcing, "It's getting late," and, as I swung my head in his direction, up near the windows, I saw he'd changed positions with Tim, who was now crouching over him, still wearing his baseball cap, ready to massage Ed in his turn. "If you haven't switched, you better do it now," Ed urged, and dropped his head on his arms as Tim leaned over him and began chopping a tattoo, slicing up and down Ed's back in swift, light blows with the sides of his hands.

I had just finished massaging the soles of Nick's feet, which had caused him to squirm in ticklish wrigglings on the blanket, and, holding his raised leg in the crook of my arm as Ed spoke, slowly laid the leg back down on the floor and waited, my hands folded in my lap, having another moment of anxiety that Nick might not want to return the favor, and, worse, the humility of the others seeing it! Like a rejection at the baths, say, I was still so trapped in habits of the old confusion that physical touch, sex-centered, could only mean that, instead of the sensual and affectionate extension it could also be.

He lay so relaxed, eyes peacefully closed as if asleep, his cheeks even redder now, cheeks as red as those of a healthy baby. Whether he was relaxed from the ministrations of my hands or from too much hash was an uncertainty in my mind at this point as I glanced down at him, waiting patiently, hating to disturb him, but prompted, too, to shake him by the shoulder, just as a reminder it was his turn now to do the massaging.

My hands no longer on him, he presently roused himself, as if awakening, opened one eye and smiled at me. He pulled himself up with a slow, indolent air, leaning on an elbow and, without warning and with surprising strength, grasping me by the hip, turned me over easy, then straddled my hips as I lay down on my stomach, pressing my cheek into the nubby blanket which still held warm within it the hidden odors of his body.

His hands, thicker, stronger, were also surer than mine, more deft, firmer (he had evidently had previous practice), as they wrung my flesh, starting with the top of my shoulders and working their way down. I began dreaming I was an animal, the rake of his hands combing my fur sleek and flat and, hearing the cold wind rattle the windows, thought of the arctic air spilling down this night from the north, and how, in the upward circlings of his pincerlike fingers, he was rubbing north into my flesh, my blood flooding northward under his upthrusting hands, as his had rushed downwards and south over his shoulders under mine; thinking how hot, wet winds from the south always rub me the wrong way, my body rubbing against the rough blanket, my sliding flesh against its skeleton the loosening skin of a fruit under the rolling pressure of calloused palms, remembering again the longshoreman in the booth this afternoon, a similar touch in his workworn hands.

True north my direction tonight, I thought, drowsily alert, has always been, the upward shove of Nick's hardy hands sparking a northward current in my blood, stretching the unleashed, scattered magnetic field of my body to align itself in the gravitational pull of the moon toward the ice-buried Pole: Tonight I am a cold blue needle of steel, lying, head pointed toward the north wall of the loft, bellydown on the floor with the others, barebacked, as we took turns kneading each other into shape, fingers unknotting the knots that tie the blood, the ties in my own becoming undone under Nick's dexterous fingers, thawing the icy clots of deepwinter withdrawal in a dance of hands over each other's skin, as deep sighs and groans of relief and satisfaction resounded in the room, louder than the breathy, thin music of a Pink Floyd record playing in the background.

I basked in the heat of his hands, hot as midsummer, making my blood balmy in this coldest night, his splayed fingers rays bathing me in a sunny lassitude of warmth, massaging me from scalp to feet, his fingers probing, for all their thickness, delicately between my toes, where the bones, of themselves, pop in delight, spread and stretch like the hollow bones of a bird's wing, making them springy and ready to fly in the dancing ahead.

In the light of the candles, the winter skins of most of us aryan white, widdershins in aryan light bleached of darkness in early religious ingrainings magnetizing the poles of my bias over dark and, since they are also males, probably of most of the others, too; aryan iron needles eternally pointing skyward in the uranium-cold land of the radioactive fathers, drunk with death, at the top of their world, in thin air, in thin light of perpetually meager suns, in adoration of luminescence in frigid pure whiteness, cricked necks perpetually stiff from gazing skyward; my childroots, exposed to such air, nipped, barely breathing, finally shriveled and atrophied gradually in the willfully denied living substance of earth that once heartily fed them—masculinist minds bent to "improve" the natural, to prove it's no longer needed, and the howl of the earth a great beast wounded. The logical end of it: silvery males ejaculate to the moon in their own weightless metallic wombs, technological hermaphrodites in suits and helmets of thinnest and lightest silver, breathing through freefloating umbilical cords plugged into tanks of rarest oxygen plugged into bellybuttons shiny as new-minted dimes; huge silverplated boots, awkward as clubfeet in an atmosphere without gravity, stomp on the face of the moon, the face of Diana, all that cold, incredibly elaborate technology built to deny her, built to swing a golf club.

I opened my eyes and twisted my head to look back over Nick's shoulder through the clear plastic over the grimy windows, longing for a glimpse of the moon, but saw only the lighted crests of the skyscrapers in a black sky studded, now the snow clouds had blown away, with a few tiny stars over Manhattan, and felt cheated, uneasy, wanting the sturdiness of the moon's face, her heartening light, to strengthen my own face and eyes, to run icy and aloof and fearless in my veins, wanting the blood river and seas of my body swept in the tides of her powerful, magnetic embrace.

The plastic sheeting snapped with particular ferocity as a renewed blast of wind smacked against the glass, setting the windows shaking like tambourines, the floorboards shuddering beneath my belly as the old building shook with the force of the gusts battering against it.

As I was looking toward the windows, I saw Ed roll out from under Tim's hands and squeeze his shoulder with a grin, then hoisting his legs from a sitting position as he kicked off his trousers and briefs, heard his voice rise above the sounds of quiet slaps on flesh and occasional drawn out sighs of contentment, as he told us it was time to end the massage and to sit up now and form a circle. Without a pause, he lifted one cheek and unselfconsciously let out a brief, loud fart, then, without losing his train of thought, resumed telling us, as though nothing had happened, that it was time to begin the next phase of the evening's rituals, the raising of energy.

There was the silent shuffle of feet and haunches sliding over the floor as we got ourselves up and rolled up the blankets and sleeping bags and shoved them against the walls, out of the way. Then each of us sat down crosslegged to form a ragged circle, most of us keeping next to the partner we had in the massage, the bodily connection still strong, so that Nick sat to my left, and now easing himself down next to me on my right was Ken, the tall blond gracious lad from Denver, who smiled at me and grasped and squeezed my kneecap for balance as he lowered himself into position beside me.

As I glanced about the circle I could see that several faces were now flushed more than before, having lost their winter whiteness, radiating a pink aura in the candlelight, while on the shoulders and backs of some, patches of reddened skin the shade and texture of strawberries glowed where the hands of their partners had heartily rubbed them, as bright as Nick's shoulders had become when my fingers untangled the knot in his neck and the blood rushed down beneath the skin.

All places in our circle the same, none higher or lower, leaderless, as I said, Ed only one of several spirit guides for the rituals now beginning, he instructed us to join hands, as we had done in forming all our other circles, left thumbs hooked to right hands, so that the energy would flow sunward about the circle, not widdershins, against it. He was speaking quietly, slowly, with emphasis, in that voice which was as rough and shaggy as the dark hair curling over his entire body.

In his wooly mane and bristly whiskers, his legs nappily covered like the hair of an animal's legs, his deepset eyes impish and serious at the same time as he surveyed the circle, seeing to it that everyone was settled before he began, he gave the appearance of some woodland creature, a totally relaxed and playful dark satyr, his hairy face earnest and amused by turns, like sun dappling dark and light among leaves in a forest, moving from one face to another, patiently waiting. I stole a glimpse of the picture of Cernunnos on the low table and saw a startling resemblance between Ed and the Horned One.

The murmurings and rustlings of the circle getting itself comfortably seated on the floor finally ceased, several of the newcomers gazing about with a look of curious expectation in their eyes. When the room was totally hushed, except for the light flapping of wind against the plastic in the windows, Ed began to speak quietly again, a slow and reassuring measure to his words:

"Close your eyes and feel the energy of the earth in your feet, feel it far below this building surging up from the ground, feel it enter through your soles, your toes, feel it coming up your calves, your thighs, into your belly, your crotch. Feel it in your ass, feel yourself *sitting* on the earth.

"Now feel the energy of the sky coming in through the roof of this building, radiating in through the top of your head, into your neck, your shoulders; energy from the sky spreading out into your arms to the tips of your fingers and back again deep into your chest, earth-energy and sky-energy dancing together in your belly.

"Feel it pulsing through us now, the energies of earth and sky pulsing one to another, pulsing into your right hand from your partner and through your entire body, and flowing out your left thumb to the partner sitting next to you on your left. Feel rooted and centered. In place. This is the place we are, where we are now is the center.

"Our energies are gathered here in this circle, energies from below and from above, from earth above and sky below, from energies all around and in all directions, so that there is no up or down, and every place is the same place, and the right place, and every direction is the right direction and the same one, like our own energies, now strong here in this circle, flowing contained and everywhere around us."

He was silent for a few moments, the room so silent I could hear behind my dark lids the light sound of our breathing as I sat motionless among the others, elbows crooked, my hands lightly holding the hands of Nick and Ken on either side of me.

Then Ed spoke up again, saying, "Now we begin the breathing," his voice huskier, even lower than before. "Breathe deeply in unison, holding the breath a second or two on the intake, letting it all the way out, holding a second or two again before breathing in again. Breathe again, see in your mind, as if you were writing in a notebook, the word 'trance,' look at it, see it clearly. Breathe again deeply together now, hold again, and when you let out your breath, let it all the way out and, again, write in your mind the word 'deeper,' see the word 'deeper,' see it clearly, breathing as one body deeper and deeper into a deeper trance," his softly harsh voice, barely a whisper, lullingly repeating the same phrases over and over, the sound of our breathing in the room a loud but restful unity like the dry whisper of wind through pines, and all the while I felt the bloodheat of the others humming through my right arm and out my left arm like an electrical current, aware of my own blood tranquilly and unhurriedly coursing through my body along with the blood of the other men surrounding me, blood no different from theirs, myself no different from them, no longer separate—in our breaths, one breath, in our bodies, one body and bloodstream.

I felt aerated with a heady sense of gaiety, a giddiness that lifted all heaviness from me, all the dark weight of the night. I tightened my grip on Nick's hand (horny palms slightly damp), and on Ken's (dry and smooth as rice paper), and each gently returned the pressure; felt that I had turned, inwardly, into the downiest of feathers, as light and playful as one of those tiny feathers escaping from my vest in the darkened backroom booth when the longshoreman had hugged me; so light I was afraid I might float off to the ceiling of the loft, skittish about that happening, reluctant for the moment to leave this solid and reassuring circle of flesh, anchoring and steadying me in a strongly connected interlacing of bloodwarm hands.

Rooted and lightheaded, as though I really had my feet on the ground, my head in the clouds, as Ed had directed us, grounded and airborne all at once, but still dizzy with that featheriness, I cracked my eyes to slits to check if I was still in the loft, just in time to catch Ed opening his mouth, a perfect pink circle in his short, fuzzy beard, uttering the mantra OM, beginning to chant in a low, strong tenor at first, leading us in the chanting, our voices joining in one by one, wavering and uncertain at the start, then increasingly louder and louder in ascending vibrations, overriding finally Ed's deepening baritone, the drone of our voices in various pitches going forth in different keys at first, our dronings an enormous human organ of sound reverberating against the walls, so mighty in the variation of its swelling chant it seemed to penetrate the bricks, move out on the frozen airwaves of the night over the frostsparkling lights of the city, rise above the topmost spires of the skyscrapers to join with other, multiple hummings, a surprising and lively hum of bees in dead winter joining in the roaring of the busy wind whipping around swaying skyscrapers, sculpting them into inverted icicles, and racing with a screaming buzz down between their icily ribbed canyons, our voices in the wind swirling up and around to the snow-laden clouds in the northern heavens, a dynamic flight of sound, breaths radiating around and around the planet, streaming in a cumulative and powerful hymn out into the cosmic throb of the night-blackened universe where the stars in twinkling light pulse back in sympathetic shine and echo along with all the sounds of our fairy breaths, our OMs a puny, tinny hint of what the universe must sing like in its breathing, including Keith's own earlier brazen speculations on Meredith Monk, bebop and bee's wings, its own far hum, crisp and merry, constantly spiraling in staggered improvisations, eccentric and centered all at once, utterly on pitch, perfectly and forever in and out of tune.

Slowly, of its own volition, our chanting faded away, the sounds of it becoming thinner and thinner, sprinkles of transparent sound, like heavy rain diminishing to a light patter, then, like the last ethereal held notes of stringed instruments at the end of a piece of music, our voices likewise evaporated into nothingness, until the room was totally still again, even the rattling windows still, the sounds of our breaths an excited lightness that was almost a silence.

After a few moments, Ed started us breathing rhythmically once more, louder inhalations and longer expulsions of breath, encouraging us to slide into an even deeper trance. Then he breathed, in a voice so quiet I almost missed his words, "If anyone has anything they want to have healed, speak of it now."

I heard the slow sough and whisper of our breathing, listened closely to my own, my body lifting out of itself, cut loose from its skeletal moorings, as I seemed to float around the circle, over the heads of the others, Ed's soft, insistent voice bringing me back down.

"Get centered in yourselves again," he urged. "Feel the energy flowing again from hand to hand, the healing energy now," and then he told us to close our eyes once more and concentrate on our breathing and concentrate on something that we wanted or that we wanted healed, and there was a long moment of silence, once more only the sound of breaths rising and falling as one breath in the room.

Presently there came a voice that sounded like Tim's (I wondered if he was still wearing his baseball cap), stammering out, "What I want is to get along better with my lover," and, amidst the steady breathing, there were several sighs of empathy around the circle, Ed exhorting us to "Direct all our energies toward the person's voice, concentrating all your energy on the need he speaks of," and there was the silence again and I felt the hands on either side of me tighten ever so slightly on my own as we all put our attention to Tim's request.

After several moments somebody asked, "Do fears count?" and there was quiet, sympathetic laughter all around, laughter which didn't break up the circuit of concentration and intensity developed within the circle, and Ed said, "Yes, they count," and whoever was speaking said, "In that case, I want to be healed of my fear of going up in an airplane—this Friday, in fact," and there was again the silence as we concentrated on it, and during it an almost inaudible voice, Jonathan's, breathed, "Don't worry, the fairies will be flying with you, under the wings, holding it up—think of that when you're up there, we won't let you fall," and soft, amiable laughter broke out again around the circle and still the cohesion of our focused energy stayed intact.

Some asked for nothing for themselves, like Ian, who wanted only that one of his daughters be healed of a "month-long virus"; and next to me, Ken's quiet voice was heard after Ian spoke, telling us about his grandmother, "in her eighties," who was ill in Denver and who wanted to get well so she could come East to visit him, and Ed each time, like a litany, reiterated, "Direct all your energies to that person's voice, concentrating all your energy on the pain or illness he speaks of, and project intense images of healing toward him and toward the one he speaks of," and again our energies beamed forth, to the West this time, focusing on Ken's grandmother, that she be well and strong soon for the trip, each span of concentration, ceasing naturally, lasting only as long as the circle, acting as one body, felt was necessary, none of it either too hurried or too drawn out, but just the right length of time given to each request before moving on to the next.

There was a longer silence and then someone whose voice I couldn't distinguish asked timorously, making it obvious that it was difficult for him to bring up the subject, that his hemorrhoids be healed, and I tried to place the voice so that I could tell him later about some healing aids I'd learned of (lots of bran and bioflavonoids with Vitamin C in the diet, refined sugar and flour products out, and consistent exercise, especially gut exercises, for writers, like truck drivers and airplane pilots and secretaries, all particularly susceptible to this condition from so much sitting); and since such a nuisance could cause a definite disruption in one's lovelife, at least in that important area, and since, I suspected, most of us sitting around the circle on our own seats of pleasure could identify with that, our energies rose and centered, it seemed, with more than usual empathetic ardor on this particular request.

Ed had us breathe deeply again, plummeting down and down as one breath into a luminous darkness, the silence lasting for a minute or for several minutes, it was difficult to gauge time now, when someone else spoke up, speaking, as several others had so far, induced by our near trancelike state as the latter part of the ritual deepened, in the formal manner of dreams, asking that "the rivers of the earth be clean again," and another voice quickly added, "And the land, too, all of the planet, healed and cleansed again," and somebody else said, "And the sky, don't forget the sky," and a last voice, which sounded like Petey's, put in, "May Kali soon show her wrath, may the goddess, stunned by these assaults on her earthbody, soon begin to shake," and I stole a swift glance at the image of Kali on the low table by the windows, her swirling arms like rotors to break the skin of the earth, to stir long-stagnant streams of blood, and bring new life. And Jonathan was heard to say, his voice trembling with passion, "Let our songs and dances here tonight be ministrations to help her heal herself, be callings to awaken her," all of it the formal language again, like the language of dreams.

"So mote it be!" several voices cried out in a chorus, like voices in deep-sleep dreaming, in another of our phrases borrowed from witchcraft, and there was a longer stillness as we concentrated mightily on the abused earth and heavens, sending our healing images streaming out into the night and over the hard frozen crust of the earth and up into the frost-shiny air, all temporarily purified in the rushing cold winds, our mute energies no more than sparrowlike twitterings beaming out feebly across the vast planetary night, but suddenly there was the image of the healing sun streaming and streaming through my mind.

And as I concentrated with the others on the healing of the earth, of its air and land and waters, the healing of the earth mother, my mother's own face appeared before me, and when it seemed no one else had anything more to say, I mustered up my courage, saying that I, too, didn't want anything for myself, only wanted to speak to them of her, of a face now seamed with fear and anguish, reflecting a mind, a spirit, suspended and wandering in a shadowland where I cannot follow, try as I will each time I visit her, can only sit with her and hold her hands and comfort her as best I can with soft, encouraging words, the shadows deepening in her cataracted eyes each time I see her. My father, her husband of 49 years, dead now six years, and her behavior so unpredictable, walking around the little town in her nightclothes in the early hours of the morning, lost, confused, knowing less and less of who or where she is, forgetting who I am, forgetting all her children, and all of those around her. Her whole life given over to others, she has none now to give herself and none of us able to give her what she needs, or know what it is we could give her. Although she cried to me in a breathless, angry voice as I helped her get undressed for bed one night, "I wisht I had my husband back!" because she is nothing without him, not ever knowing any other way—so that my sister and my other brothers, having tried to keep her and look after her as best they might, could no longer handle her, nor the one brother now living with her, and decided, after many family meetings, she must be in some safe place, each of us finally facing that hard decision and agreeing to put her in a nursing home. And I knew she understood this without understanding, knew what was coming, even though she didn't know, and can see the fear grow larger in her eyes each time I visit her, as the time approaches for her to go, and the light gradually drains from her eyes as she slips deeper and deeper into the twilit place of shadows where there are no more names, and I can no longer follow, having stepped out of my own shadows, for this day, anyway. Much as I want to, it's hard to comfort her and make her feel less alone, less frightened in her going, which isn't just her going into the home, we both know that. I try to see her gathering darkness, which I know will also someday be my own, so that I might give her stronger solace and understanding, however awkward or useless, in this growing lightless place she's in in her mind, where she's screaming out the truth of her life at last, an illumination, as I listen, and listen hard, not wanting to forget any of it. And the best I can do for her most times is get her to sing fragments of songs she still remembers, because she always loved to sing, and help her along with forgotten words, phrases, the two of us singing "Oh, You Beautiful Doll" and "I Found a Million Dollar Baby in the Five and Ten Cent Store," sitting side by side on the front porch of the house where I grew up and where she has spent much of her life, songs I heard her sing as a kid, and learned from her, following her around as she did the wash or cleaned the house, and still remember.

And what I said to those in the circle is just as I've written here, and when I finished the silence lengthened in the room and there was the light thwack thwack thwack of the plastic sheeting in the windows as the wind moaned in around the cracks. I asked the others to help her, asked, the healing working through us, that she not be in pain and not be too afraid when she goes into the home, which I knew now would be in a few short days when the bed of a dying patient became vacant and there would then be a place for her at last.

There was a brief silence, then Ed's hoarse whisper was heard, saying, "Keep centered in ourselves, keep centered in the circle,

138

concentrate all our energies toward this mother, that she not be afraid or in pain. Concentrate, concentrate, many minds, many spirits, concentrate as one, and heal."

The room was so still I could hear the light beating of my heart, the crackle of candle flames twisting in the draft on the low altar by the windows; sensed the circle of the night turn above our little circle, our breath the rhythms of its turnings, experienced once more the currents of blood energy passing through us one to another about the circle, just as the sun swings unseen above us in the night, our chanting pulling down its light through darkness, brightening our blood. Slowly, I began to feel a terrific warm rush of energy everywhere in the loft at once, and everywhere in myself as well, in every nerve and fiber, a warm, tingling sensation, like I had just run a mile, like I felt after my run from the West Village tonight. I became lighter, as before, lightheaded, felt that heavy sadness being pulled out of me, like a suction, and a hidden darkness dispelled, and a yellow aura was in the room, different from the light of the candles, a steady, peaceful effulgence like the golden light gathered in the air just after a rainy sunset, and I was suddenly bouyant in that place where sadness and concern for my mother had been, and hoped that she was feeling it, too, at that very instant, knew that she must be, and concentrated all my energy with renewed vitality, along with the others, sending it South to her through the bitterly cold night, to the house where both doors had to be locked so she couldn't get out to roam at night. Hers is a story I will also someday tell.

As the radiance lessened, I sensed a pleasant afterglow of ease and drowsiness, a relaxed pink spirit enveloping me, as if all the arms in the room were cradling me, and presently heard Jonathan's voice say, "I hope your mother knows centeredness, like a flower, and won't be afraid."

And another voice, which sounded like Ian's, spoke up, saying quietly, "May she be held in the arms of the Great Mother."

And I was bathed in a tremendous wave of comfort as each one spoke, thinking, because all that could be done had been done and what might have been done was now too late, and pray to the Mother as I might, there was no hope for her, almost saying it aloud, "May the earth soon hold her." And was joyous for her that she might be with our Mother again, as she was now, wandering childish in her mind with her own mother, back among the cobblestone streets and brick row houses in turn-of-the-century South

Philadelphia, crooning wisps of barely remembered songs.

We continued sitting in our circle, breathing deeply, no one speaking, and after a while Ed said, "Whoever it is that spoke of his mother come stand in the middle of the circle to be cradled," and I let go Nick's and Ken's hand and got up and stood as he said to, closing my eyes, as you were supposed to do, so that I couldn't see those who had offered to take part, but could hear them rise, their bare feet approaching me across the floor from several points of the circle, and could see in my mind's eye, from past cradlings, what they were doing, two men crouching behind my legs, feeling their forearms as they crisscrossed their wrists and joined locked hands at the backs of my knees, while two others, standing either side of me, with hands similarly crossed and locked, pressed them against the small of my back, while a fifth person stood close behind me, his hands placed at the base of my skull, ready to cup it for balance and support.

When I heard Ed murmur, "Okay, easy now," I went limp, felt the locked wrists at the back of my knees begin to slowly hoist my legs, as always, when I'd been cradled before, with surprising ease off the floor; felt my body tipping backwards—my heart fluttering with fear as I leaned back for the fraction of a second in unsupported space—and then the locked forearms, like crossed lances, of the pair standing either side of me, caught me just above the small of the back, my skull instantly clutched, as in a bowl, in the waiting hands of the person standing at my head, heard his barefeet scuffling on the boards as he moved back a few steps, heard the whispery barefeet of the other four as they gained a firm footing, and I was lifted completely off the floor in a horizontal position in a balanced and even distribution of weight, my hands folded across my belly, held suspended in midair a moment on the reinforced strength of their crossed wrists and enfolding hands, not even feeling the tiniest twinge of uncertainty now, feeling my bones, every nerve in my body relax, felt my heartbeat slow, as I let myself sink into their firm yet easy support that had no hint of even the slightest exertion in it.

They began to rock me, a slow and easy head-to-toe rocking at first, working in harmony, their arms like one pair of arms, and I knew, from participating in past cradlings, that the weight of my body would soon become negligible, like air, in their hands, in their rhythmic unity. As they gradually increased the arc of the sway to wider and wider swingings, they began to hum, a soft, murmurous humming that the others sitting around in the circle soon joined in on, so that I felt like a child being rocked in a cradle of arms, their softly crooning voices like mothersong in my ears, felt myself swinging back to the origins of all, learning song, then words, learning speech, watching her mouth, learning the face of my mother, learning it again this night in primal beginnings, in listening touch, as the singsong humming of the others increased as their rocking increased, their rustling lullaby lulling me, dropping me deeper and deeper into paradoxically tense but utter slackness, stirring a quiet and jubilant humming in my breast. Dreaming, in the slow, easy rhythm back and forth, that I was a papoose strapped in a bark cradle swaying in the arms of my crooning mother, or riding up and down on my mother's back as she worked and sang, and now I was suspended in the low branches of a tree, the breeze, like their hands, catching and swaying me idly back and forth at first, and then, as the breeze increased to a rolling wind with the more strenuous and wider swinging of their hands, the ascending hum of their voices became the purr of a rapidly rising wind, the crooning my mother's voice had been, which I, feeling it rise in my throat, spontaneously sang back to.

Gradually the arms slowed in their rocking, their humming voices falling lower and lower, the voices out in the room growing softer, like the wind at the windows falling, descending to a barely audible whisper, and the arms ceased their motion and I lay quiet, hearing nothing but the even rhythm of their breathing around me, feeling so light I sensed myself levitating to the ceiling, then slowly floating down again, my body a silken plume again, aware once more of their crossed wrists and clasping hands beneath me like sturdy straps of flesh, holding me supine til my body adjusted to the stillness, and when they sensed that that was accomplished, after a few moments, with no jarring or jerkiness, I was eased upright on my feet again, the solid floor feeling strange beneath my bare soles til I took a first few tentative, stumbly steps upon it, like an infant learning to walk.

I blinked open my eyes and saw those who had held me, Ian and Tim and Bob and Bert, with Daryl at my head, all beaming at me, and I went from one to the other and embraced each one, not only thanking them for the cradling, but feeling as if I had just returned from a long and distant journey and was terrifically glad to see them all again.

We sat again in our circle, taking hands once more, right hand joined to the left thumb of our partners, closing our eyes as we drifted once more into deep breathing, so easy now to fall into it, to breathe as one, to breathe as one pair of lungs, beat as one heart, a steady even tempo of breathing around the room once more, time passing without passing, time stretching and shrinking as if it did not exist at all, only this instant, on the sharp edge of which I felt totally vibrant, totally alive.

Presently, I heard a stir out in the little kitchen and, opening my eyes, saw that Jonathan had slipped out there and was bending over the stove, and I wondered if he was going to brew us some herb teas as he had at other circles: yellow dock, witch hazel bark, and mandrake root—but this time he was holding a poker over a gas jet as he prepared to mull some wine in a carafe at his elbow, the tip of the poker ingot-red, Jonathan's pallid freckled face, solemn in concentration, bathed eerily, like an intent wizard in his alchemical laboratory, in roseate blue from the reflection of the intense heat of the metal in the gas flame, his thin lips curling in a smile as he stuck the poker into the wine and there was a loud hiss followed by a puff of steam.

Carrying the carafe in one hand and a large platter in the other, he moved quickly to the table where the food was, his fingers busily flying over the fruits and breads there, as he filled the platter. When that was done, actor to the core and so as not to rush things too much, he waited a beat in the shadowy wings by the blue votive lights on the wine table, where he snatched up a goblet. Then, at the exact dramatic moment, when several men began surreptitiously opening their eyes, glancing about curiously with a distant sleepiness, wondering what was coming next, restlessly rearranging stiff legs to more comfortable positions, Jonathan, Hermes-quick, stepped swiftly and elegantly in long-legged strides into the center of the circle, clutching the carafe and the goblet aloft in his thin bony hands, and immediately filled the goblet to the brim, set down the carafe, and lifting the glass above his head in both hands, spoke, saying, in his clear, flutelike voice, "We ask that this wine be blessed first by the benevolent spirits of the Winter Solstice, with thanks to Bacchus and the Bacchae, and to all the gods and goddesses of the vines, and to Mother Sun who darkened the grapes. Blessed be."

And several voices answered within the circle, "Blessed be."

Then he passed the goblet from hand to hand among us, each

taking a sip, except myself, and Ken on my right, plus one or two others, those few of us choosing instead a drink of the pulp-thick apple juice from the jug Jonathan went and got to pour for the abstainers before he followed the goblet of wine about the circle, replenishing the glass when it was drained, busy, intent, quietly and steadfastly absorbed, moving in and out of the circle with his wine jug, a bee in flight, a bee alighting, pouring nectar, flying off again, moving from one to another as if we were flowers to be nuzzled, which we certainly were, rosyfaced blossoms of flesh he kissed as he circled and poured, and missed not one of the purple-stained mouths.

Bits of food were shared next, Jonathan now standing in the center of the circle with the platter he'd made up earlier, filled with slices of apple and tangerine sections (it pleased me to think some of the portions might have come from the fruits I'd brought) and cheese and pieces of the whole grained cakes and breads, all golden brown in the candlelight, like loaves of sun, and again Jonathan spoke, holding the platter high, his deep red hair burning bright at the ends in the glow of the candles, saying, "We give thanks to the green spirits of this summer past, and all summers past and to come, to Demeter and Cronus, to Ceres and Saturn, for their gifts we share tonight in this Fairy Circle, for the fruits and grains that sustain us, that give us life. Blessed be."

And again several of us murmured, "Blessed be," in response.

He swung the platter down and moved about the circle once more, darting in and out, offering each of us something to eat from the plate, a few of us feeding each other, putting bits of cake or slices of apple into the mouth of the men sitting either side of us, a laughing, joking communion of sharing in nurturance, far more exciting and meaningful swallowing live fruits shared from living hands than any Holy Communion I'd ever remembered receiving on the tip of my tongue in church as a child, and recalled those dry, stingily thin wafers, bleached of any sustenance, held pinched between the bloodless thumb and forefinger of a thinlipped priest on a Sunday morning, a faint mothball scent clinging to his vestments, the parchment-dry skin of his fingers smelling antiseptically clean; thinking of that as I slipped a succulent section of tangerine between the parted lips of Ken beside me, his curled tongue, pink as a prepuce, flicking the slice of fruit deftly and expertly from between my fingers and into his mouth, driblets of the bright orange juice running down his chin, to his and my delight, the two of us giggling like kids as he rubbed his chin dry with the back of his hand. And when Petey bit into a fat black plum—which must've cost somebody a pretty penny at Balducci's at this time of year—he squealed in surprise as its juiciness spurted over his cheeks in all directions, even into the eye of his neighbor, Tim, and we all laughed at the slaphappy, crosseyed look of astonishment on Petey's face.

At this point, Bert lumbered forward, a teasing grin barely discernible in the folds of his heavy beard, and, motioning us all to get up, herded us together in a close circle, shoulder to shoulder, telling us to raise our hands at the ready, while he briefly explained to the few others who hadn't participated before, the object of a game called "Trust," while those of us who had played it at our other gatherings, began to laugh in anticipation, a few of us groaning at the prospect.

When we were set, he tapped Petey on the shoulder as a signal that he was to be the first in the center of the now tight circle, choosing him probably because Bert knew Petey had played the game before with us, and also because he was one of the lightest among us, and would start us out easy.

Bert looked around the circle and asked if everybody was ready and when we all nodded yes, he said quietly, "Okay, Petey, shut your eyes and let yourself go," and his voice grew even quieter, repeating, "Let yourself go," and then he added, "Have trust in us, we won't let you fall, have trust," his words ending in a gruff, hypnotic whisper.

Petey, standing in the middle of us, our shoulders pressed around him, his eyes closed, his slim body utterly relaxed, like a ragdoll, began swaying and falling, as loose and out of control as possible, and as he swayed and fell around the circle in every direction, he was caught lightly and held momentarily in our hands before being eased off in another direction to other supporting hands, just as Bert had directed. Then, as his trust grew, and we catchers got used to the rhythm and pattern of his fallings, Bert motioned for us to move farther apart, and the circle expanded slowly, opening up, like a flower, each of us moving a few more feet from the partner standing on either side of us, so that the drop of Petey's body fell in a longer, and scarier, stretch of space before our hands reached out to catch him. Every few moments Bert signaled us to move out a step or two in an increasingly wider ring, so that Petey's lithe, pale body fell like a long blade slashing among us in extendedly daring and breathtaking falls, his silken blond hair flying straight up as he dropped, and was caught at the exact instant before he hit the floor, his thin frame held again and again for the briefest moment in our supporting hands before being passed along to the hands of others.

There was a wonderful sense of revolving movement, like a dance; we became one dancing body dancing in place, moving and working in harmony, a waving, cylindrical flower of flesh with Petey at its center its corolla, the hands of the rest of us cupping petals sprouting around him as he tipped and sliced among us.

One by one, at a light tap on the shoulder from Bert, we took our turns in the center of the ring, my pulse quickening a bit in expectation as the time wore on and I knew my turn would come, as it had before, trust hardest for me, then as now, but something I was slowly learning in the Circle, in games such as this, giving up control, and isolation, trusting others and myself.

Some of us were light and pliant and totally laid back about it, like Petey, and Keith, too, when it came his turn, so that they were easy to shore up and easy to move with, while others, like Bob, chewing the ends of his reddish-blond mustache, were visibly nervous and unsure, and heavier, too, so that it was harder when such a person faced me directly and I had their full, frontal weight falling against my upthrust palms. Several times I had to strain against Bob's chest to hold him back, and a few times lost my balance and had to back up a pace or two, struggling to support his weight, tensed and made heavier by his fear, to regain my footing.

Whereas Daryl, when it came his turn, though slim, was, surprisingly, because of his being so totally inert, like a deadweight against our hands so that a few times I had to grip him by the front of his sailor's pants to hold him; he, of all of us, was the most trusting and yet, paradoxically, the least supple, like a leaden marionette without strings.

But there was, throughout, that sense of rhythmical support and strength in the shared efforts of the ring of men, eyes alert and attentive, focused in eager and wide-eyed concern on the person swaying and collapsing in our midst, our arms poised, hands up, palms out flat, always at the ready to gently but firmly, with a slight nudge, send him upright again and weaving, bending around the ring in another direction, to the waiting hands of others.

When I felt Bert's hand on my shoulder and knew it was my turn—perhaps, because he was a considerate man, perceiving the

145

uneasiness in my eyes, he had chosen me last so I might gather strength from the example of those who had gone before me—I closed my eyes and silently breathed a swift prayer to Kali to tear this fear from me and let faith grow in its place, then moved into the center, the warm and steadying shoulders of the others immediately closing around me, so that I began to feel a surge of confidence, as if Kali had heard me and given me courage in the firm closeness of their flesh.

As I stood among them, eyes shut tight, their bodies so near I smelled their heat, their sweat, my arms against my sides, legs straight together, I tried to relax as much as possible, thinking of Petey looking limp as a ragdoll. At first, still a little mistrustful, I let myself only sway in small, careful arcs, but then, feeling their strong and encouraging hands grasp my chest and back and shoulders in sure, almost caressing bolsterings as I swayed, I allowed my body to lean and drop in wider and wider headlong plungings as the circle broadened, myself now the corona of the flower our flesh made, the arms of the others grasping me like branches in my free falls, their hands cupping my body like protective, nesting petals.

More and more I let myself be taken by their hands, turned from one to the other in a gentle and pleasurable turning, only once or twice having a flicker of doubt, when the mind asserted itself, wanting to take over again, the fear of losing control returning and I wanted to take back my will, which made me instantly lose my footing and stumble into their arms rather than sliding easily in and away on the palms of their hands. But I called on Kali again to help me, her picture among the candles vivid in my mind's eye, and got my feet centered again, felt centered by her, placing them firmly on the floor, imagining, instead of my ego ruling, the suppleness of a snake coiling into my limbs, for the second time this day, letting myself drop again in lazy, rubbery loops, a black snake weaving its body around and through and from limb to limb of a yielding and sturdy tree of flesh, their arms the human branches I dipped and wrapped around in my snake-hipped gliding, trusting myself to the certainty of their vinelike hands, having renewed confidence that their waiting fingers, like tendrils, would be there to catch me, and they always were, hands and arms as excellent snakehandlers as they were limbs of trees, and knew then, in that moment of total surety and trust, the game was over, and stopped my swaying and falling and stood perfectly still with eyes closed for several moments til I sensed the circle begin to move apart, and opened my eyes and saw the others looking at each other and grinning, and I grinned myself, particularly at Bert, and we all burst into spontaneous and gleeful applause, like children will, in exhilaration after the game, several of us hugging and clapping each other on the back in an equally impromptu sense of high-spirited camaraderie.

It took a little while for us to get settled down again, and in the meantime, Keith stepped forward, setting a small wooden cradle-like basket on the floor in the middle of the circle. In it he placed a plastic bag of what looked like hashish and a small, bluntly rectangular hash pipe made of dark wood, tossing over it all a green silk handkerchief as a coverlet. He then stood up, waving his hands for quiet, and asked those who had brought "dope to share" to place it in the basket, and several men, including Ken beside me, scrambled up to search in the pockets of their discarded shirts or reached into their trouser pockets and tossed loose joints into the center, while some threw out more of the small plastic bags, all of it scattering around the base of the little ark of a basket, a few of the joints rolled in rainbow-tinted papers. Ken leaned over and whispered in my ear that what he'd thrown out on the floor was "some really dynamite Hawaiian grass."

An impish, exaggeratedly greedy smile on his face, Keith stooped over and gathered up the offerings and, lifting the silk handkerchief, placed the joints and bags inside with the hash already in the basket, and, with his long, thin fingers, carefully smoothed the folds of the cloth over the top again. He stepped back as Ed, in his position as guide again, came to the center and, kneeling, his dark curly head bowed, spread his hands over the green-covered basket, intoning, "I call on the spirits of cannabis, on night-flying witches whose bodies are rubbed with herbal hallucinogens, to bless this marijuana which, in this Saturnalia, in this night of the winter solstice, we will use only to increase our conscious contact with the spirit-beings of the cosmos, within and without. So mote it be."

"So mote it be!" rose our voices in an answering chorus.

Then he lifted the silk coverlet and reached into the basket, bringing out the pipe and a bag of hash, and shaking a loose chunk from the bag, carefully packed the bowl, tamping it down firmly with his index finger, and scratching a kitchen match with his thumbnail, lit the pipe, puffing to get it going, then closed his eyes and inhaled deeply, holding his breath, and went and sat down in his place in the circle. After a few moments, he forced the toke out of his lungs in a thin, gray mist, his voice choked and high as he quoted, " 'I have tasted the things within the holy basket,' " then passed the pipe to the person on his left, fiery-bearded Bob, following the previous direction of the circle in the generating of energy, the direction of the sun, Ken leaning again against my shoulder with a sly smile to whisper, *"All* baskets are holy!" and I looked at him and smiled.

When the pipe reached me, I abstained, as with the wine, not needing or wanting any of it, nor minding that the others did, high as I was from the potent punch brewed so far by the games and rituals alone, and after taking it from Ken, who inhaled deeply on it, handed the pipe on to my left, to Nick, who took it readily from my hand and, closing his eyes in dreamy expectation, placed the thick stem between his teeth and sucked in a long and leisurely toke before passing it on to Danny, seated on the other side of him, Nick waiting a few long moments with bulging cheeks and tight-shut eyes to get the fullest effects of the smoke before expelling it from deep in his lungs in a loud, hissing wheeze, more forced than the sighs escaping him during the massage.

Several of the joints, the rainbow-rolled ones in particular, were now taken from the basket by Jonathan and Keith and lighted and also passed from hand to hand about the room, smoked til they were no more than tiny coals of roaches gleaming in the dim light, the air itself now so blue and drowsy with marijuana smoke that just by inhaling it my body floated in a pleasant cloud, like a swarm of feathers caressing my senses, gently tickling me inside and out in a silent merry dusting of laughter.

When the pipe had gone around the circle, followed by the rainbow-colored reefers, the only smoking the smoking of grass, since I'd never seen anyone smoking cigarettes or anything else at any of our circles, Ed shut his eyes and said, "Now let's join hands again and close our eyes and breathe again in long, deep breathing together, and for those of us who feel moved to do so, call down the gods and goddesses, the fairy spirits, and all the spirits we want to have present here tonight to bless and strengthen our circle and to celebrate the winter solstice with us."

After a long and awkward silence, as if each of us was waiting for someone else to speak first, joined hand to hand once more, only the sound of our breaths in even breathing in the high and empty space of the loft, I heard a voice within the circle say in a hoarse uncertain whisper, "I invoke the spirit of Saturn, god of golden abundance."

There was another long silence, then another voice spoke, one not so hesitant this time, a clear tenor voice which was clearly Petey's, "I invoke Ceres, sister-goddess of fruits and grains."

In a hushed voice, someone said soon after, "I invoke the Great Mother."

And another, almost immediately after, "I invoke the spirits of the winter solstice."

Each invoking whoever he was moved to invoke. The silences in between, after a particular spirit was asked to bless the circle by its presence, were like respites giving the spirit time to appear, giving us time, too, to sense and recognize its being there, before the next one was called forth.

Then one more voice, faltering, breaking with emotion, a voice that sounded like Ian's, saying, "I invoke the presence of my dead father, who my mother recently told me was gay."

I wanted to open my eyes to peek, to see who had spoken, to see if it was really Ian, seeing his bright red flared trousers in my mind, moved by the evident feeling in his words, the effort it had cost him or whoever had spoken to say it, but decided not to, that it was better not to know, in this moment, and kept my eyes closed, concentrating on bringing among us the living spirit of the dead gay father.

"I invoke Laverna, goddess of thieves, in the spirit of the pardoning of all so-called criminals," came another voice with a distinctly Southern slur to it, so I knew it had to be Keith speaking. "Especially from Rikers Island," he added, "as was done on this day for all prisoners in the ancient Roman Saturnalia."

A long pause, and someone else spoke, "I invoke Isis, goddess of all," and smiled to myself, perhaps the pot floating in the air getting to me at last, thinking sillily, 'Isis, on this icy night when ice is in the air,' thinking, too, in a more distant connection, of the poet Charles Olson telling me he'd had a dream once on Black Mountain of the two of us approaching the temple of Isis together, and wondered now how Charles would have enjoyed being here tonight, suspecting he would love it, and realized, in silently evoking his name, he was here with us already, and smiled even more broadly at the welcoming thought of him.

"I invoke the horned god of blackness, the goat of the underworld, son of the goddess of night," came another voice, which I was pretty sure was Jonathan's, and saw again behind my closed lids the picture of Cernunnos propped up on the altarlike table between the windows.

"May the Animal Spirit be with us," asked another. "May it soon free all the chickens, cattle, pigs, all animals tortured and mutilated and slaughtered without care in animal factories for profit and gluttony."

"I call on Kali to be with us," piped up an excited voice immediately, "Goddess of destruction and new growth. May she break down the doors of the slaughterhouses and free all the imprisoned beasts," and hearing this, this time squinted my eyes toward the windows and fuzzily glimpsed Kali's likeness once more on the low table, her zigzagging arms, bent and extended like swords, seeming to spin like a wheel in the dancing leap of candle flames.

"I call down the presence of manitous in the Great Spirit."

And another: "I invoke Mawu, great black mother of all."

"I call forth the spirit of the Great Faggot and the Great Dyke."

And another: "I call forth the spirit of Sappho."

And then they began to come thick and fast, in voices of breathless excitement:

"I invoke the spirit of Gertrude Stein."

"And the spirit of Emma Goldman."

"And the spirit of Susan B. Anthony."

"I invoke the Great Sissy," came a giggling voice which sounded like Petey's again, and several others laughed and exclaimed, "Yes! Yes!"

It was pleasant being silent, meditating on the gods and goddesses, the fairy sprites, the room, with all the invocations, getting a bit overcrowded with them all, I grinned to myself as I got, however much I tried to resist it, even more of a bit of a buzz just breathing in the hash smoke which was also crowding the room in a heavier cloud. Enjoying the hand-held silence of the other men, their strength and affection; breathing, in my deep breathing along with theirs, that peculiar male odor of ourselves, the lure that signals us, that calls us one to another from some inarticulate threshhold deep within, a salty odor of glandular sweat exciting the nostrils, red membrane swelling to that funkily musky scent, of ferns, of woods ripe in autumn. Even a misty trace of it out on the air of this dark, frozen night, a scent of spores acute enough to indirectly bring us together in a circle in these longest dark hours of the year. Enjoying the buzz of their blood-strength pulsing in my veins with the strength of my own blood, its bubbles fizzing in my ears like the gladdest champagne.

I heard someone saying, his voice cannabis-high, so that he was almost singing, "I invoke the power of the fairies," and there was a pleased ripple of affirmation around the circle.

It may have been just my highly attuned aural imagination, made even more sensitized by the haze of blue smoke in the air, but, after several moments of intense silence following this particular invocation, I swear I heard a sudden and distinct scurrying noise up near the ceiling, like the quick, insistent scratchings of mice, followed by low and mischievous gigglings.

Startled, I looked up but saw nothing, saw only the curlicued design in the embossed tin ceiling high above my head. Yet, as I glanced about me, I sensed a strong, gleeful aura awash in the room—it had the feel of the color of ripe nectarines—and was sure I heard, like tiny splashes of sound, the faint tinkle of wind chimes in a playful breeze, even though the room was perfectly still, the plastic over the windows sagging without movement, no wind for the moment stealing in through the crevices.

Perhaps it really was mice, I thought, or tricks being played on my ears by all the pot wafting through the loft.

I peered around the circle to see if the others were aware of it, but if they were, they made no sign: each sat, lids shut fast, left thumbs still hooked to right hands, breathing easily and deeply, entranced, as if everyone was contemplating the host of visitations we'd invoked. I shut my eyes again, too, and let the energy of the other men and the energies of the spirit presences course through my body once more. To my right, Ken gave my hand a sudden squeeze as if he had sensed my moment of surprise with its brief interruption of the flow of circular power passing between us, his quick, small gesture like a reassuring signal, pulling me back.

Or perhaps that slight pressure on my hand meant he had heard the fairies, too, perhaps it hadn't been mice or my imagination after all; or maybe it *was* mice, or even cockroaches, what was the difference? the fairies and fairy spirit being extant and ecstatic in all living things.

Spooked by these uncanny manifestations, a change, a sudden shift in mood came over me, so that I shifted in my place, felt an urgency to speak. "I invoke Diana of the moon," came a voice from within me, cracking a bit in the hot, dry air, so that I hardly recognized it as my own, it sounded, in a swirl of increasing excitement, so strangely different in my ears from my customary voice.

An icy brilliance brushed my shoulders, as if the moon itself was bending in at the windows, sending in upon us its frozen beams through the glass, through the plastic sheeting, and for all I knew it may very well have been doing just that. But this time I didn't look, trusting to its presence in the darkness of my skull, splashing the deepest shadowy coilings of my brain with silvery light, feeling the delicious shivers of the moon's rays ripple over my scalp and down my spine, the light of it blue and electric in my hair, its shimmer between my bare shoulder blades like a thin mountain stream, sparkling and icily clear, realizing the moon, like the sun now in its netherness below the rim of the earth, didn't have to be over Manhattan to touch us in invocation, for us to feel, to bask in, to be filled by, its generous and powerful attendance.

"The scientists are going to dye the moon green," someone said.

And somebody else said, with a tinge of anger, "Leave the moon alone."

" 'Raw is the moon that sings in me,' in the three-quarter moon of my life," I sang, quoting Arthur Wilson's poem, and thought of the drunken woman who had staggered up among the garbage cans outside the backroom, and prayed that Diana's protective rays still washed over her, wherever she was now, and clapped my hands, applauding the invisible moon, like a genuine lunatic, loony in lunar ecstasy, a sudden report so startling in the silence, the others snapped open their eyes to look briefly, questioningly, in my direction, a few smiling, all seeming to understand my spontaneous outburst—anything seemed to go, as long as it harmed no one.

We closed our eyes again and resumed our steady meditative breathing, focusing on the circle, on the palpable presence of the unseen powers, essences, visible and invisible, forces from the cosmos in ourselves, held in dynamic tensions of balance.

A long silence in which no other spirits were invoked, and during it I sensed again a golden glow in the air, its light current tripping from hand to hand, the gleam of it powdering my closed eyelids like yellow motes of pollen sweeping lightly through the loft in wave after wave; and then after several more long moments Ed's cracked, husky voice saying simply, "We're all avatars," and then another moment's pause followed by a whispery sound, and when I looked, saw Ed getting to his feet where he lifted his eyes to

152

the ceiling as if it were the sky and announced, " 'I consecrate this circle to the powers of the sun and moon.' So mote it be!"

"So mote it be!" all answered.

There was an even more extended quietness this time, only the deeply rising, deeply falling breathing again, which Ed, after some moments, seemed reluctant to break by the hint of regret in his voice as he told us to stand with him and gather in a closer circle, saying, "Let's begin the touching now, let's begin by touching each other's hair," himself the perfect hirsute guide, his skin a fur of dark hair, his elf-black eyes the eyes of a small, sharply alert animal.

"Shut your eyes," he told us, as the stragglers among us, blinking awake with self-conscious smiles, pulled themselves slowly to their feet and joined the rest of us gathering around Ed in a tight-knit cluster. "Feel the difference in texture and shape and length of hair. Move around. Touch the hair of as many as you can."

Eyes shut, I reach out in the close press of shoulders, hands lifted, groping, placing my fingers on the first head of hair they touch, my fingers sliding down strands of it, crisp as corn silk, smoothing it, my fingers now stiff brushes, now raking combs, clean hair squeaky as I pinch it between my fingers, the protective and decorative hair.

Still learning the sight of touch in blindness, as in the booths in the backroom, my hands nightflying wings, like bats, reach out again and graze and catch the hair of another, this time a coarse and curly bush—I wonder if it's Nick's, but don't cheat, instead lean to smell strands of it coiled about my fingers, and am pretty certain it's Nick's. Whoever it is, I let my fingers stalk through his hair like stealthy explorers in an unknown jungle, my palms, surprised, absorb the tropical heat of his scalp. Smiling to myself, growing even more fanciful, I imagine the pads of my fingertips the paws of small beasts, lightly, curiously, padding through the dense hairy brush. Hands, like other nosing, rooting animals, sometimes two pairs of hands at once, explore my own hair, tufts of it rubbed between unseen fingers, the roots of it probed and pried into as strenuously as the nattily dressed redbeard with the briefcase had done back in the booth that afternoon, so many strange fingers like tiny feet tracking over my scalp in my second massage of the day, slicing myriad parts like trails through my hair, while my own hands continue to reach out in darkness, moving around in the compact milling of bodies, sometimes at the peripheries, sometimes pushing myself into the center, not lingering, as Ed instructed, other hands reaching out ceaselessly for my head, caressing it, my own hands touching as many heads of hair as I could, some silky, some coarse, some bushy, like Nick's; others thinning, like my own; a few balding; wondering what the other balding ones felt like—especially those quite young—in the clone-locked world of Christopher Street, where a full head of hair, like cocksize, youth and looks, however narrowly and wrongly defined, is imperative.

My swiftly flying hands alighted next on a nest of curly, unkempt hair that had the curious texture of moss matted with thistles, when suddenly the head spoke, my fingers again surprised, picking up instantly, like seismographs, the sensations of sound resonating up through the top of the skull, the vibrancy of vocal cords like wire brushes whisked lightly over the skin of a drum as the scalp speaks through my hands. Hearing, feeling, his voice, without opening my eyes, I knew it was Ed, the image of him like a dark-haired goat leaping so powerfully into my mind, I could actually feel the pointy nubs of horns sprouting up through his thick, shaggy curls.

"Move, move around," he was urging, in a voice that had a soft, sandpapery feel to it as my fingers played over his scalp in gentle massage, "reading," rather than hearing, his voice through their sound-sensitive tips. "Touch as many as you can, don't linger. Now move down to the face. Lose your ego. Don't linger with anyone, move on to the next. Touch everyone with your eyes shut. Don't judge. Don't compare."

My fingers disentangled themselves from his thick and snarly locks and now searched out the faces of those around me, spanned high and low foreheads, some dry as bone, some slick with oil and sweat so that my fingers slid easily down the brow; touched the sharpness and bluntness of noses, one so puggish I wondered if it had been broken, perhaps late at night in some deserted cruising park or alley; the surprise of hairy faces, again noting the differences in coarse and fine hair, its flatness or curl, as I stroked beards between my caressing fingers, thinking of Bob's, its coppery tint, loving the feel, the differing shag and nap of each; touched cheekbones prominent in faces arrowsharp as well as those blunted in broader faces padded with jowls; brushed with my hands the incredible tenderness of lips, skin on mouths as tender as the lips of the anus; touched occasional eyeglasses (Ian's? I wondered, Bert's?), their metal frames like tiny amazing windows on the face; discovering, too, in the closed eyes of

154

others, the delicate skin of the eyelid as satiny soft and finely sensitive as the skin at the eye of the penis, as whispery smooth as the under integument of the foreskin.

Hands on my own face like the caressing hands of grandmothers, fingers like feelers brushing my cheeks, antennae searching, mirroring their own features in the sweep of hands.

The hone of our faces like prows shaped against wind, against weather, against imperative usage, bare, sheerskinned, sensuous faces fronting, in their defenseless nakedness, in all seasons, in numberless bitter nights like this, in simply looking up at the sky, the vastness of millions of miles of space with all the insupportable weight of its atmosphere bearing down on that trusting oval of an upturned blossom of flesh. The wonder is that this shy, gelatinous speck of an eye peeping out in all its vulnerability on the endless spatial outer reaches of the universe isn't squashed flat by such enormous cosmic pressure, or shriveled instantly to a cinder by the staggeringly hot volcanic eye of the sun; or, at the very least, in total despair, have its vision clouded by the immense and immeasurable loneliness of the heavens—toughly tender faces shaped, once crawled out of the salt-electric currents of the sea, in the fierce and loving ionic winds of the cosmos.

Finding all of it open and susceptible human flesh as we moved close among ourselves, shy and courteous and careful with each other, totally exposed and trusting, I discover all of it new again, the feel of it unbearably lovely beneath my newly sighted fingers.

And always beneath my fingers the realization of the incredible delicacy of flesh, the smoothness of it defenseless in response to touch, strains out for it, eager to have it, so that the unseeing hands on me, my own blind hands on others, could just as well have been the hands of women as of men, the smaller ones the hands of children; and, in imaginative extension, the hands of some becoming the roughly caressing paws of animals.

Ed had us move down to the touching of the neck, my fingers slinking down, garter snakes with a volition and life of their own, curving and coiling easily around equally serpentine throats, slender and thick; press bony discs of buttons at the top of spines, moving from throat to throat, thumb on one side, fingers on the other, feel the varying heartbeat pulsing in each, each stretching gullet beating in a quickened tempo, mutely eloquent of an excitation no words were needed to express from those same taut and silenced vocal cords; the flesh at the base of the neck so pulpy and exposed; feeling all around the sinuous stand of gristle and muscle; aware that these same fingers which stroked the throat in exploratory delight could also slowly choke off the breath feeding through this narrow passage, this miraculous swivel of tendon and bone.

And then, again, Ed suggesting we next move on to the arms, and I worked my hands around, touching flabby and muscular ones in turn, some bonesharp thin, others heavily fleshed, fingers slipping into mine, boned rings curling blindly, the unbelievable hook and bend in them, tugging, as if they were udders, down the length of each of my fingers in a milking motion, my own doing the same to theirs, their incredible grasp and small-boned flexibility, filed, clipped nails blunted claws in atrophy; round flat elbows like heels grinding at me, while others jabbed my ribs, my chest, with the sharpness of knives, elbows flapping like wings as arms crooked and uncrooked in the slow circular thrashing and rubbing of elbows in intimate and anonymous hobnobbing around the tightening hub of our circle.

And out of the sepal of our turning calyx of flesh, turning with the winter solstice night, each body curling out of its whorl a petal pink with excitement in the heat of our closepacked bodies, the rippling core of stamens we formed emitting an unfolding scent of perspiration and the dry fragrance of ourselves, startling and keen and alluring in my nose, like the salt bouquet of the sea off there in the blackness of night framed even blacker in the dirty windows, night-sea roiling beyond the sawtoothed skyscrapers, beyond the bristling shores of Manhattan island, dark, frozen-foamed waters rolling in stiffly under the stiffening air.

Smoothing my hands over breastbones now, guessing I'd touched the chest of a very light blond, like Ken, if the hair was sparse; surmising, perhaps falsely, the thicker the hair the darker; peeking once, curious, because of its density, to find my fingers buried deep in a mat of chest hair the shade and richness of buckwheat honey, and peeping, spied the face of Hal from San Francisco sneaking a look back at me, both of us busting out in grins as we caught each other at it, myself more pleased then anything to know my fingers were growing sensitive to light and dark; each of us growing aware, through all we touch this night, in steady accretions of loveliness, like seashells rainbow-sprayed in the long curl of waves in that phosphorescent sea beyond the windows.

Placing my hands against sides to feel the breathing, breaths now increasing in hurrying tempo, I tripped my fingers lightly down ribs of scrawny physiques—Keith? Petey?—poking in more strenuously on fleshier chests—Bert perhaps? Or Bob?—my clasping hands now still, cupping each ribcage like a tabernacle of bone, protector and container of the truly sacred heart, each one of which I could feel leaping within as I moved around the circle, each breast pounding like a sacramental drum between the listening palms of my hands, my eardrums reverberating with the thump of my own heart in strong and steady beating with their own.

And exploring next the tits of all, vestigial nubs from when we first were female in the womb, as we were, earlier, in the lost pink mists of amniotic paradise, when the world was a woman; shrunk dugs only useful for kisses now, and I made good use of them, of each chest in turn, brushing the nipples of each with my lips, delighted to feel the tips of them hardening under my tongue in arousal; nipples responding in blind response, like a woman's breasts to a baby's mouth, or the mouth of a hungry lover, udders equally generous, generous to all.

My index finger burrowing next into belly buttons, silently merry to probe fuzzy lint cupped in a few like tiny nests for microscopic birds; sticking my finger in deeper ones, a couple large enough to comfortably fit a walnut or an egg-sized ruby; some tiny enough to hold no more than a grain of rice or the chip of a diamond; and one or two "outies" the size of plover's eggs; the innermost surface of each having the same nubby feel of a hard, impacted bud about to spring into blossom, a tightly curled hood of an eye in the belly of self, umbilical eye of the mother seeing inward and outward in the center of flesh in blind and radiant sensual wisdom at the jointure of wholeness.

And we, that night, in a circle, baring the button of our bellyeye to breathe and see in the suneye of the mother, melting snowblind visions of the fathers from the top of the earth in restoring the sight of the nethereye in the sun of the solar plexus; my fingers hot in each knot of motherblood burning there, lighting my fingers like brands with sight as I move around the circle balanced on the nub of her lifeline, her center in me keeping me centered, intact and lively to all around me, brighteyed to these creased eyes winking at me in midriffs twisting and bending everywhere I turn.

In our bunched flesh we are a ring of sensuous mountains.

The shudder of a rill of a spine as I traced it delicately with the tip of my forefinger, the tremulous flesh parting under it like splashes of shivery water, the buttonbones of the spine like stones my fingers skipped down in the sinuous bedrock of bloodstreams, each of us standing cataracts of blood.

My fingers gliding now down humped and angular muscles of shoulders, down slopes of backs, shoulder blades jutting, triangular boulders perilous to fingers which, fanciful again, transforming backs into Tetons of flesh, were skiers racing down snowy whitenesses of skins icily smooth in the lift and fall of curvaceous lines, to the base of the small of the back where, always, in small surprise, no matter how sparse, a tiny cluster of hairs sprouted, greeting my fingers like welcoming nosegays glistening with tiny beads of sweat like dew.

Surprised to touch rough denim and ribs of corduroy in levi and trouser tops, to encounter the leather of close-fitting belts, the cold metal of buckles, barriers to the body below, to the further push of my forefinger as it pinched itself frustratingly between coccyx and heavy cloth just at the start of the enticing declivity of rounded buttocks, unable to explore further, held back by the tightness of belted trousers and snug elastic bands of briefs.

My hand brushed a series of buttons on smooth wool fabric and, without opening my eyes, I realized my fingers had grazed Daryl's old sailor bell-bottoms, their flap jutting out in a 13-button salute my own hand caressingly saluted before moving on. And it was the same each place my hand alighted, tight, resistant threads stretching over imprisoning flies, taut across butts swaying and grinding everywhere my hands flew, disappointing, after so much fingering of naked torso flesh, the rub of clothing like an alien thing, my own levis suddenly burdensome, constricting, their washworn, pliable fabric suddenly too tight everywhere.

At this point I longed to take off the rest of my clothes and gazed again with a pang of jealousy at Ed in his comfortable nakedness. He, too, was aware, as he cocked an eyebrow and grinned teasingly around the circle, that we'd arrived at an impasse in continuing our ritual of physical exploration, since most of us still had our trousers on, and Daryl, his gray sweatshirt as well. Ed's puckish eyes continued to twinkle under his thick brows as he said in an offhand manner, "You'll all feel a hell of a lot better if you take off as much of the rest of your clothes as you want to. And remember, nobody has to do anything they don't want to do."

That was all I needed to hear. I grabbed my shirt and T-shirt off the floor where I'd dropped them earlier during the massage, and along with a couple of others, stepped out of the circle and went along the narrow hallway to the desk where our coats were heaped, found my jacket and vest and placed the clothes I was carrying on top of them, keeping them all together so I'd be able to find them again later. Then I unbuckled my belt and quickly shucked off my levis, adding them also to the pile, straightened them out and plumped them up a little, making them comfortable, like they were old friends, which they really were, I'd worn them so long that even without me in them they retained the shape of my body like a rumpled, abandoned second skin, and in their deflated folds and creases looked so much like they were sulking at being left out of the rest of the party that, when no one around me was looking, I gave all my secondhand rags a couple of affection-ate pats to let them know I'd soon be returning to claim them.

Taking off my watch I stuck it in a side pocket of my levis and, standing in nothing but my frayed briefs, wondered if it was too early to take them off as well, too soon to be completely naked, even though Ed had been so right from the start, no doubt as an example to embolden the rest of us. But I didn't feel all that bold about it, not wanting to be the only other one in the buff, and stole glances at those undressing around me in the narrow hall to see how much they were taking off, and, for additional clues, checked back over my shoulder where I could see, through the smokily dim air of the candlelit loft, that a very few of the men were still turning from one to the other, still exploring each other's backs in a slow lift and fall of hands, the circle, or what was left of it, turning in a slow and smaller everchanging configuration of bodies, but each of these men was still wearing his trousers.

Others, however, also heeding Ed's words, were lying on their backs as they kicked off their pants; while Petey, his fair hair flying up and down in the candle-sheen, and Tim, who had his baseball cap now clapped on backwards, were each hopping about on one leg and laughing uproariously at one another as they struggled to kick out of their straightleg denims—all of them as frustrated no doubt as I had been wearing the last of our clothes, all moving again to the center of the floor to regroup in the circle, stripped now to the shorts, scratching at their thighs and chests in the first few moments of unaccustomed nudity with each other, since we'd never stripped quite so completely before in any of the other gath-erings of the Circle.

The only two remaining holdouts were Danny, barechested, but his plumpish legs still encased in his tight, satiny dance pants, those soft gray eyes, the color of fog on the sea, still following Keith everywhere, when he wasn't glued next to him in the circle, his dreamily stoned face like a dimmed spotlight following every move he made; and slim, delicate-wristed Daryl, who, for reasons of his own, kept on his sweatshirt and bell-bottoms; each perhaps still too modest, unsure, not yet fully trusting themselves naked among us, or trusting the nakedness of the others, perhaps knowing from past experience that among most males, there's nothing more defenseless than a naked body, not ready yet to see, as I was learning here tonight that, paradoxically, and depending on the company, there's nothing more protected.

Then, just as I was about to go out and rejoin the circle, I saw Hal, at the outermost rim of the group, pointed beard sticking straight up, giving him the air of a haughty satyr as, eyes closed under lifted brows, like an exacting connoisseur of flesh, he continued to fan his hands out over the backs of those nearest him; saw that he, too, along with Ed, was now totally bareass, glimpsed the curve of a beginning erection swaying between his downy thighs like a pink and ripening banana, before he vanished into the innermost hub of the growing cluster of men.

That moment's glimpse of him gave me the nerve, and I wasted no time sliding down my shorts, in my eagerness forgetting about the exposed rubber in the legs and snagging a few hairs on the way, which stung only for a moment or so. The second time today, I laughed to myself, remembering again the rough, impatient hands of the longshoreman in the booth, as I stepped out of my shorts and tucked them in a pocket of the levis so they wouldn't get lost, giving them, too, a little friendly pat, touching them more for luck I think than anything else.

I walked back slowly into the main part of the loft, stepping carefully on the balls of my feet, standing at first near the fringes of the circle, where I was relieved to see no one appeared to pay any attention to my nakedness, as if it was the most natural thing, which of course it is. But even so, I stole a wary glance out the uncurtained windows to see if any of the tenants across the air shaft were looking in at us and wondering what we were up to. But most of the windows now were bathed in the cathode-blue sheen of television sets, all the neighbors evidently staying at home on a night like this, their attentions absorbed in video screens and not at our goings-on in the windows of Keith's loft.

Unencumbered now, totally free to move, nudity naturally superior to any garments, however sheer and loosefitting; encouraged at having gotten over my trepidation of baring myself to the others, I stepped into my old place in the circle between Nick and Ken, both also stripped down now to their shorts, having discovered again, a traitor to my old and faithful clothes, what every child knows: What better skin to move in than one's own?

Now that three of us were totally nude, most of the others also became braver and, before the last of the touching ritual resumed, shorts and briefs of every imaginable color and shape were being peeled off hurriedly, like so many snakes shedding the last remnants of old, restraining skins, underwear flying through the air, kicked back or tossed over shoulders amidst a flurry of unrestrained laughter, to join the clothes already taken off and dropped back out of the way against the wall like so many castoff nuisances, no penis envy here, as in the backroom, no one sizing another up with anxious, jealous eyes.

To my surprise, the sharp elbows of his crossed arms stabbing the air as he lifted his sweatshirt over his head, Daryl, too, at last stood barechested among us, lowering his nicely shaped eyelids with a slightly embarrassed expression as he let the shirt fall on the floor behind him, his sparsely haired, lean triangular chest, with clavicles as bonily prominent as my own, looking so vulnerably exposed, an exposure enhanced by his genuine shyness as he hunched his thin shoulders and folded his long, slender arms across his chest and slipped back into the circle, still keeping his sailor's pants on, however.

Ed has us all join hands as before, telling us to remain standing and, with a satisfied smile as he glanced around the almost totally nude group, said to close our eyes as he started us off breathing deeply in unison again for a few minutes, to reconnect ourselves to each other and to reform the circle.

When we were only a few moments into it, abruptly, without warning, Jonathan shoved his way boisterously into the midst of the group, grasping us firmly by the shoulders, smacking hands apart, jabbing at us with his elbows, the fine, delicate skin of his brow wrinkled in consternation, his eyes large with anger.

I stared at him in bewilderment as he roughly shouldered me out of his way, at first thinking he was kidding, but seeing that he wasn't, my own eyes grew large in amazement, as did the eyes of the others, shocked at the abrupt change in him, from his gentle and playful impish nature, a spasm of fear coiling in my gut that maybe he had suddenly taken leave of his senses, had become psychotic, perhaps, from too much pot or wine, or, judging by the vehemence of his actions, both. I looked at Nick and Ken beside me and they shot puzzled glances back at me, just as baffled and at a loss to understand this inexplicable change in behavior as I was. We all looked to Ed for an explanation, but he stood quietly, with a set, unsmiling face, watching, and then ducking out of the way as Jonathan stormed by.

Turning sharply on his heel and marching back again among us, his skinny arms still flailing out at us on either side, scattering us against the walls, he opened his mouth in a contorted twist up one side of his face and began to sing in a loud, unmusical voice, raucous with ugliness, a voice which surprised me, coming from one who was so soft-spoken:

"Get out of here!
You're not allowed!
Get out of here!
You're too much of a crowd!
Faggot freaks!
Faggot geeks!"

Watching him retrace his steps, slamming his arms through the empty space he had cleared in the middle of the room, listening to him repeat the lyrics of his song in the strident, mimicking tones of someone he thoroughly despised, communicating his intent by now to the rest of us as we stood hanging back against the walls, separate from each other where only a few moments before we had been so close, our circle broken up by Jonathan's sudden crazy departure in mood, it slowly began to dawn on each of us, as we glanced apprehensively at each other, then back at Jonathan, that his outburst and accompanying song of rage had been planned ahead of time, and was sprung on us unannounced, for maximum dramatic effect.

He stalked next to the windows and stood stiffly at attention between them, in front of the low table where the candles and joss sticks burned amid the icons of Kali and Cernunnos and the earth mother, the red globules bubbling up in the lighted lamp behind, their rippling reflection suffusing his sharp face and bare chest in a brickred flush, reddening more brightly the crisp waves of his chestnut hair, as he stood silent awhile, as if meditating, his thin

162

naked back defenseless in the candleshine, pimples sparse over his shoulders, his arms dropped at his sides, all eyes watching him, uneasy, not knowing what to expect.

After several long moments, he turned slowly to face us and began to sing again, his voice quieter this time, a pleasant tenor, and I felt a sense of relief, could feel it in the others too, since the tone of his voice, the expression on his face, was once again the Jonathan we had come to know, not the stranger's face twisted with the anger and raucous shouts of only minutes before.

His clear, pure voice, in a chant half talked, half sung, rose in the hushed room as he sang a song of his own, one we learned later he'd written especially for the evening, singing homage "to loiterers and dancers / to cruisers and lovers / forced into darkness on old, unremembered grounds / in amnesia America," singing homage to all those who had striven, and were striving, "as we were this winter solstice night / to uncover and remember / re-membering ourselves into / whole creatures again"; sang of " 'Adam and atom' / split and fragmented / the first and last / of death-centered life," of the one long death of lives "split from the sustaining and nourishing / roots of wholeness;" split from animals "slaughtered without reverence / killing their spirit in us," their meat turning "vengefully rancid / and cancerous / in our guts;" split from women "murdered in mind and body"; split from the earth itself "and the man-made death of the earth / in a loss of the sacred / in a mindless and murderous / sleep of ignorance"; sang of "being alive to all / learning again treetalk / and beasttalk / and the speech of birds and stones / the singing of the grasses / of earth itself / in mothertongues everywhere," lost voices our forebears "heard and knew / and conversed and were fluent in," especially ever more keenly on this "long night of the ingathering close / of blood-wakefulness / the season of the sleep of seeds," the night of the winter solstice "lively with their spirits / which are also ours"; singing, finally, for us to "take life back into our own hands / from those whose hands are dead."

When his arhythmic, unrhymed plainsong ended, everyone stood still, visibly touched, as I was, touched deeply somewhere in some old and forgotten place of feeling, of knowing; his song like the fragment of a teasing tune, half remembered, obsessing and tantalizing memory, and which I struggled to recall, to make a total melody, but couldn't, hard as I tried. Perhaps in the days to come it would return, I told myself, and deeply hoped it would. In the meantime, there was the rest of the evening still; maybe I would learn something more of it, of its words and music, in the hours ahead.

Jonathan, his face faun-sharpened, letting his hands drop again at his sides, stepped away from the windows, joining us once more, hands reaching out to caress his neck, his shoulders, clasping his fingers, more in relief, it seemed, than in praise, though there was that, too; that shy, sly grin of his creasing his features once more, the old gently mocking, pixieish grin of the familiar Jonathan intimating, Fooled you, didn't I? as Ed—in on it from the start—came forward and hugged him, congratulating him on his acting, which others also chorused, laughing now at the joke he'd successfully pulled off on us.

After several minutes, when everyone had simmered down at last, we found ourselves drawn again into a circle, as if by instinct now, without Ed having to speak to us, and stood quietly waiting until Ed finally announced we would continue where we left off in the ritual of touching.

Now, for most of us, without constraining or identifying garments of any kind, not even socks to tag us, the circle pulled into a tighter conflux as we began the last part of the ceremony of exploration and awareness of each other's bodies, from the toes up this time, Ed saying, "Now let's pick up where we left off and move down to the feet and lower legs and work our way up."

Feet encased in boots or sneakers or running shoes, uncalloused soles and insteps protected, imprisoned, in leathery darkness, flesh kept pale and delicate there—now free at last and breathing, bare soles splayed flat on the slick floorboards, the scuzzy, sweaty odor, like mushrooms in dank shady woods, as toes wriggle free, toes like little bulbs, like small tuberous roots, some misshapen and turned under from pinched footwear since babyhood, cramped toes spreading and sprouting now in this barefoot winter ritual.

As I stooped and ran my fingers over toes, I envisioned, out in the darkness, deep-frozen in northern earth, roots, buds, bulbs, seeds, encased in hard pods, in winter slippers, all benignly numbed in narcotized needles of frost, deep sleeping in a dream of spring.

Toes spread and splayed in exquisite tension as I pry among them, the torsion of tendons spread wings of the feet I expect to fly out of my cupping hands, feet readying themselves for barefoot dancing. I saw swift-footed Hermes in each pair, knew he flitted cheerfully and mercurially about our ankles and thighs in silvery streaks reflected from the moon down under. In most of the feet I touched, the surprising length of toes, the curl of the small toe under, like a shy leaf; most feet smooth-skinned, but on a very few pairs, tiny tufts of hair over the instep, hairs like threads of roots; the hard crust of heels against my palm.

I embrace shins and calves, thighs, a million years of forebears standing in our legs, some hairily rough as oak, some smooth as birch bark, a stand of legs like saplings. I move, hunkering along with the others from one leg to the next, imagining myself creeping in a close-packed grove, brush my cheek down the downy bark of flesh that tenses and hardens under the caress of my face, smelling goat musk in the shaggier hair, bark musk-rubbed by hides, by lifted legs, muscles that become bark in sturdy and flexible legs that are tree-limbs whose sap is the blood I feel racing hot against my cheeks, my head, crown of the tree I also feel myself to be, rising and standing now among them as I hear, in the shuteyed dark forest of my head, Ed say in his quiet rasp, "Move up now, move up to the ass, and then to the crotch. Do whatever you feel like doing, if the other is willing—anything goes, so long as nobody gets hurt."

I stand and stretch my legs to get the kinks and cramps out from so much crouching through the thicket of limbs, leaning a moment against crotches that are forked inverted branches; and others who had also crept as I had, doing the same. Parting my legs as wide as I can and stretching my arms above my head, I fling them about slowly, feel my arms, my spread legs, like branches waving, my snapping fingers and flexing toes like twinkling leaves, my torso a sinuous trunk bending in a breeze my thrashing body creates among other thrashing bodies. Green buds pop in my blood. I expect my smooth and barklike skin to explode in a riotous profusion of flowering branches. Evershifting smokelike textures curl beneath my lids. I am a green bush burning with green fire in this deadest night. My fingers emerald flames, I dare touch no one now for fear of singeing them. I turn and turn at the outskirts of the circle, laughing silently to myself, primed by green sap skipping in me inwardly from limb to limb; all around feel a gleam of green luminescence. The compass in my center swings true north. I am northern needles of pine. I burn, I burn green fire in the white freezing night. The faces, the bodies, of the others in the circle, light up in my turning as I turn among them, lighting the loft, outshining all the candles in my burning.

Beneath the roots of my feet I feel the wheel of the year turning, the earth groaning on its frozen axis, revolving the vast trunk of its planetary tree, sacred oak festooned with mistletoe, raised once more in ceremonies of winter, turning again; I, too, am turning, a dancing tree, raised in our tiny ritual of the winter solstice, my branches holly, fir and pine; as I spin, the candles scattered about the loft, now flickering in among my limbs, are microscopic tongues of sun.

In the branching arms and legs of the others, I no longer fall separate from the tree of the earth, am one of its leaves, am one of its branches, an unfolding twig on its global trunk, the bones of my feet, my toes, like roots, reconnected in this bare-limbed ritual in deepest winter. The planet in its farther tilt now—shadows of its dying grasses lengthening as the days shorten—the globe a yule, a hoary, ancient wheel, far, far beyond memory, spinning its eighth turn into glacial winter, darting beneath its crust, like spokes, needles of black frost in the kindest sting of somnolence in this brief whirl of a day.

I totter now, my drowsy tree-arms, tree-legs, heavy with cold, tip from side to side as the earth tips now in winter-weight farther and farther away from the sun; ourselves below in this box of a loft with its whitewashed walls, in tiny radiance forming an infinitesimal circle of the sun. I stood still, drooping, yet felt the trunk of my body rotating, tilting as the planet tilts, tilting all of its trees, the ball of the earth pushed farthest out in black galactic space on this longest night, yet tipped at an angle closer to the daystar source, the mothersun.

I am my mother's son, I see, which is the best in me, the woman in me.

My fingers glide from one ass to another, cup sleek roundnesses, some too large to fit into my hands, hardy flesh spilling in a more than ample generosity through the stretched net of my fingers; while others are just right, firm, spherical fruits, silkily fuzzed, that fit snugly into my palms, like those of the wheat-haired youth in the backroom booth hours earlier. Hairless and hairy posteriors, no two alike, the flesh-pink heat of them radiating, as before a fire, through my outstretched palms and up my arms and throughout my body, unsagging me, making me snap to spry and erect attention; snap open my eyes as well, where I see all around me huge dimples catching pools of bruised light in the slanting flames of the candles, as buttock muscles squeeze in perturbation at a particularly sensitive caress or touch, dimpling indentations of flesh when the unseen hands of others glance like breezes over trembling behinds, like the withers of a racehorse shivering with excitement and anticipation as the wind she'll run in slips delicately along her sleek and glossy haunches. My own hands sweep the cushiony softness of hair carpeted lightly there, the thicker, more wiry thatches in several crevices more resistant to my inquiring touch; while on the cheeks of some my hands slide away on buttock-flesh as smooth and hairless as glass.

I shut my eyes, pick up, like Braille, amidst the down, the tiniest buds of gooseflesh, and on what feels like tougher, older hides, small leathery patches of skin the size of half dollars, callouses worn on points of buttocks from years of sitting. The responsive tips of my hands fly over melon-shaped mounds of flesh which now read back to my rapidly translating fingers nothing but intimations of snug and succulent pleasure ahead, my nostrils suddenly aware of an aroma like overripened peaches in the room, heady and dizzying. An invisible fingertip circling into me from behind — I hear myself murmur dreamily, cant my hips against it, the magical wand opening me.

The curl and crinkle of pubic hair crisp with shine in candlelight. We offer our mouths, our hands, our bodies, to any and all who want them. The light rush of hands on me the way a rose must feel when the leaves around it brush against it in the wind. I am blown open, the bursting pod of my cock sprouting rosily pink among the other swelling roses. I feel a slight stinging sensation and opening my eyes, see, with surprise and puzzlement, sudden rakes of red lines down my chest, my arms, bewildered, not knowing how they got there, not remembering the thorny dig of any overzealous nails—does the rose feel its thorns? Perhaps a few of us had already sprouted invisible beast claws; perhaps the mysterious marks were the playful and painless furrows of the fairies I'd heard earlier, descended from the embossed ceiling unbeknownst to me as I played among the buttocks of the others, flying down and around to leave their tiny clawlike rakings as souvenirs of their astral visit on my earthly body, leaving me tickled pink, so to speak, and I laughed outloud just thinking of it.

Our contorting, intertwining bodies, one body; our varied and supple strengths, one strength; our differing degrees of bodily warmth one heat radiating male odor and arousal, by this time the sweat of our hairy skin smelling like beast-hide, whiffs of crotch-odor like fontina cheese, excited male musk of sex released in the air in an agitated spray of sudden sexual perfume. We are on the scent, the scent of self, of each other. Mouths on mouths, kissing, tongues down throats, erections naturally, shamelessly, rising, red as the oily bubbles rising in the lamp between the windows, balls of lava red as verbena squeezed up from the bowels of the earth, our nuts swinging pinker in its heat and light, quivering, wrinkled sacks like wattled throats of turkeys—a rounding tree of flesh wild cocks and turkeys roost in, and that I'm now a branch of, turning in the middle of the candlelit loft, turning with the night in the concentric rings of winter, in the three concentric rings of golden Saturn, turning even in the rings of winter-stiffened trees slumbering behind rough bark in Marble Cemetery across 2nd Street, in all the ginkgo trees throughout the city, and in the trees uptown all over Central Park.

Turning in the current of our searching fingers, we search for each other, blindly, imperatively, on the loft's hot-pink floor; my needle, now an ingot, points due north still, a fiery arrow intense enough to melt icebergs, glaciers—I am all fire now, the floor under my feet burning, the heat coursing up from far below the cellar of the tenement, from far below the frozen rock of Lower Manhattan, from deep in the belly of the globe which bubbles pitchblack lava splashing in rings of unmeasurable heat up from the earth's core, the heart of the earth pulsing, shimmering up molten billows of heat, scorching the soles of my feet, a planetary hotfoot to shimmy my hips, making me dance.

The goddess is the pulse at the heart of the earth.

I dance with her, standing still, held in the cradling and over-arching arms of the circle of men, impelled by their heat which is fire lit from the same unseen forge of whitehot fires leaping far beneath the frozen crust of earth, burning up through the crusts of the soles of our dancing feet.

The lamp by the windows reddens the walls of the loft like the inside of a blast furnace. I leap in their flames and dance with them, my feet tapping over the bloodred floor, red as coals, red as the everchanging orbs in the lamp, making my legs drummers on the winter-taut skin of the earth; feel the bud of myself, long hidden, nipped in the perpetual winter of the fathers, emerging tonight along with the rosebud tips of other cocks, merrily bright, the nether-eye, the weather eye, alert to changes, shy eyes peeping out of turtlenecks, wrinkled hoods like crushed petals of roses, a stand of pricks in a lively stretch of greeting to the sun above the night and the nether sun boiling in the fiery womb of the middle of the earth, out of the suns our bodies are, alight with sweat and the flush of blood in the dim room made bright by our luminous skins, pink auras dulling the candleflames, our radiance in the room, radiating out in spiraling rings into the night, pulse north to shimmer with aurora borealis fanning up over the winter-desolate sky, and streaming back in return, through the plastic-sheeted windows, through the clouds of hash smoke, the sickening sweet smoke of joss sticks—the shine of Diana is suddenly all around us dancing on the white brick walls stained flickering red like hearth flames, sprays of her rainbow nimbus over each our heads in cold and crackling fire, as we sway, moved in her light, her darkness, our faces pink and black by turns in the fast-changing light, a garden of fleshy, bobbing roses suddenly sprung in a third floor loft in a decaying Lower East Side tenement in the midst of deadest winter.

We are our mother's sons, protecting night, protecting wildness.

The room grew dim again, the candles burning in straight, thin flames, the wind outside momentarily still so that even the loose windows were silent, the only movement in the room the lighted lamp on the low table, the tomato-shaped globules still slowly moving up and down in the sheen of its golden, oily light. There was a slowing down among us, a sense that the first part of the ceremonies in our Saturnalia had ended and another was about to begin, though what it would be we didn't know, at least those of us who hadn't been at the planning session, and we stood about exchanging shy half-smiles, suggestively graced with the intimacies we'd shared.

Almost imperceptibly, however, there was an air of feverish expectation in the loft. We grew quiet, yet were restive, moving a little apart from each other after so much closeness, waiting with flushed, anticipating faces, each of us glancing now and again at Ed, who stood silent with a crafty smile curving in his beard, waiting for him to speak, to learn where he, or the other guides, Keith or Jonathan or Bert, planned to lead us next, guides to awaken the guides in ourselves.

Then, at a glance from Ed, Keith leaned back on one elbow and began scrabbling among the clothes he'd taken off and thrown on the floor behind him. From a pocket somewhere within their folds he withdrew a thin sheaf of notes and, from his place in the circle, began to speak, glancing down now and again at the scribbled scraps of paper, which looked like blank restaurant checks (was he a part-time waiter, I wondered, to support himself as a dancer?), as the rest of us flopped back, relaxed but respectfully attentive, curious to hear what he had to say.

" . . . Saturn . . . the Roman god of agriculture . . . the god of all . . . Saturday named for him . . . " I heard him intone in his pleasant North Carolina drawl, and thought to myself, Saturn must be rising about now, since it had to be close to midnight, due to rise at 11:43 p.m., to be exact, according to this morning's paper, but my mind tuned out, drifted, being lately uncomfortable with all-male gods and male-identified heavenly bodies, trying, in my personal life, to get out from under what I thought of as their smothering sacrosanct privates ensacking the air of earth and heaven in a fetid cowl for far too many centuries. On this, my first Saturnalia, which I chose now, secretly, to call my first "satyrnalia" (and from the looks of it, in the rosily pink sensuality of our carryings-on so far, nakedly goat-hoofed and shaggythighed, it had become just that for all the others as well), I preferred the mischievous highjinks of us lesser imps with more of a sense of mortal humor and a bit of gay sparkle, to the heavy testicular solemnities of braying, thick-bodied Jehovahs and Joves, or even Saturns, with their stolen names of women; preferred the prancing goat-dancers of forest and field, long only capering in the wilderness of my head, but who were very much like the men gathered around me now as we sat like furry-legged satyrs, mussed hair whirled up into cones on the heads of a few like horns, our ears sharpened in careful listening, sharply attuned to each other, as Keith's voice continued, a pleasant sound in the room, my own ears lax, though listening, occasionally tuning in again, picking up on a phrase here and there: " . . . During the festival of the Saturnalia in Roman times, celebrated around this time, December 17, in the old calendar, all criminals were pardoned. . . ." and remembered it was Keith had spoken up earlier evoking Laverna and the pardoning of all prisoners on this night. " . . . At root . . ." his soft-toned voice murmured on, " . . . all such rituals, which are outgrowths of more ancient rites in the winter solstice, enact the rebirth of the sun, are prayers for its return. . . ."

My mind wandered again, agreeing in a pleasantly lazy way with his words, but not taking them very seriously, not taking in their substance, their import already seeming to be an inarticulate essence in blood-memory. I leaned back on my elbows, eyes half closed, feeling my blood push through my veins like sluggish sap, wondering if this was the drowsy sensation bears felt just before hibernation, when winter closed in. I began dreaming of caves, of their dark, furry warmth, feeling myself grow heavy and sleepy with ancient, unthinking knowledge bred into all our bones in these northern climates with the shrink of the day and the stretch of the night in deepest winter, beginning in this brief flicker of a day when women and children and men and animals huddled around long-ago fires in childlike uneasiness, sharing gathered roots and grains, telling stories and laughing and dancing, singing—just as we were doing, ourselves a small circle of fire, here, this evening—to ward off the vast and impenetrable cold night beyond their tiny circle of warmth, their instinctual rituals of solstice, of equinox, closer than ours to the rhythms of earth, ending in propitiating prayers for the return of the sun, as Keith had said, in brave and lively ceremonies of chanting and singing—as we, their sons, were doing tonight in lesser intensity and drama—making themselves light in the fearful and narrowing darkness of winter, with all seeds and many beasts, like bear, quiescent in the earth, worshipers of northern and midnight light, children afraid of the dark, needles of the heart fixed inexorably north, afraid of all that is dark, dark skies, dark skins, an inherited fear which is a needle in my own bleached heart, and perhaps in all the others in this circle as well, right up to this very night and hour, as we huddle in each other's warmth, feeling kinship, feeling millions of years of ancestors in my blood, in all our bloods, drawn together for heat and solace on such long, dark nights of the year, their spirits gathered in this room, in me, swarming multitudinous corpuscles warming and enlivening me in a dance-span of millennia.

My attention continued to waver in and out. Perhaps it was the smoky, incense-laden air, a pleasant tiredness stealing over me from the day, or my own expectations of what was to come, but I felt so physically contained and at rest as I reclined comfortably on the floor in a loose circle with the others, my mind resisted listening too attentively to Keith's succinct and evidently well-prepared notes, read in a clear but increasingly self-conscious, hurried voice as if he, too, realized this was not a time for the exercise of our intellects but a night, without reserve, for the full and uninhibited play of the senses.

" . . . Dionysus, the horned god . . . god of wine and frenzied revelry . . . " I heard him murmur in his quickening Southern drawl, and at the name my ears pricked up, my eyes darting to the picture of the god in one of his earliest manifestations, Cernunnos, propped among the candles on the low table by the windows, " . . . who drove women mad, made them tear their own infants apart and suckle wild beasts instead. . . ."

Not him! Not that part of him here with us tonight! I wanted to cry out. Not that toxic, intoxicated side of Dionysus, poisoning women's minds and the womanmind in men; poisoning me, rightly, in my ignorance, in my misuse of his gift for all those years when I was sitting, in my arrogance, on the throne of the universe while at the same time crawling blind in the gutter, without moderation, without respect for the spirit's spirit-enhancing sacred uses, such as here, tonight, these seasonal eye-openers increasing conscious awareness of the cosmos within us. Not Dionysus the trickster priest dressed in drag in the stolen skirts of the priestess, seducing, controlling, the cerebral maddener, the monstermaker of crazy ladies in the name of cathartic "sanity"; women tricked out of their roots in womanearth and womansky in a froth of the blood in frenzied rituals that made them beside themselves, no longer with each other—Kali—I looked imploringly over at her icon among the candles—Kali, the detoxifier and awakener, even her name and regenerative powers, stolen by thugs; crooks, too, stealing the caduceus women once carried within, Hermes' rod topped with the wings of the healing heavens, entwined with the snakes of the healing earth (men kill snakes as they kill women as they kill the earth), suave male-mothers in business suits masquerading as the healers in wholeness women once were and, despite enforced amnesia, still secretly are, protectors and inspiriters of all sentient life on earth.

Mutilated women taking back what has been stolen from them in primal awe and envy, beginning with their bodies, their minds, bodies and minds deformed in ugliness by lies (the truth seems ugly only because the lie is so hideous); and faggots burn no more in the same fires that consumed their sisters, and burn us still, the brand on each of us, marked for death.

Upend these murderous monsters in this longest night, I prayed to Kali, drive them out of our circle, back into the vacuous no place they sneaked from, the shadowland of the undead where nothing is seen or sensed for what it is.

The healing presence was with us, her radiance shimmering in the room amid the haze of hash and incense, her shine on the whitewashed bricks, like Diana's, an iridescent aureole gleaming just over our heads. She speaks in my ear in rustling whispers, stealing my heart in healing thieveries.

For centuries our circle broken, the backs of women broken, under the marching feet of those who have forgotten how to dance. Now at long last, in this long turn of the year, our circle is whole again, these thirteen sons, faces like thirteen moons, remembering forked root Cernunnos and the best of leaf-trembling Dionysus, in wine-drunk sperm-ecstasy entwined among each other, in senseless and sensual celebration of the grape-dark vines between our legs, in celebration of the shaggy musk of loins, of pot-high, the sweetly intoxicating singing of seed like the roar of a sea in our ears; that roaring loud in a room suddenly transformed into a huge prismatic conch shell in the inner spiralings of which our ears, held fast, are listening; hearing news of women truly loving one another again, and that's a revelation and a revolution; and news of some men now, as here tonight, beginning to have love for one another, too, feeling totally alive in our bodies, and that's also a revelation and a revolution, and not the same old turn where nothing changes: Changes everywhere in the air like pollen flying.

Beneath my breath, to be double sure, I called on the fairies to banish that aspect of his presence from the circle, the selfish and egocentric drunken god of the bondage of self, god without respect, and suddenly felt an absence in the room, like one enormous exhalation through the windows as the plastic sheeting flattened against the panes, and as it died away, Keith's words again emerged out of it in a soft monotone, drawing my attention, as he spoke of Hermes " . . . the quick, the connector of synapses. . . ." and Hermes was in the room, replacing the brief negative charge of Dionysus, Hermes suddenly lightning-swift in my blood, the quick, ingenious dancer connecting rapidities faster than light, the twirling threader, the weaver, the dancer through obstacles, his energy joining each of us here in a roseate garland of quickening, affectionate flesh, mindflashing.

I felt a lively urge of dancing in my feet, surging up my legs, spontaneous rhythms from the earth itself in the beat of the goddess at the heart of the earth, and had to seize my ankles to keep them still, knowing the time for dancing would come later.

I glanced across at Jonathan, my eyes literally dancing across the room to where he sat, slim back erect, listening mindful to

Keith, himself Hermes-quick, Hermes-light, personifying in the sly and merry gleam of his eyes, in the movements of his lithe and supple body, in his feathery ankles, all the slithery, quicksilver qualities of the mercurial god and goddess within.

I longed to dance with him, my arches bucking, coltish ponies eager to leap, and hugged them to the floor with my hands, begging them in a whisper to be patient.

" . . . Wednesday . . ." I heard Keith intoning once more, the sound of his voice bringing me back, puzzled as to why he was talking about Wednesday on Monday, " . . . Is the day of the week named for Hermes. . . ."

He was finished, and there was a moment of silence as he tamped his notes together in an even pile and tucked them back in the folds of his discarded clothing crumpled in a ball on the floor behind him. He stood up and, standing in that erect, formal stance of a dancer, said with an engaging, wide-eyed smile, "Now let me lead you all in a few warm-up exercises," adding, with a flash in his eyes, "For the very *intense* amenities to come."

We all struggled to our feet, forming a ragged circle, Keith suddenly focusing his body into an intense physical concentration of his own, the formal poise of his bearing bespeaking the trained dancer, and the pleasure he took in it, his obvious assurance evoking, by the dour looks in a few faces, the immediate envy and pique of some of us clumsier ones.

He began to take us through a series of simple dance steps and gestures, pliés and bends and squats, exhorting us in his mild but firmly encouraging voice to stretch our arms and legs and torsos as far as we could. In contrast to his own litheness, I noted, with some envy of my own, that even the high and supple curve of his instep had a studied and elegant grace, my own less elegant insteps, squeezed in upon themselves, were still straining for release, ready to spring, and I let them gambol and gallop as much as they liked as I hopped from foot to foot, in place. Noted, too, with relief, that most of us were awkward but sportingly willing to learn the rudiments again—although several, especially the light-haired Danny in his electric-blue pants, and the wiry-bodied lad from San Francisco, Hal, were agile and polished in their movements, perhaps having taken some lessons, particularly Danny from Keith, or perhaps they were dancers, too.

As for the rest of us, except for Jonathan and Petey and one or two others, we appeared hulking and confused, our watchful, uncertain eyes fastened on the willowy figure of Keith as he tick-tocked his buns around the floor in elegant small twitchings and bowed and turned with sylphlike ease and confidence; even his eyes, though closed, were closed, in the lift of his delicately fine brow, with a graceful and dramatic intensity, while in the harried, wide-open eyes of the rest of us as we watched his every move, struggling to follow, was a look, the opposite of the one in Danny's completely adoring eyes, of confusion mingled with flat resentment at the prospect of making fools of ourselves in our elephantine stiffness.

Mercifully, the exercises lasted only a brief time, and ended with Keith having us jump up and down, like kids, which was more to our liking.

"Aim for the ceiling!" he cried, leaping himself like a gazelle, arms flung upward. "Reach for the sky!"

Most of us began to laugh as we bounced up and down as hard and as high as we could, my own feet bounding at last in unrestrained freedom. I scrunched my shoulders and squatted down as far as I could to push myself higher, enjoying the lift of my body as I sprang up toward the ceiling, exulting each time in the birdlight, weightless sensation in the splitsecond leap, even enjoying the flat smack of the soles of my feet as they hit the glossy boards again and again; delighted, too, in the weight of myself as I crouched before springing.

The others, from their wide grins, were enjoying themselves, too, and throughout the loft rang a jubilant sound of laughter interspersed with the whisper of bodies rising and falling and the thump of feet whacking the floor in a steady and insistent drumming, the soft grunts of our breath as we landed.

Here was something simple and direct that all of us could do without feeling graceless or inadequate, and so the body exercises ended with a lot of good feeling and high spirits, not to mention heavy breathing. I glanced across at Bert, big-shouldered, large in the paunch, puffing a bit, but his dark, moody eyes were smiling behind his wire-rim glasses, his round cheeks above his beard having the ruddiness of pomegranates.

There was a deliberate pause for rest now, most of us just standing around, loose-limbed, arms akimbo, getting our breath back, slight smiles still on our faces as we eyed each other, a few, like Petey and Ken, sprawled flat on their backs on the floor, arms and legs spread out, wearing dizzy grins, Petey's tongue hanging out one side of his mouth in exaggerated fatigue.

After a few minutes, Ed walked among us, softly clapping his hands, playfully shooing us all back together in a close pack, telling us to stand with arms about each other's shoulders. When those on the floor had hauled themselves up and we had pulled ourselves into a tightly interlocked ring again, Ed said simply, "Make animal noises," and started us off himself, making thin, hyena yappings fluttering deep in his throat, and presently the rest of us followed with timorous and scattered yippings of our own at first, our barks and howls soon increasing in frequency and volume, bouncing noisily off the walls of the loft, so loud, in fact, the vibrations, ringing almost painfully in my ears, must have echoed throughout the entire building, perhaps even out over the entire block, and up through the roof to the cold and listening heavens.

I was sure the neighbors must have heard us, and had a momentary rush of fear: What if they became frightened, hearing, in the depths of Manhattan, such unaccustomed beast-howling blasting through their apartment walls, and one of the tenants called the cops? And what if the police broke the police lock (who will protect us from the protectors?) and barged in, guns drawn, to find a dozen or so stark naked men barking and yowling in a tight circle like a pack of wild animals?

But my apprehension dissolved and I took delight in the imagined scenario as I felt something playfully tugging at my hair, like the tiny claws of mice. Thinking it was one of the men teasing me mischievously from behind, I brushed my hand above my head to reach for his fingers to give them an affectionate squeeze in return for ridding me of my moment of fright, but was baffled when I only swiped at vacant air. The fairies again, I said to myself, realizing their spirit was jolly in the room once more, tantalizing me anew, and grinned to myself, thinking—bitten by infectious fairy-humor, where everything is possible and, as Ed had said, anything goes— if the cops pull a raid, maybe they'll lay down their guns, strip off their uniforms and join us. Fat chance, I knew, but it was fun to think about it.

And what with the visitations of benevolent energies in the room throughout the night, and also remembering the stone mythic beasts and stonefaced women on the front of the building when I'd entered, like guardian creatures protecting the place, protecting us, too, I was sure, I felt immediately safer, thinking surely they would let no harm come to us, or let anything harmful enter through any of the windows or doors.

Assured now, the muscles of my throat thickened as I joined my voice to the baying chorus, our heads lifted, mouths stretched wide, baring our teeth, the back of our throats. Seeing inward in beasteyes, the eyes of most of us were shut tight in the strenuousness of howling, neck muscles fattening with blood, veins corded and swollen from unaccustomed strain. I felt a collar of fur suddenly bristle on my neck, tufts of hair on the ridge of my spine stood stiff; felt my teeth lengthen, grow to points incisor-sharp; my fingernails and toenails grow into the hard black claws of a wild dog, a coyote, a wolf; my throat stretch into the lean raw gullet of a beast swelling joyous in the rough power of the sound of its own howlings roaring raw out of its black belly and up its quivering larynx, baying out through the long curled lip of my wide-open canine muzzle, pink with blood.

Baying among the others, our voices a beast-chorus, harmonious, thrummed out of our joined animal-spirit, in touch with and sounding off among all other animals howling from pack to pack in a faint far call from the distant past across the long night of the year, my ears pointed and furry now, our earsplitting yowls—louder than the singing of the hounds I used to hear up in the Black Mountain hills—crowding up through the roof, up to the invisible moon, cascading down to the sun below the darkness of earth, circling up in widening rings of sound to the signal-flashing stars.

Keith had, in the meantime, slipped out to the long-silent phonograph to put on a record, and soon music, a wild and delirious tempo of flutes and drums, blared from the loudspeakers at the front of the loft. The dancing began, at first singly and in pairs, moving in threesomes, then each of us joining more often than not in configurations of four or five men at once, shifting to form other clusters of dancers, a kaleidoscope of unpredictable formations, swirling and weaving, arms now lifted high above our heads, fingers snapping; now our arms falling in lazy descent to curl, like leaves, around shoulders, waists, clasping hips, buttocks, all of us swaying nakedly, even Daryl, I saw now, rocking rhythmically over the shiny hot-pink floorboards, involuntary hardons sprouting everywhere among us, clear, tiny pearls, like early dew, glistening at the tips of a few in the candle-gleam.

Never having danced in the nude before, except as a child with other children, stealing off into the woods surrounding the little town I grew up in, and dancing naked among the sassafras trees, dancing innocently for each other, kids, left to themselves, being natural pagans, natural fairies; the sudden realization occurred to me with something of a shock, that that had been the last time, and as a result, I delighted in the embrace of arms about my shoulders and waist as I gyrated around and around, enjoying the sensuous brush of other naked hips and the bristly rub of hairy thighs, of groins, against my own, punctuated now and again with the impetuous capering, in high leaps with heels clicking, of frisky colts, of kids, our barefeet pounding and pawing the floor like hoofs, myself bouncing among the others like I had springs in my heels.

I was dancing, danced by rhythms in and out of me, no longer dancing in a rigid and monotonous copulative beat, in flailing, cockcentered jerkinesses of disco, rock—down, up, down, up, in ingrained linear thrusts imposed by tumescent electronic music on the subsumed body of sound—but swirling and twirling and spinning my body to another music, ragged and raw, and subtly delicate, too, in improvised riffs and rhythms, my flying arms and legs spinning out in curls and tendrils of movement, surprising even myself at the shapes my body was taking, surprised as well at the fantastic convolutions of the others strutting and reeling and bending around me.

Dancing naked at last, all of us dancing now, in calmer, swaying circles of three and four as the music slowed and grew low, a murmurous drone humming up unforced from the depths of our throats, filling the smoky air of the loft with the low dynamo buzz of bees, a glad, dry hum the color of honey, and as sweet in the throat as it rose, filling the room in a higher and higher pitch, sparking an aura like the sight of yellow butterflies fluttering about each other in sunlight, our humming gradually diminishing, then rising again, like the whir of cicadas clinging to the bark of trees in early spring, the shrill rise and falling away of their pipelike singing, singing for mates, singing for light after years of darkness, singing for the sheer hell of it; the chords of our droning plucking an accurate and corresponding chord in my own breast, drawing me, willingly, closer to all those dancing around me, all of us cicadas, I saw, sprung up now from underground after many long years, and spreading our long-shriveled opalescent wings in dancing in deepest winter, making a spring of it, in the air of the loft, in our heels, an unknowable energy, a vast, pulsating rhythm we touched in our deepest place, pulsing unconsciously with it, alive in its galactic flash and vibrancy, our dancing limbs fluttering like the whir and flash of the red-eyed cicada's wings.

Again the brimming goblet of wine is passed by a grinning Jonathan, skipping faunlike among us; the wooden pipe of hash is also passed around by Keith, who is gliding everywhere at once like mercury. The wine and hash, along with the quickening music, increases the tempos of our dance, the emanations of our chants, the hum of our singing, all of it like heat rising, lifting the roof of this aged, lopsided tenement, thawing momentarily the frozen, clamped lid of the night.

And I, once more, turn down the wine and pipe, those cosmic eye-poppers, when they're passed again around the dancing circle, still intoxicated as I am simply with the singing and dancing, the alluring odor of other males, drunk in the energy and heat that carouse through my veins, Hermes-swift, energy streaking out again one to the other of us, linked still in our dancing, aerated blood tingling with a silvery oxygen more effervescent than any champagne I'd ever drunk, drunk on the liveliness of death, on the promised life in its whispery kisses, so cold on my mouth on this coldest night they are the hottest of kisses. I careen among the other dancers, eyes tight, a closepacked, drowsy seedpod, equinox-dreaming, our lifting prick-prods greeting each other like rising suns.

I know we are noticed dimly among the stars seen dim through the sooty windows, star-eyes seeing our prancing bodies in homage, star-ears hearing the chants from our throats, tin-eared and feeble for the most part but resonant in celebration of starpower and moonpower, songs not heard from our backwater earth in this off-the-track galaxy in thousands of years.

The cosmos always in tune, I listen, danced by its rhythms.

Over the rooftops of the Lower East Side, stars visible in the grimy panes of the loft windows wink back at us across immeasurable, cold galactic distances, wink sparklingly at our little Fairy Circle, our pathetic and foolishly brave rosebud-in-winter of a Saturnalia (satyrnalia) celebration under the tarpaper roof of a dingy tenement in a neglected and littered part of the city, neighborhood of the poor and abject, shunned and substantial survivors— how at home we are among them!—who have become hard, gleaming with a stubborn sparkle in this long night, in all the long nights of persistence, like the carapace of seeds, of insects, fabulous armadillos, defiant tears freezing eyes like diamonds on fiercely determined faces, stubborn to live, substantial and ingenious as the cockroaches seething beneath the floors of the building, seething throughout all of the neglected, rundown buildings in this forgotten lower portion of Manhattan island. Voices from other generations back, tough and sturdy Jews, Poles, Puerto Ricans, Blacks, voices in the walls like the low, soft sighing of the nightwind at the windows, like the scurrying of mice, whispering other impulses, other directions, speaking the single, insistent word: *resist, resist*—survive and bloom in secret, in moonlight, in the stink of sour hovels; you are meant to live, however you can— pallid fairies frisking in moonshine of our own radiation, hidden behind tenement brick walls, behind a stout police-locked door for safety, surviving, dancing, tending our fire, stoking and mending the forgotten fires of heartier, livelier forebears as we strike our own, touch backwards and forwards over the long years gathering energy in tongues of flame, kin with all the other inhabitants of these walls, living and dead.

The unerring compass of our earthcentered selves points the eyes in our heads, points our cock-eyes, moonward, starward, cockeyed with glee, energy of earthrock surging up through the cockroach-ridden floors (those other cunning survivors!) into the soles of our naked feet, blackened from dancing; feel the rotating tremors of earth pulsing up through my limbs as I dance and turn with it, the blackness out of which we spring in a kick of dancing (tiny cocks erect), the blackness that pulls us back into it with the embrace of a lover in the place of starts and rests where all is a circle within circles and there is no end; as tonight the creak of the continent settles in winter, resting, only a rest; its grains and fruits buried among root cellars under earth, seeds in fat blackness sleeping, waiting—the flames of the candles, swirled and blown flat in the gusts of air eddied up in our dancing, dimmed, as if the door had suddenly opened and the blackness of the solstice-night itself slipped into the room like a huge sable cloak lining the walls of the loft in fur-gleaming darkness.

Caress me, blackness, I am your lover, I sing to myself as I weave among the others. This night I have known your contours as my blind fingers, in sensual intelligence, have stroked and touched the curves and planes of flesh of these strangers, no longer strange, who are now as familiar as my own skin, as I, with theirs, along with your presence, which is as enveloping as the skin of a black snake sheathing me snug and intimately close as a second skin.

At the lava-black heart at your roots, I kiss you and embrace

180

you, beloved of the long night; dispel all the lies spread about you by the frightened fathers of the evil in light without darkness. Acquaint me with darkness, beloved of the long day, bestower of starts and stops, of the seed that sleeps and the seed that wakens, rest in me and dance with me in the volcanic stretch and arctic shrink of your planetary spin. I spin with you. Your darkness is friendly, your cosmos friendly.

Blackness, the mother I spring from, on whose grasses I dance with care not to hurt them, for that would be hurting the skin of the mother, and the skin of the earth is the skin of me, the dark my body belongs to, blackness I sag back into in a dozing sleep, the blackness of death not death, but only the revivifying blackness this night, my mother, is, that envelops me in a seedpod of darkness, enfolding me again in her collective light, down in the blackness of the beginning of things, a seed with a kernel of sun at my core, spring-dreaming, benignly stung, learning to be dumb, in this harsh, freezing night that's only a tiny sleep at the start of the solstice slumber.

The dancing continued without letup for an hour or more, our faces glistening with sweat in the candleshine, the room filled with breathless laughter and the muffled sound of our naked feet beating, slipping, across the floor as we circled and careered about the loft, our swaying nut-sacks swelling pinker, our dancing shadows, caught reflected in the candles, thrown in long, huge silhouettes up on the walls and ceiling.

Gradually, the intensity of the dancing subsided, easing off, like so much else this night, of its own artless volition, the dancers now coming together in a closeness of open and affectionate hugging and kissing, caressing each other all over, all of it in an easy, trusting manner, with no one excluded, none left untouched or unkissed, with one group eventually breaking up and joining another, new clusters forming now and again in natural, slow and unpredictable movement. The music quieter now on the phonograph, a soft droning cello in long, sustained notes, eerily spatial, while mingled with it, and occasionally rising above it, that curious involuntary murmur of content we continued to hum intermittently to one another in the smaller circles, heads pressed one to another, arms locked about each other's shoulders, hands now and again sliding down in deft brushings of each other's flesh, fingers as lightly murmurous as our humming voices, clouds of bee-sound buzzing in seductive, trilling octaves out of throats so relaxed they are elongated with the satiety of pleasure and contentment; the exact same sound as the buzz in my blood, the humming all around me in my ears, like the hum of the womb of the cosmos itself out of which we are constantly born and reborn.

Finally, only one hardy, more energetic trio with stronger lungs, Ed, Ken and Tim, standing near the narrow passageway leading to the front of the loft, were left still humming and hugging in a close head-to-head huddle, while the rest of us, one by one, dropped to the floor to sit or recline on the blankets and sleeping bags and pillows several of us had spread out again, or sat slumped back against the walls, resting from the dancing, sitting silent for the most part, or gazing about with rapt smiles, a few talking quietly among themselves in excited whispers, others going off into the hallway space to help themselves to the food, a couple making games of it, laughingly, prankishly, feeding each other like kids, as Ken and I had done earlier.

I landed on the floor near the windows, and beside me Hal was lying tucked inside one of the larger sleeping bags, eyes peacefully closed, the delicate skin of his lids, his fine, still-damp brow, appearing translucent in the gleam of the candles. I sat, legs drawn up, arms folded over my knees, gazing down at him, then looked about the room, then back at Hal's face, which was the color of peaches in the guttering candles, and felt a quiet sense of satisfaction. The loft had cooled perceptibly by now, the ancient radiators no longer hissed and clanked, the heat had gone off before midnight. I could feel on my bare back the chilly drafts blowing in through the loose, wind-shook windows, and shivered a little. It seemed a good idea to get beneath a blanket, or into a sleeping bag, perhaps with somebody else, and, without a moment's hesitation, uninhibited, still loose and open from the dancing and the evening's rituals and games, I did, easing myself down and slipping myself in beside the San Franciscan, pulling the flaps up snug around our shoulders, nestling close to him.

He turned his head and opened his eyes a bit to see who it was had burrowed in beside him, then seeing me, smiled, unprotesting, shutting his eyes again and lying quietly on his back as before.

Carefully, I lay the tips of my chilled fingers on his chest, teasingly, and to warm them a little, too, a tremor quivering his pectorals for a fraction of a second, and felt his heart, the beat of it, as I spread my hand flat, slow and muted under my palm, like the atmosphere of the loft itself now, a slackening and quieting air, as our Saturnalia was slowly winding down to a close.

I began to caress his breastbone, then let my fingers skip down to run lightly over his belly, beginning to massage it, taut muscles there loosening, kneading it in a friendly way, nothing sexual really, just content to touch the skin of another, despite all the skin I'd touched that evening, enjoy the closeness of his warm body in the feathery warmth of the sleeping bag as the room grew cold around us, blue curlings of smoke here and there from candles snuffed in burning themselves out.

I felt blissfully serene.

We began to talk quietly, he with his eyes still shut, about San Francisco, where he'd lived for six years—"The average time we all seem to spend out there," he said with a rueful grin—myself curious to hear what it was like now, the Castro area, or ghetto, depending on how you looked at it, and the somewhat greater freedom there today; and how Polk Gulch and North Beach had changed; and told him something of what it was like in the fifties when I was out there—I've already started to write about those days, in a book to be called, appropriately enough, *San Francisco Days*—the extreme openness and closedness all at the same time, city of ocean light and ferment of poetry and jazz excitement, and a paranoid-heavy police city, too, particularly for lesbian and gay people. He expressed surprise at how much police entrapment there was in those days, and also hadn't known, being considerably younger than myself, that here in New York, Mayor Lindsay had put a stop to such practices, for the most part, back in the sixties, although, as I thought again of the tearoom up in the George Washington Bridge bus station, they still go on here and there.

Presently we grew still, my hand resting quietly on his stomach, no need really to talk. The panoramic vision of San Francisco panned across my mind as I remembered the brilliantly sunny day, soon after I'd arrived in 1956, when, having paid my dime at the turnstile for the privilege, I stood on the pedestrian walkway out at the center of the Golden Gate Bridge, the bridge swaying in the strong winds blowing in off the Pacific, and gazed back over the roiling deep blue waters of the bay at the city, thousands of white buildings clustered up its hills so bright in the sun it hurt my eyes to look at them.

My hand reached lower down, brushing the pencil-thin line of hair extending from navel to pubic bush and, cupping his genitals, began to massage his cock gently, remembered it swaying vivid between his thighs, all rosily pink, the first time I spotted him naked from the hall, a cock I'm certain I had already stroked in the circle earlier, and now touched again, my fingers equally blind, hidden beneath the slippery nylon of the sleeping bag, its inner lining smelling of old sweat and hair oil, my hand moving more in a gesture of simple affection and friendliness than anything else. Erotic without feeling compelled to act on it, I sensed that he, too, seemed content to leave it at that, my roots, cock-loving, wonderful in itself, but knowing that's not the be-all and end-all of any of us, not the totality we are. The others apparently felt the same, since I could see no one indulging in intimacies any different than those I've already revealed, which seemed satisfying enough to all, for now, although our revelries could easily end, when we got our second wind, in a great and glorious tumblefuck, and that would be wonderful, too.

By this time, we were all pretty well settled down, several of the others sitting around wrapped in blankets, except for the three some still hovering close together near the front of the loft, their low voices and laughter, their occasional humming, a pleasant, additionally relaxing sonorousness in the room. Now they began to go through some of the simple but elegantly measured steps of Celtic country dancing learned at an earlier gathering of the Circle, with Ken's light, silvery laughter, bright as the moon, as he executed a neat turn, first under Tim's arm, then under Ed's.

I watched them leisurely, totally at rest, buried up to my nose in the downy softness of the bag. It was enough just to be lying close to the warm and comforting flesh of this young man whom I had not known before this evening; felt so open and comfortable with all the others, too, none of whom I'd known either exactly a month ago this night, and some, like Ken and Keith, not even before this night; felt suddenly a deep vitality, an enormous surge of hope that something tremendous could grow out of this nucleus, a real force, an affectionate and caring power among males, a change in the way we are with each other.

A profound and satisfying peace fanned out over my entire body, like slipping into a warm bath, my mind lulled and yet alert to even the slightest movement in the room; at rest and alert, at one with all, and alive to everyone and everything about me.

I guessed it must be close to one now. The atmosphere in the smoky loft exuded an air of rapturous fatigue. I was beginning to nod off when, out of the corner of my eye, I saw Ed slip out from under the embracing arms of Ken and Tim, having finished their country dances, and step once more into the center of the floor.

184

"It's getting late, why don't we bring things to a close," he said, and had us all gather in a circle again as we had at the beginning of the evening, our movements slower this time, less enthusiastic. I resented leaving the comfort of the sleeping bag, and particularly the comfort of Hal's summery body close to mine, but the two of us shoved out of the bag's toasty interior like newborn twin butterflies struggling out of a chrysalis and, rolling it up and sitting on it, using it both as a seat and insulation between our bare bottoms and the rapidly cooling floorboards, joined hands with the others, Hal sitting on my right this time, and Ian, with his gray beard, his blurred eyes crinkling in a smile at me behind his steel rimmed glasses, on my left.

Clasping the lifted hands of those seated on either side of him, Ed closed his eyes and started breathing deeply in the now slow, familiar rhythmical pattern, the rest of us following, our breaths rising in volume as we slipped gradually back into that near trancelike state again, for myself, finding it easier this time, listening only to our breathing, the soft whisper of air in and out of my nostrils, concentrating only on that, as we recentered ourselves, recentered ourselves in our little circle, and in the vast circle of the night, breathing out and out in rings to the edges of the wintery heavens themselves, and the strong winds of the heavens breathing back in us, invigorating our lungs once more, their playful tremolo bubbling gaily in our blood.

Lifting his head, exposing his pale, strong throat beneath his sparse beard, Ed began to speak again, quickly, almost in a whisper, and this is what he said:

"And now we sit again in our circle, this floor, the ground again, and feel the energy of the ground in us, feel the energy from the molten center of the earth come up through our feet once more, up our legs, our ankles and calves, into our knees and thighs, radiating up through the ass and into the crotch, feel the energy from the core of the earth radiating all through your legs and into your belly. Now feel the energy of the sky come down through our heads into our necks, our shoulders, coming into our chests, our hearts, our lungs, breathing it in, feel sky-energy radiate out along our arms to the fingertips, feel it coursing back into the body, back into our ribcages and down in our bellies; feel it in the solar plexus, feel it meet there in the sun of our bellies with the energy coursing up into us from the core of the earth, feel ourselves grounded and centered and sunlit and moonlit and lit from within as well by the fires from the heart of the earth, and feel a oneness with it all, here in this circle, where all energy is contained; feel the flow of energy from one to another through our hands, feel the energy moving in the circle, moving as our blood moves, circulating in the circle of our veins, the circle of our bodies, feeling the energy of your blood running in your body and the blood running in the bodies of those on either side of you, all our bloods flowing here in the energy of the circle, and feel the roundness of the circle and the roundness we are within it."

At a nod from Ed, Keith got up and brought a lit candle from the low, altarlike table by the windows and set it on the floor in the center of the circle, a white votive candle in a clear saucer, and then Ed asked us to focus on the flame for a few moments as he began the ritual of the moon:

"The flame a tongue of light, a tongue of the moon in a round candle in a round plate. Now let's close our eyes and see a sliver of the moon like the shaving of a fingernail, a maiden moon, in the roof of our skulls, which is the sky. And see the thin moon and see it grow now to quarter-size, a quarter moon, and now it waxes to a half moon, the mother moon, and see it in the roof of your head, which is also the firmament, and see now the three-quarter moon in the sky of your mind, three-quarter full between mother and crone, and the energy from the earth and the energy from the sky is still flowing in us, with our bloods, is still flowing around the circle. And see now in the mind's eye in the mind's sky the full moon now below the earth, the crone in its roundness, the circle of the full moon like the circle we are, the sphere the full moon is, the perfect and beautiful hag of the full moon our open eye out into the cosmos, the cosmic eye. And the energy is still flowing around us in the circle, and all is a roundness, the sun a circle and a roundness, and everything a globe, a sphere, the stars a circle and a roundness, like our circle, and we're touched by the stars as we're touched by the moon, the sun, in their roundness, and the earth on which we sit is a circle, a globe in roundness, a woman in roundness, our round mother, and the energy of the earth is in our circle, in the blood of each of us, circling here, circling as the energies contained within our circle—and everything is a round-ness, ourselves a roundness, without beginning or end or top or bottom, and every point and everything upon it is alive and every point upon our circle is the right place so that wherever we are upon it is the right place to be; and we are the circles of the cosmos within us and the cosmos without, and the moon and sun and stars are within, in our bloods which are racing rivers, oceans; and we are meant to be here and we are wanted here, and all is a roundness, complete and whole in the eye of Diana, eye of the daughter-mother-crone in the cosmos of the night, she has her eye on us, now and forever; gleaming, protecting, cool eye of total magic and mover of tides of the rivers of earth and the rivers of our blood in the night and early morning; the sun her other eye in double-seeing, hot, unblinking eye of the mother in loving, seductive flirtation to grow in, nurturing, beaming, in unending heat and light.

"So that we walk in the roundness of the cosmos in the roundness we are, at home and in place wherever we are, centered in our bellies as the heavens are centered in the eyes of the moon and sun, centered on earth, centered in us, the eye of the ogling cosmos on us also flirtily urging, Live! Swirl! Change! The energy of the blood of the cosmos coursing round us everywhere as the liveliness of our blood here in the circle courses through our bodies, and they are all one and the same. And the energy from earth and sky is still strong here in the circle, and the energy of our cosmic selves flowing from one hand to another is strong, and even when we drop hands, the energy will still be with us, the energy contained here in this room, and our circle won't be broken, no more than the circle of the moon or sun, the earth, are broken, but will remain intact wherever we go when we leave here tonight, for the moon stretching to roundness is in us, and the roundness that every living thing is, and everything is alive and changing."

He was silent and there was a long pause, and rest, our eyes still closed, the pointed flame of the candle in the center burning red against my lids, the only sound in the room that of Ed's excited, rapid breathing with its faint raspy whisper, myself feeling a rapturous wholeness of the in and the out, very much *here*, in the circle, and at the same time being at every point upon it, as Ed had said, centered here and everywhere at once in ever widening rings out to the vast rotundity of the planet itself, out to the round moon and sun, the round stars, to the incomprehensible rounding breath of the expanding cosmos breathing in me, breathing, in one breath, in our tiny circle.

After a few moments Ed said quietly, "Blessed be," and the rest of us answered, "Blessed be," and we sat silent for several minutes more, unmoving, reluctant to break the spell, to separate from each other, Ed's breathing quieting gradually, and finally someone stirred, and then another, and opening my eyes, saw most of the others were looking about the circle and smiling, like sleepers just awakened, a few stretching and yawning, some already pulling themselves up, like they were getting out of bed. Ed, a pink aura about his face and shimmering up and down his naked body, standing too now, motioning for the rest of us to arise, to stand close and put our arms around each other, "To get ourselves warmed up to get up a good head of steam for the cold streets outside," he grinned, and we formed our hugging circle, just like the ones we made at the end of other fairy circles, before we parted from each other for the night, except this time, instead of partial undress, the majority of us were blissfully, unself-consciously naked.

With arms thrust about each other's shoulders, we squeezed together as close as we could get, so close that our heads touched, brow to brow. And hug each other we did, a compactly joined ring of male flesh in one huge encircling embrace of inter-woven arms, each of us struggling to buss the two or three caught and held laughing in the center, Petey, Jonathan and Keith forming the axle we kissed around, their arms forced straight at their sides so they couldn't move, Petey's pale lips the stain of crushed straw-berries from so much kissing; then, craning around them, stretch-ing our shoulders and necks to reach across the circle to give a smack on the lips to those directly opposite us on the perimeter; then kissing all those around the rim of the wheel of the circle, some of us, myself included, kissing the mouths of several more than once in the confusion, and everybody laughing about it, peals of laughter rising up in light clouds of sound that filled the room in a merry congeniality of our contentment with the night, with each other, in these final minutes of our hours-long Saturnalia. We broke into spontaneous song, singing lustily and cheerfully a song Bert taught us, which we sang at all our other circles, and as we spiraled in an ever tightening circle, we continued to kiss as many mouths as we could, singing:

"*Listen, listen, listen, to my heart's song*
Listen, listen, listen, to my heart's song
I will never forget you,
I will never forsake you
I will never forget you,
I will never forsake you."

While all the time we were swaying, a tree of flesh again, our limbs and trunks, in the low, sputtering candle flames, were shadowed with blood coursing richly at the surface of our skins, bloodsap, over the long evening, pumped up by our hearts out of roots of flesh unknown to us, our cheeks darkly red as winesap apples, scrotums as darkly empurpled as Italian plums, flesh the color of coppery leaves of beeches undulating in a sunshine that makes each leaf more darkly gleaming, and like a dry, autumnal wind whirring through those same trees, we began once more to make our familiar, unpremeditated humming, a murmuring of quiet delight, the rustle a tree makes in pleasure of being stroked by the wind, pleasure taken in our closeness to each other as the close-packed leaves of a beech caress one another in windplay, delighting in our lively, receptive flesh, accepting of each other, with no more thought of it than the acceptance leaves have, fluttering brightly among each other.

Then Ed began one last OM, a thin, high note starting deep in his throat, then reaching deeper and deeper into his belly and bowels til it became a husky basso of sound in which we all joined, our voices spiraling up, ragged at first, in a drawn out and hearty timbre, sent, heads bowed, first earthward, then, lifting our heads, directed heavenward; next, pointing our heads in each direction of the circle, projecting our rising OMs east and north and west and south, each head turning in one last turn in our one-note hymning with the circling of the invisible sun in the winter solstice night. Again, the alert and spine-thrilling vibrato of the droning as it increased in pitch and variation, vibrating strenuously in the room, awakening me to a sharper awareness, our droning voices becoming one huge harmonious bagpipe of sound, lifting higher and higher, sounding depths, becoming the vast keening bellows of the lungs of blue whales singing to each other over a thousand miles of ocean, the lively drone and humming song of the genial, lightstreaming sea of the universe itself.

As Ed's voice dropped lower and lower, the rest of us, taking his lead, also gradually reduced the pitch of our droning until the register of his and all our voices struck the same low note of the OM we had begun the chanting with, our voices diminishing softer and softer to long, drawnout breathy whispers, ending finally only with the hush of our breathing, steady and sure.

The loft was utterly still. We stood, shoulders pressed, heads bowed again, heads close and touching, in our small circle of embrace, transfixed for several long moments, the guttering spangles of candle flames dancing against the stark walls and ceiling in bursts of light the only movement in the room.

Then Ed said simply, quietly, in his husky, ragged voice, in a tone of finality still edged with the exhilarated energy of the night and of his own last words in the ritual of the moon, "Blessed be," and all of us answered as one voice in our swaying, airy flesh-tree of hugs, "Blessed be." And then some moments passed again before, reluctantly, unwilling to break the mood, the total stillness, we dropped our arms from around each other, began to move apart, separating ourselves, began to move now to other parts of the room, no one speaking, each of us bent on searching for our clothes, our circle broken.

Not really though, I thought, as I went down the narrow hall with several others to the desk where our clothes were piled, glad to see my plaid shirt and levis again as I pulled them carefully out of the heap, smoothing them a bit by way of greeting, since the room was really getting chilly now and I could feel goose bumps breaking out up and down my chest and arms. But within me, I felt the pull and force of the circle still, strengthening me, magnetizing me in a direction that felt right on target, one that encompassed all the directions in as unbroken a circumference as the hoop of the globe itself. No matter where I turned I was turned in the right direction, the sense of the roundness Ed sang of, still powerful in me, our circle not broken, as he had said, but only temporarily interrupted, as we each carried its connecting energy away with us, til we gathered next time.

The thought cheered me considerably, and as I pulled on my levis I began to whistle softly to myself, my body filled with a new resiliency, a renewed energy, like when I was that kid I remembered earlier, dancing naked with the other kids in the woods at home a long time ago, a wiry and receptive flexibility akin to that, supple as a sapling in spring and as raw and heartbreakingly green again.

As we put on our clothes, the others jostling around me, we kidded each other, and laughed good-naturedly as we kept bumping into or jabbing one another with our elbows, all of us shivering, trying to get dressed at the same time in the scanty space. But despite our high spirits there was also an air of delicious tiredness and, in myself, a feeling of sadness, too, that the highly animated evening was drawing to an end.

Well after one o'clock, I noted, strapping on my watch and turning my wrist toward the dying flames of the votive lights still burning in a blue glow on the food table nearby, where, scattered over the top, nothing but crumbs and bits of the cakes and breads remained, a few orange peels, and apple cores, too, turning brown in the dwindling candlelight.

Someone I couldn't recognize was standing at the toilet off the darkened kitchen, his naked torso visible above the broken mirror-screen set up beside the bowl; and someone else, Ken, it looked like, wearing nothing but an unbuttoned shirt, was standing behind him, waiting; then Petey, wrapped in a sweater, wandered up behind Ken just as the person who'd been pissing gave a yank of the chain and there was a loud growling of water flushing. Just like the lineup outside the toilet in the backroom bookshop, I thought to myself, but in a totally different atmosphere, for sure, this time, those in line here cutting up and joking with each other in a friendly way as they waited their turn. I needed to use the john myself, after the long night, but decided I could wait til I got to the baths, which was only a block away on First Avenue.

Fully dressed now, I slung my duffel bag over my shoulder, kissed and hugged and said my farewells to those around me who were finishing dressing, then moved out to the loft where I went about the room kissing all the others one last time, putting my arms around each, giving and receiving strong embraces, especially thanking Keith for his hospitality.

"Yawl cum back agin, now, hear?" he drawled out in a camp, deep-down Dixie accent, as he clasped my arm.

At the door, I took one final look about the room, the place having a cold, smoky smell, sickening sweet incense and stale reefer mingled with the clean and snowy odor of winter blowing in at the leaky windows, what little light there had been growing more dingily dark as the candles burned low all about the loft and began to sputter out one by one, the main source of illumination now the soft electric Lava Lamp with itscrimson bubbles still floating up and down inside it.

I opened the door and strode out into the even chillier hallway, air as cold as the fluorescent lights in the ceiling, glaringly harsh brightness so abrupt a change from the warm and mellow candlelight of the loft, I narrowed my eyes in a painful squint as I headed down the stairs.

Despite my fatigue, I was so light in my body, that feeling of feathers fluttering within me, just as I'd felt after all our other circles, I practically floated down the flights of stairs, not one footstep alighting on any of the steps, it seemed, and at the bottom, all but flew down the long hallway, feeling so transparently fluffy, I just about had myself believing I didn't need to open the vestibule door to let myself out but could pass right through the glass with the greatest of ease.

In the cold entryway, colder, I noted, with an immediate shudder, than the upper halls of the building, I yanked down my face mask and slipped on my gloves before I opened the street door and, bracing myself, stepped out into the night once more. The sudden icy wall of air that hit me felt, in the still-raging wind, well below zero now, causing my eyes to smart instantly, then stiffen just as quickly into what felt like bits of frosted glass, blurring my vision for a long moment or two, giving the block, briefly, an icily crystalline iridescence in the beige light of the streetlamps.

Bundled up now, I hoped my puffy down vest under my ski jacket made me look huskier than I actually was in case I met up with some stray preying male, toxic and dangerous, some mugger or homophobe who wanted to mess with me, one far different from those males I'd just left, who were far more dangerous in a way; so much so we were only safe to dance our celebrations of love among each other out of the way and out of sight behind the thick brick walls and heavily locked doors of a dingy, anonymous loft building in a Lower Manhattan slum.

Slapping my hands together briskly, I trotted down the steps and onto the pavement, swinging east down 2nd Street to the all-night baths, luckily, just around the corner, where, as planned, I would rent a cubicle and put up for the rest of the night, leaving for home early in the morning to get back to my writing, as soon as the sun rose, which wasn't too many hours away, 7:15 a.m., as a matter of fact, if I remembered correctly from yesterday morning's paper.

The street had an even more bleak, deserted look than when I'd walked up it several hours earlier. Yet, inside myself, there was a color and warmth as bright as the red in the vest I wore, which was protecting me nicely from the blasts of arctic air funneling in high force between the narrow slot of buildings, the temperature of these cutting winds reaching an intensity that made my exposed skin ache and constantly brought quick tears to my eyes, moisture which froze instantly into tiny beads on my lashes.

As I scurried away, I glanced up over my shoulder to take one last look at the grimy stone faces of the goddesslike women jutting out from the even grimier facade of Number 67, and the fierce-looking animals, too, embedded in the brick, all of them bathed in the blond light of the streetlamp, glowing with that same color and warmth I felt burning in my own blood. They all seemed to be gazing down at me, beasts as ferocious guardians, the unsmiling faces of the women in strong and serene protection, as I hurried down the lonely street, feeling safe under their gaze, and gazing back up at them, thanked them silently, not only for their reassuring presence now, but their presence guarding the building during our rituals through the night.

I hastened on, no longer bothered by the late hour or by my being alone on an abandoned city street—with my ski mask close down around my eyes I must have looked, anyway, like the only possible mugger on the whole Lower East Side that night—the very low temperature undoubtedly making the streets relatively safe, the crime-rate low, for this night anyway. My body still glowed with the energies generated at our Saturnalia, held the heat of it, the closeness and warmth of the bodies of the other men. As I rushed along, head up, shoulders back, moving energized in its force, I continued to feel weightless, as if I were striding two feet above the sidewalk, and inside my head echoes of the tuneless and potent humming and chanting of the circle continued, including Jonathan's song weaving in and out, invigorating me so much that in spite of the stiffening cold I sensed my mouth beneath the mask curve in a smile as sharp as a sickle moon.

But when I reached the corner at First Avenue, passing the Manhattan Wine & Liquor Store, recognizing it as one of the places I used to buy my booze in when I lived briefly in the neighborhood years ago, its heavy metal doors rolled down tight for the night, I staggered backward from a slap of wind that hit me in a frontal assault that almost knocked me off my pins. I swung away, out of it, regained my footing and, hunching my shoulders and lowering my head, pushed across the empty sidewalk, the intersection, the avenue itself, unusually deserted, even for this hour, with no traffic for several blocks in either direction, so that when the wind died down I could even hear the clicks of the traffic lights—the loneliest sound in the world at that hour—and was able to cross the wide avenue, in spite of the flashing DONT WALK sign, with no trouble at all.

I was beginning now, for the first time since leaving the loft, to long for, in this shriveling cold, the tropical, humid heat of the steam room at the baths (a place I couldn't stand in my book on

193

the baths, but since I quit smoking, I've been able to stay in longer and longer, making it well worth kicking the habit, if you get my drift), already luxuriating in my mind in the dry, marrow-toasting warmth of its sauna. The bars would be just about beginning to empty out now, so I figured, despite the weather (eros ever more hot in the blood on nights like this), the baths would start to get crowded, as they usually did, no matter the night, right around this hour. But I didn't get too excited at the prospect of prowling the maze of corridors or of desirable strangers paying me visits in my cubicle, I felt such total satisfaction from the night at our Saturnalia, and would leave any such chance encounters in the capable hands of eros, trust to its unfolding for any further amorous adventures.

For now, a hot shower would be pleasure enough, not forgetting the use of the john, and, most alluring, a few hours sleep, and thinking that, in a sudden spurt of running, I reached the other curb and galloped toward the entrance to the baths a short distance from the corner, its globes of light either side the door warm, welcoming beacons in the shuddering winds of the dark and empty avenue.

Credit: Bob Goff

Michael Rumaker was born in Philadelphia in 1932, grew up in Southern New Jersey, and was educated at Black Mountain College and Columbia University. His books include *Gringos and Other Stories* and *The Butterfly* (a novel). His one act play *Queers* was published in West Germany as *Schwul*. A second novel, *A Day and a Night at the Baths*, was published in 1979.

Other Grey Fox Books

Daniel Curzon — *Human Warmth & Other Stories*

Guy Davenport — *Herakleitos and Diogenes*
The Mimes of Herondas

Edward Dorn — *Selected Poems*

Lawrence Ferlinghetti — *The Populist Manifestos*

Allen Ginsberg — *Composed on the Tongue*
The Gates of Wrath:
Rhymed Poems 1948-1952
Gay Sunshine Interview (with
Allen Young)

Howard Griffin — *Conversations with Auden*

Richard Hall — *Couplings: A Book of Stories*

Jack Kerouac — *Heaven & Other Poems*

Stanley Lombardo — *Parmenides and Empedocles*

Michael McClure — *Hymns to St. Geryon & Dark Brown*

Frank O'Hara — *Early Writing*
Poems Retrieved
Standing Still and Walking in New York

Charles Olson — *The Post Office*

Michael Rumaker — *A Day and a Night at the Baths*

Gary Snyder — *He Who Hunted Birds in His Father's*
Village: Dimensions of a Haida Myth

Gary Snyder,
Lew Welch &
Philip Whalen — *On Bread & Poetry*

Jack Spicer — *One Night Stand & Other Poems*

Samuel Steward — *Chapters from an Autobiography*

Lew Welch — *How I Work as a Poet &*
Other Essays/Plays/Stories
I, Leo—An Unfinished Novel

I Remain: The Letters of Lew Welch &
*   the Correspondence of His Friends*
Ring of Bone: Collected Poems
Selected Poems
Trip Trap (with Jack Kerouac &
*   Albert Saijo)

Philip Whalen   *Decompressions: Selected Poems*
                                 Enough Said: Poems 1974-1979
                                 Scenes of Life at the Capital

Allen Young   *Gays Under the Cuban Revolution*